The Wool Over Their Eyes

DIONE MARTIN

Inspired Forever Books
Dallas, Texas

Inspired Forever Books™
"Words with Lasting Impact"
Dallas, Texas
(888) 403-2727
https://inspiredforeverbooks.com

Library of Congress Control Number: 2021901324

Paperback ISBN 13: 978-1-948903-53-0

Printed in the United States of America

For *my daughters – Sofia and Ava. The loves of my life.*

Summer

"We are healed of a suffering only by
experiencing it to the full."

—Marcel Proust

Chapter 1

At eighteen, Natalia knew seven things about her biological father, Joe. He was a tall, dark, handsome Italian. Although he was married when he met her mother, he wanted to leave his wife (that's what he'd said) and run off to be with his mistress—in Mexico, where fresh air gave new life and the Caribbean waters washed away the heavy burden of guilt. Never mind his three children. Never mind his wife. Never mind his morals.

Now, ten years later, she would soon know eight. He was dying of cancer.

She was enduring yet another date. Ted. She knew she shouldn't have agreed to meet him. That damned Pamela. Her best friend since first grade. Pamela was always ready to try something new—new food, new drinks, new shoes, new men. Taking chances was her elixir for happiness.

"You need to venture out," she'd encouraged. "Stop moping and looking for perfection. Stop looking for another Tyler."

Natalia had reluctantly set up a profile on a dating site where she faced a barrage of messages and winks from men who hid behind dated photos and wishful thinking. You will know what I want you to know, she thought.

Ted seemed attractive enough and the dating site professed they were a match. But he was mechanical—every question, every response clipped. Each word enunciated with the utmost care.

"So, you like hip-hop, R&B, alternative, and rock music?" He seemed surprised.

What was she supposed to say?

"I'm not big on alternative and rock, but I like some of it," she replied. "Red Hot Chili Peppers. Coldplay. And you like jazz, right?" She scanned the menu, though she already knew what she wanted.

"I do. Wynton Marsalis, George Benson, Jason Moran. How long have you been a runner?"

"Since college. I ran track. Were you an athlete?" She didn't recall anything sports-related on his profile.

He dodged the question. "What events?"

"The 200 and the 400. Now I run distance—a couple of miles every other day or so."

"Were you any good?"

What kind of question was that? She was grateful to see their waitress.

"I'll have a hot green tea and a chicken wrap, please."

"That sounds good. I'll have the same thing," Ted said.

Five questions later, she watched the steam escape from their cups and wished she could follow it up and out. Away from the tiny table where Ted sat entirely too close. Instead of settling in the booth across from her, he'd chosen to box her in against the brick wall. They weren't at the side-by-side-in-a-booth stage, but what choice did she have? She had to crane her neck to look him in the eye.

She thought about the last time she'd sat in a booth this way and felt herself falling back to that moment as a memory of Tyler barged in. They were sharing a pizza and sipping sweet teas at their favorite hole-in-the-wall on a cold Friday night. She hadn't needed to crane her neck because her head had rested comfortably on his shoulder while his muscular arm curved around her waist. There was security in his embrace and comfort in their silence.

Pushing those thoughts aside, she tackled Ted's deluge of questions as they waited for their chicken wraps. Her left foot involuntarily shook as she fiddled with the white cloth napkin on her lap.

"What's your issue with cats? Why don't you like them?" Ted asked after their waitress delivered their food.

"I'm allergic to them," she said, sighing.

He seemed to be operating off a software program. If he asked her one more predictable question, she was going to scream. She could see him mentally checking off items on some internal list. She didn't think she could stand to hear another word come out of his mouth. And though she had no interest in his responses, she tried to deflect the attention off herself and throw a couple of questions at him. She stared at the two artificial white carnations leaning toward the chipped brick wall as Ted droned on about his siblings, his divorced parents, and his favorite pastime, playing chess.

As they waited for the bill, she found an opportunity to escape to the ladies' room. "I'll be right back," she said with a fake smile, mentally urging him to stand up so she could scoot off to freedom.

A moment later, she reapplied her lip gloss and took a deep breath before walking back to their table. She'd rather design a concept board for a new client than let this dead-end date continue. She could do better. She could find another Tyler—or at least come closer than this.

"I have to get back to work," she announced. "It was nice meeting you." She hoped he caught the hint that they wouldn't be seeing each other again.

"Well, um . . ." He paused, unsure of what to say as she stared blankly at him. "Okay, well, let me know if you want to have dinner next time. Lunch feels rushed, you know?"

"I'll do that," she lied.

She hurried to her car, thankful to be alone again. Thankful she'd had the good sense to decline Ted's invitation to pick her up from her office. He would never know where she worked, much less where she lived.

She'd just turned the key in the ignition when her cell phone rang.

"Hey, Ma," she answered.

"Hi, honey." The "honey" held an unusually heavy weight. She knew something was wrong.

"Are you sick again?" She braced herself for the worst as her stomach galloped. A couple of years earlier, her mother had suffered a bout of something the doctors never diagnosed—a spell that stole her ability to sleep and left her weighing fifty pounds less. Natalia lived in fear it would return to finish the job.

"No, no. *I'm* fine," her mother assured her.

"Then what is it? Tell me." She clenched the phone in her hand.

"Well, it's your father. Your *real* father. Not your stepdad."

Ah, the man Natalia had dreamed about so often. She pretended it didn't matter that she'd never met him, that she'd grown up without a real father-daughter bond. She pretended it didn't affect her relationships with men, and that she didn't despise him for what he'd done. But she did.

He must be dead. She'd never have a chance to meet him.

She dissected her one muddled memory of her real father. She was five years old and wore a blue sundress that flared out at the bottom. Her hair was in two puffy ponytails with large blue ribbons tied at the top of each. Standing on a corner with her mother, she stared up at a man she couldn't quite see because the sun shone brightly just behind his head. She'd raised her hand to shield her squinted eyes and get a better look, but the sun's power and glare were too strong, and she'd stared down at the concrete instead. She could have sworn he nodded in approval before giving her mother a white envelope.

She'd asked her mother who he was. "No one, sweetie," she'd said. But Natalia couldn't shake the feeling that the man was Joe, her real father. She lived with the regret of not moving her body just enough to get a better view of him. The three of them never stood on that hot corner again. It could have been her only chance.

"Is he dead?" she asked. She was numb as she watched an elderly couple leisurely walk into the restaurant she'd just abandoned, holding hands.

"Well, Barbara called me the other day and told me she ran into a friend of Joe's," her mother began. Barbara was her mother's best friend and typically knew everything about everybody. "He told her that Joe had been having really bad headaches for months, but he wouldn't go to the doctor. A few weeks ago, the pain was so bad, he was vomiting and couldn't see clearly." Then she delivered the bad news. "He's very sick, sweetie. He has brain cancer."

The light and air disappeared around Natalia as she struggled to inhale.

"He can fight this, right? He'll have chemo, and he'll live, right?" She willed her mother to say yes. There could be no other alternative. He had to live.

"They've given him a few months. Probably less."

A few months. The words banged around in her head, reverberating from side to side, and then beyond as though she were in a canyon, the echo penetrating her chest. She trembled as she tried to suffocate an intense ache. Her heart cracked open and released her long-held, secret desire.

I have to meet him. Hold his hand, touch his face. Look into his eyes. Where is he? Who is he with? I have to see him. Now.

Chapter 2

Time had taken advantage of Rosa. It had stomped all over her face, leaving its fine tracks to prove not only its remarkable strength but also its ability to demolish beauty. She knew she was the opposite of that now—a shriveled flower, dried out and brittle. She'd accepted this ragged and wrinkled version of herself many years ago. Her once long, dark, luxurious hair, now thin and gray, hadn't been washed in days. Her once luminous eyes were worn and tired.

Like her aging skin, she felt fragile. But she knew she had to be strong for Joe and their three children.

Her dear Joe. The love of her life. She'd been working as a waitress at one of the most popular Italian restaurants in New Orleans—Pascal's Manale—when they met. He walked in, boisterous and charming, with a group of six other men. All dark-haired and tall, with olive skin and well-defined, muscular bodies sculpted from their years of military service in the Vietnam War.

As she made her trancelike way to their table, he was the only one she saw. The connection was instant. The chemistry palpable.

She could see a lifetime of happiness in his gray eyes. There had been no doubt in her mind that Joe was the man for her.

Their summer wedding at St. Mary's Church a year later was still the happiest day of her life. Her youth and beauty were accentuated by the most exquisite dress she'd ever worn. In the gown's long lace sleeves, demure high neckline, fitted bodice, and flouncy, tiered skirt, she felt soft, subtle, and sophisticated. She could still remember the sound of the dress as it swished with just the slightest movement.

Now, thirty-four years later, she watched Joe lying before her, thin, pale, and struggling to breathe in an uncomfortable hospital bed. A shell of the man he'd once been.

How could there not be more years for them? How could they only have a finite number of days left with each other?

Recognizing their own limitations, the doctors at Touro Infirmary in New Orleans told them MD Anderson Cancer Center was their best chance—the center specialized in cancer research, treatment, and prevention. They used words like "multidisciplinary," "chemotherapy" and "prolonging life." But they were tentative as they spoke, folding their arms, taking deep breaths, and angling their heads. "He has a slim chance, and there are no guarantees."

It was worth a try. After several conversations with center doctors who had reviewed Joe's medical file and scans, she packed their bags and they made the five-hour drive to Houston.

She'd spent the last several weeks in this mauve-colored room. She'd memorized everything about it—from the gold-framed photos of muted flowers and pecan-colored hardwood floors to the diamond-patterned upholstered chair and tiny bathroom that Joe could no longer get up to use on his own.

As she held his cold hand, sadness surged through her, taking over her mind. A lifetime of love now reduced to an indescribable pain. Joe's gold wedding band hung loosely on his boney finger. As Rosa pushed it up, it slipped back down just above his joint where loose flesh gathered. Soon, it would fall from his finger and land on the floor with a ping, circling and tilting until it came to a stop.

Rubbing the smooth metal, Rosa thought about its meaning. This small symbol of eternity—no beginning and no end. And yet there was a beginning and there would definitely be an end—at least in this life. He would live with God forever in the kingdom of heaven. Later, she would join him.

Her thoughts were interrupted by a light tap on the door. The nurse peered through the gap before she entered.

"Hello, Mrs. Russo. How are you?"

"Oh, I'm hanging in there," Rosa said. She couldn't answer the question honestly and didn't understand why they bothered to ask. Probably out of habit.

She continued to hold Joe's cold hand as she watched the slow, steady movement of his chest rising and falling.

She'd never heard of glioblastoma, the tiny, inoperable tumor whose fingerlike tentacles were reaching far and wide into Joe's brain. None of the doctors could explain where it had come from. There was no gene to blame. No one poor choice Joe had made—too much alcohol, smoking, a poor diet, lack of exercise.

The doctors had said the tumor was an aggressive one. After they removed part of the abnormal growth, the pathological exam confirmed his fatal diagnosis. Chemotherapy was futile.

Now, Joe had all of two weeks to live, but he seemed to be declining more quickly than they had predicted. How could something so small wreak changes so big and permanent?

"Nancy, with our palliative care team, is ready for you in the conference room down the hall," the nurse said as she checked the machines near Joe's bed. "Your children are also there."

Rosa already knew this. They'd arranged to meet in one of the conference rooms near the end of the hallway several days ago, and her children had stopped by a few minutes earlier to let her know it was time.

She walked slowly, feeling the weight of her flabby legs. Varicose veins had taken over, creating green winding paths up and down and back and forth—a map of misery as they tingled and throbbed. Her knee-high support hose merely dulled the aching, never fully alleviating it.

Oblivious to the activity around her, she walked past patients in wheelchairs. She approached the tall, ominous door of the designated room and pushed the lever downward to open it. This was not a conversation she was ready to have. As she stepped into the room, Catarine jumped out of her chair and rushed to her mother's side, holding her bent elbow to steady her steps.

"Hello, Mrs. Russo. I'm Nancy Hall," a young woman said as she stood and took Rosa's hand between both of hers.

Rosa stared briefly at Nancy, a petite woman with auburn hair and green eyes, and managed a small smile. She hugged each of her children tightly before she sat down. Impending death had a way of sharpening the edges of everything surrounding life.

Catarine took the chair next to Rosa's, scooted it closer to her mother's side, then reached for her hand. Her oldest son, Joe Jr., sat stoically, skilled at keeping his emotions in check, while her youngest, John, looked tormented, his face like gnarled roots.

"I'm a nurse practitioner on the palliative care team," Nancy began. "I understand you've had some discussions with Dr. Duplessis about alleviating Joe's symptoms. My goal is to make sure we discuss all of the options available to you, that I answer all of your questions, and that you all agree with the decisions you make for him."

Solemn nods and silence.

"Tell me a bit more about Joe. What is important to him? What does he value?"

Everyone expected Joe Jr., the new head of the family, to speak. They stared at him, even Nancy.

"My dad has always been a provider. God has always been first in his life, then family—us," Joe Jr. said. "No matter what happened in our lives, his chin was always up."

"What do you think Joe would choose in terms of treatments to prolong his life?" Nancy asked. "Would he want to be on a feeding tube or a ventilator? We want to customize the treatment to meet his needs and make the most of his final stage of life. Much of what we'll do now is try to relieve any pain."

"My dad is a proud and stubborn man. He would want to go with as much dignity as possible," Joe Jr. said. "He would be much more comfortable at home than here. I think he could go more peacefully at home." He dropped his head, blinking rapidly.

Nancy continued to talk about how the family could help each other, and she read off a list of resources that could help them cope emotionally: support groups, family meetings, referrals to mental health professionals. Soon, she was shuffling through papers as she brought up the financial side. Joe had decent health insurance, but the family would still face medical bills.

She was mentioning advance directives when Rosa slid her chair back from the table and walked out without a word.

"Mom, wait," Catarine called. "We're not, she's not . . ." But Rosa kept going.

Chapter 3

Natalia walked through the door of her fourplex. She wasn't sure how she had even made it home. The whole drive was a blur.

She felt a brief sense of comfort as she closed the door, dropped her purse, and slid to the floor. From the moment she'd first seen the place four years ago, it had felt like home. Built in the late thirties in the heart of Montrose—an eclectic neighborhood in Houston—the brick building was surrounded by a mix of other fourplexes, bungalows, and small apartment complexes on a heavily tree-lined street. It was framed by tropical landscaping in the front yard, and fig, pomegranate, and pear trees surrounded a pool in the back.

She knew she'd wanted to live in the area after she got her degree in interior design. Like other art enthusiasts, she was drawn by the neighborhood's boutiques and small galleries featuring work from local artists. She could walk to nearby restaurants, run at Memorial Park, and hang out in the museum district.

She found the energy to head to the nightstand in her bedroom. She carefully retrieved a blue box, then reached for the key on the top window ledge. As a young girl, she'd kept a diary, and she still did. Not one to readily trust anyone other than Pamela with her thoughts and feelings, she released her pain onto the pages. The journal was her confidante. Pressing her fountain pen down, she began, the blue ink varying the thickness of her loopy writing.

My heart is heavy and sad. My world will never be the same. I thought I knew longing before. I thought I knew emptiness. I thought I knew sorrow. But this unbearable feeling has settled around me. I can't even imagine what my dad must be feeling right now. I can't help but wonder why I didn't know or have a premonition. He's my dad, after all. And I can't help but think we share a special connection despite the fact that we've never met. All I can think right now is that we will. I don't care if his wife is there. I don't care what my mother says. I'm done with her telling me what to do. I'm done paying for her mistakes. I'm done living by a rule book I didn't write. I know that if I don't do what my heart tells me to, I'll carry the constant pain of regret followed by the question, what if?

What if I'd had a real father—instead of a stand-in, a stranger who kept his distance and openly showed contempt for me because I wasn't his flesh and blood? What did it even mean to have a father? She slammed the journal shut and stared at the ceiling, contemplating the question. She thought it meant having someone who loved you unconditionally. Someone whose heart ached when yours did because he knew when you were hurting—and he held you in his arms so you wouldn't have to turn to undeserving boys or men. Someone who intuitively knew when you were anxious or overwhelmed. Someone who made you feel beautiful so your confidence level could soar, giving you a buffer between the harsh realities of the world, of people, of life. Someone who cared more about your success and happiness than you did. Someone who believed in you more than you believed in yourself. Someone who would die for you.

Soft heaves took over, her chest shuddering. She blew her nose and composed herself enough to call her mother.

"Where is he?" she asked.

When her mother didn't respond right away, she demanded: "Tell me where he is."

"Oh honey. I don't think that's a good idea."

She had expected this response and was ready with her own. "I know. But I'm going to see him anyway."

"But his wife and his family are there with him. If they see you, they will know," her mother said simply. "You look so much like him. Your eyes alone—"

"Well, that's not really my problem, is it? All my life I've followed all of the rules. Lived by the book. Done what you said. It's not my fault I was born under these circumstances. You did what you did. And he did what he did. Why am I the one to bear the brunt of the consequences?" She knew her voice was getting higher and louder as she felt the anger swell inside her. She didn't like using this tone with her mother, but enough was enough.

Her mother was silent for several seconds.

"I promised your dad that I would never do anything to disrupt or destroy his family. He was good to me. Good to us. There's no reason for that. Our past sins are behind us. I've told you this before." She sounded almost robotic. "It was bad enough that you were born this way. But they're white, and we're black. And that just makes it—"

Natalia had heard all of this before. Being illegitimate was bad enough. But being the Black or mixed-race child of a white man with a family of his own was just deplorable.

"Well, *I* didn't promise him anything," Natalia yelled. Why was she yelling? She felt out of control as the tears returned.

"I know," her mother said calmly. "But do you really want to hurt his family? Ruin his reputation? Destroy his legacy? They would never see him the same way if they knew."

She thought about each question, about his family.

"But he's dying, and I want to meet him, to see him. All my life I've dreamed about him, wondered what he looked like, what he sounded like. And you and your husband kept me from him."

For years, they'd led her to believe her stepfather, James, was her real father. No one told her otherwise, and she'd been trained to call him "daddy." But when she looked in the mirror and saw her gray eyes, her curly hair, her lighter skin, she knew that wasn't possible. She and her sister looked nothing alike.

When she started asking questions, her mother told her a partial truth, revealing the seven precious pieces of information she knew about Joe. Her mother ended the brief story with a finishing blow: Joe and his family had moved to Mississippi, and she gave Natalia all of the reasons why she shouldn't disrupt their lives. "They don't know anything about you, and they don't need to. There's no point in talkin' about him, so stop askin' questions about him," her mother had said.

She was sick of living a life dictated by her mother. Why had she lived this way for so long? Why didn't she do what should have been done years ago? She was sick of being suppressed. Sick of being the secret.

"I may never have a dad, but at least I can have a few last memories. And how do you know what Joe wants? Don't you think he would want to see me, too?" she pleaded.

Her mother relented. "MD Anderson in Houston."

MD Anderson was just a couple of miles from her apartment. Surely this must be a sign. She would drive there tomorrow on her lunch break.

18

Natalia followed the blue parking signs to garage number two on MD Anderson's campus. Her hands trembled on the steering wheel as she navigated her vehicle into a small space on the second level designated for compact cars. She grabbed her purse off the front seat and speed walked down the stairs and across the street toward the main building.

Once she was inside, an elderly receptionist looked up at her pleasantly. "How can I help you, honey?" Her Southern drawl was sweet and soft.

"I'm here to see one of your patients," Natalia said breathlessly.

"Okay, do you know what floor you need to go to?"

"No, I'm not sure. He has brain cancer, and it's terminal."

"I'm so sorry to hear that," she replied. "You'll need to go to the seventh floor."

She nodded and walked across the shiny tile floors toward the elevators. The heels of her shoes clicked, echoing off the high ceiling. She arrived at the elevators, pressed the top button, and squeezed her hands together as she watched the red numbers above the metal doors count down from seven to three, then pause.

What was taking so long? *I could've climbed the seven flights by now.* She finally heard a soft ding and looked expectantly at the doors.

When the doors opened, an elderly white woman stood before her, ready to exit before she could step on. She seemed rooted to the floor, unable to move. *Does she need help getting off?* She considered helping the woman, but she'd read somewhere that elderly people didn't like others to assume they needed help. *But she needs to get off so I can get on.*

When the woman finally decided to get off, the doors were beginning to close, and she had to reach out her arm to stop them. The woman opened her mouth, then closed it before stepping off. She turned back to look at Natalia, who smiled absently—an involuntary response. But the woman didn't return the smile. Instead, she looked confused. As the doors closed, Natalia wondered if she was lost or had gotten off on the wrong floor.

The ride up felt like an eternity. Her limbs were beginning to shake. When the elevator reached the seventh floor, her feet felt like they weighed a hundred pounds. Fear anchored her to the spot.

The sign for the Brain and Spine Center was the first thing she saw, and she forced herself to walk toward it. Intimidated by the long, dimly lit hallway, she stopped at a nurses' station to ask which door would lead her to Joe's room. One nurse was on the phone, the receiver resting on her shoulder. She listened intently as her fingers skittered across a keyboard. Another was talking with a couple.

She felt compelled to speak in a hushed tone when another nurse appeared behind the station and asked, "Hello, how may I help you?"

"Oh, hi—hello. I'm here to see Joe—Joel Russo." She recited the words as if she were reading from a script.

"And you are?" the nurse asked, her chin dipping down toward her chest, eyes peering above her glasses.

"I'm his . . . I'm a friend of the family," she replied, her eyes begging for the room number. *I just need to know where to find him.*

"Just a moment, please," the nurse said as she walked away.

When Natalia heard the elevator ding, fear called her toward it. She watched a family wheeling a patient through the steel doors. Just as she turned to retreat down the hallway toward safety, she heard a deep voice. "Hello, Ms. . . . ?"

She pivoted to face a tall, attractive African-American man looking searchingly at her with dark eyes, awaiting her answer. At first, she couldn't speak; her mouth was ajar as she looked up at him. She felt like she was on a stage with a glaring spotlight shining on her, but she had no lines.

"Hello?" he asked again.

"Hi. I'm Natalia Foster, and I'm here to see Joel Russo." Her gaze darted toward the lapel of his white jacket, where his name was embroidered in blue: DAVID DUPLESSIS, M.D.

He massaged the stubble on his chin and furrowed his brow as he stared at her, clearly contemplating his response.

"Hello, Ms. Foster. I'm Dr. Duplessis." He extended his hand. "Forgive me—but are you a relative of the Russos?"

Dear God. Was it that obvious? Or did he ask everyone that question?

"Well, do I have to be a relative to see him?" she asked. Damn it. This wasn't the time to have a smart mouth. Perhaps she could have said it more nicely, but she couldn't shake her fear. She had to see him. If she was forced to reveal that she was a relative, so be it. For a fleeting moment she thought about running down the hallway toward the patient rooms, yelling his name and hoping he would respond.

"Well, you . . . Never mind," he said. She sensed he was exhausted but also confused. "I'm sorry, Ms. Foster. I don't know how much you know about Mr. Russo's condition, but he went home—his home in New Orleans. He's not very coherent and doesn't have much time left. His family wanted him to be as comfortable as possible before—"

"When did he leave?"

"Just a few minutes ago," he said. "His wife and children were with him."

She thought she was going to collapse. How could she have come so close? She was just a few minutes away from seeing her dad. Tears began streaming down her cheeks.

21

When the doctor touched her arm lightly, his fingers were warm against her skin.

"Why don't you sit down for a few minutes?"

He led her to a small waiting room at the other end of the hall. His hand on the small of her back kept her steady.

"I'll be back to check on you," he said as he closed the door.

The weight of Dr. Duplessis's words pulled Natalia down into a dark abyss. *Not very coherent. Doesn't have much time.* Her mother had said a few months, but now it seemed he had a few weeks, possibly even less.

She paced back and forth, and as the truth settled in, she stopped abruptly at a window at the end of the room. She pictured Joe surrounded by his real family as she studied her own blurred reflection in the glass. Her high cheekbones and full lips were her mother's, but her gray eyes, curly hair, and light skin were the telltale signs of the mixed blood that coursed strong and hot in her veins. A wave of jealousy washed over her as she bit her lower lip. The taste of blood, rusty and metallic, filled her mouth and she swallowed hard.

Dr. Duplessis entered the small waiting room. "Ms. Foster?" he asked, quietly closing the door behind him.

"You didn't have to check on me," Natalia said as she continued staring out the window.

"I wanted to," he replied, handing her a box of Kleenex.

"That's very nice of you," she said. "I'm sure you have patients who need you more than I do. I appreciate you telling me about my—about Joe. I know you didn't have to and probably shouldn't have."

She managed a small smile. Joe would be in a better place soon. She hoped he'd already asked God to forgive him his sins: conceiving a child with a woman who was not his wife *while* he was married; not helping to raise that child; not claiming—or being allowed to claim—that child.

"I don't mean to pry, Ms. Foster, but how do you know Joe? He's been under my care for a couple of months, and I don't believe I've ever seen you."

"I don't know him—well, I didn't, but I wanted to," she said. "All my life, I thought about him. What he looked like. How he talked. How he walked. How he laughed. I'm his daughter."

"Aha," he said, slowly. "I see the resemblance now. I don't know how I missed it before. Joe's age and illness obscured it, but I definitely see it now."

"Please, don't tell anyone," she said. "They don't know about me."

"I promise," he said. "I'm so sorry. I wish I could do more to help."

"You've done more than you realize. I'm going to New Orleans," she said, nodding decisively.

"Well, I'll be checking on him through his family. If I hear anything, I can call you—if you like," he added quickly. "You are family, after all."

"Of course. I would like that very much." She scribbled her number on a small notepad he pulled from his pocket.

Buoyed by a morsel of hope, she felt lighter as she walked back to the elevators. She had a new plan.

Chapter 4

Rosa held the silver cross hanging from the delicate chain around her neck. Feeling the smooth metal had become a habit. She prayed and recited Psalms daily. She knew God could grant them a miracle. But as each day passed and Joe continued to decline, her hopes diminished.

The nurses were helping her sons gather his belongings so he could die comfortably at home. Catarine had already gone back to New Orleans to get their house ready for Joe's final weeks.

"I'll meet you downstairs," she said to no one in particular.

"Where are you going?" John asked. "We're almost done."

"I need to do something first. I just need a few minutes, and I'll meet you at the main entrance."

She couldn't bear to watch them lift Joe, frail and weak, and place him in that wheelchair. She couldn't bear to watch them gather his things—a Bible on the table next to his bed, his toiletries, his slippers, his robe. She couldn't bear the finality of any of it or what it meant. The doctors had done all they could do. Hope was tiptoeing away from her.

God can heal you, she thought as she walked toward the elevator. She stepped on, pressed the number one, and vaguely listened to the soft classical music—a strumming of harps and pressing of piano keys—until she heard the soft ding and the silver doors opened.

A young woman with dark, wild, curly hair and gray eyes stood before her, wringing her hands. Rosa was unable to move or breathe, arrested in a way she couldn't comprehend. It wasn't that she was surprised to see someone standing there. It was something else. A feeling of déjà vu. Knowing but not knowing.

She tried to collect her haphazard thoughts before she stepped forward, thrusting her arm out to stop the doors from closing. The young woman brushed past her, stepped inside, and quickly pressed the button. Rosa turned back and paused just in time to see the young woman nod and smile sadly before the doors closed.

Rosa inhaled the fragrance of lotus blossom and dewy lilac the girl left behind. There was something about her she couldn't shake. And she realized the girl reminded her of Joe. She had been looking into eyes just like his. Was the girl real or had she imagined her? Was she an angel? Was it a sign?

But a sign of what?

They were not supposed to leave the hospital this way. Joe slumped heavily in a wheelchair but weighed only a hundred and fifty pounds. He'd shopped at the Big & Tall since he was fourteen. His feet were so wide—a triple wide—he'd resorted to having his shoes custom made.

Rosa had imagined the two of them walking out of the hospital holding hands, Joe healed and cancer-free. Instead, John and Joe Jr. were gingerly placing their father into the back seat of his black Lincoln Town Car.

"Wait," she yelled as her sons lifted him.

26

The dark leather seats would be too hot. Joe wouldn't have the energy to sidle about in the seat, and she didn't want his delicate skin to feel any pain. She removed a folded blanket from the trunk, carried it like a newborn, and covered the seat from top to bottom.

She walked to the other side of the car and leaned against the door as she stared at a row of evenly dispersed shrubs across the paved driveway. The smell of wood from recently spread mulch drifted in the air.

"Come on, Mom. We have to get going." Joe Jr. gently pushed Rosa to the side and opened the back door, waiting several seconds before she slid into the back seat. Joe was already asleep from the daily medical cocktail—a pile of pills in bright colors.

"This is not at all what I imagined," Rosa said as she buckled her seat belt and double-checked Joe's to make sure it was secure.

"I know. It's not what any of us imagined," John replied.

"Catarine took care of everything?" Rosa asked as she began flipping through the pages in the blue folder one of the nurses had given her. The "plan of care" listed all the caregiving tasks Joe would need: instructions for medications, dosages, doctors' orders, and contact information for the home health care agency they'd chosen. The words dissolved into meaningless marks she couldn't bring herself to decipher.

"Yes, she should already be there waiting for us," Joe Jr. said.

She closed the folder. Her emotions vacillated from one extreme to the other. She relinquished all control and let them do as they willed. She inhaled deeply and dug her fingers into her palms as her anger rose up. She retrieved her Bible—brown and leather bound with HOLY BIBLE embossed in gold. She flipped through the worn pages, many of them with notes on the sides, and slipped the ribbon marker out, fiddling with the smooth, satiny fabric.

They were pulling into traffic, horns blaring, exhaust rising from an eighteen-wheeler just ahead.

John was turning the radio knob in search of a station they could all agree on—and a song that might lift their spirits—when she heard a snatch of Nat King Cole.

"Go back!" she demanded. Nat King Cole was singing "Smile."

She closed her eyes as his soft, silky baritone voice enveloped her. The strings and piano pulled her into a fluffy world where she thought of Joe's soul and took comfort knowing he would be in a better place soon.

With her hands settled on her Bible, Rosa closed her eyes and slept for nearly the entire drive—five hours full of fitful dreams that involved Joe. In them, she saw the girl from the hospital elevator running toward her. She was trying to tell her something, but though Rosa watched her lips moving, she couldn't hear a word. Soon, the girl was yelling. Rosa only knew this because her face was contorted and twisted, her mouth wide. But she still couldn't hear a word she said. Then she was shaking Joe, trying to wake him. His body moved easily from side to side in the small bed, but he wouldn't open his eyes. She was still shaking him when Joe Jr. turned into their neighborhood in Old Metairie.

She turned to look at Joe, his head leaning against the window. He was asleep but not peacefully. His labored breathing reminded Rosa of a wounded animal, his chest rising and falling, rising and falling. But at least he's still breathing, she thought. He's still alive.

She glanced at Joe Jr. He'd begun to drive slower and slower the closer they got to their neighborhood, filled with stately mansions.

Rosa knew he was admiring the manicured lawns, eyeing the luxury cars parked beneath porte cocheres, and relishing the exclusiveness. His chin tilted up and he smiled proudly as he waved at neighbors here and there. He acts like he's the mayor or something, Rosa thought as she rolled her eyes. She hoped he was also thinking about his father and postponing the inevitable: delivering Joe to his preliminary resting place.

She eyed their stucco home warily. Having been away for several weeks, she expected the place to look different—run-down, unattended—the way she felt. But the hedges were trimmed, the grass mowed, the blinds open. Life appeared to go on as it had before. No one would look at their home and see the pain and suffering of its inhabitants. On the surface, it was splendid.

Before they reached the front door, Catarine opened it, and she stepped aside to let them in. Rosa waited on the front porch as Joe Jr. escorted his father in, practically carrying him—his right arm holding Joe securely around his waist, Joe's left arm dangling around his son's neck.

They hobbled slowly, like infantrymen leaving the battlefield, past the spiral staircase, through an arched doorway, past their den, and into a guest bedroom on the main floor.

Thanks to Catarine and the home health service, the room had been transformed into a hospital retreat. Oxygen equipment. A shower bench, convertible commode, and foam risers in the adjoining bathroom. Extra pillows on the hospital bed. Throw rugs removed. Practically childproof, Rosa thought. She hoped Joe could move around for a while before he was confined to his bed.

Rosa knew he would be more comfortable now. He would much rather look at these soft blue walls, with their metal and wood crosses, and these windows adorned with silk drapes puddling on Berber carpet.

"Maybe we should sit outside later this evening when it cools off a bit. I bet Joe would like some fresh air," she said to no one in particular.

Joe had always enjoyed their lushly landscaped backyard, a scene of serenity with its cascading fountain, magnolia trees, Mary garden, and view of the golf course. Wrought iron patio furniture with deep cushions surrounded the turquoise ripples of an in-ground saltwater pool.

Rosa had spent years tending to yellow lantana, globe amaranth, gardenias, and star jasmine so her family could enjoy the intoxicating aromas. She wondered if Joe could still identify their scents.

As heavily medicated as he was, she wasn't sure if he even realized he was now home—but then, there it was. A moment of recognition, a brief glimmer in his still beautiful eyes—a lighthouse beam directed right at her—followed by a thin smile. Her heart warmed as she held his hand and helped him into bed with Joe Jr.'s help.

"Did you see that?" she asked almost excitedly.

"See what?" Joe Jr.'s brow seemed to be permanently furrowed these days. His face was a reflection of his anger at God, his defeat, his lack of control.

"He smiled! He knows he's home!"

Joe Jr. nodded somberly, leaving his mother to tend to Joe's demise.

Rosa wanted to save Joe. To hear his laugh again—that deep chuckle that was always waiting to come out. To see his amazing smile—teeth so perfectly aligned, his dentist had been jealous. To feel the security of his strong arms around her. To run her hands through his now completely gray—but still thick and wavy—mass of hair. To look into his beautiful gray eyes. Eyes that he would soon never open again. How would she continue living without Joe?

His decline had been so rapid, she'd had little time to prepare herself and accept it. As she watched him sleeping now, a mere shadow of the man she adored, she knew he would soon be relieved of his suffering. While hers continued.

Chapter 5

As she threw clothes in her suitcase, Natalia thought about what she would say at work. She had no idea how long she would need or how flexible her boss would be.

The thought of taking time off from work triggered sharp, nauseating jabs in her gut. She'd been hired as Shelly's assistant designer at D&D Group after she finished her MFA in interior design. She knew from the start that she'd landed her dream job. Her career counselor's words echoed in her mind: "Do what you love. Something you have a natural talent for. Something you would do for free. If you follow your passion, the money will eventually follow you."

Shelly was one of the most enthusiastic people Natalia had ever worked with. As the team lead, she'd built a name for herself not only within the design firm but also within the industry. Under her wing, Natalia's talents and her confidence blossomed.

"You're a natural with colors, fabrics, and textiles," Shelly had said after her first couple of weeks. "And you have a great eye for spatial arrangements."

Natalia absorbed as much as she could, adopting the senior partners' terminology ("creating contrast," "functionality of the space," "better balance") and mannerisms (talking with your hands was a necessity), along with working long hours (no one left the office before six).

She accompanied Shelly on meetings with architects, structural engineers, builders, and clients. She listened closely and asked smart questions to understand their goals and how the space would be used. With ideas already churning, she would begin sketching out her concepts. Reading blueprints became second nature, the intricate lines, symbols, and abbreviations leading to a vision she would help bring to life.

She'd worked hard to gain her bosses' respect and admiration, and she was working toward her second promotion. During her five years with the firm, she'd never asked for more than a couple of days off.

"Hi, Shelly. How are you?" she asked, gripping her cell phone tightly.

"Good, good! You're calling me? This is a surprise. Is everything okay?"

"Well, no it's not," Natalia replied. "I have a family emergency and need to head out of town right away."

"What's going on? Can you talk about it? I totally understand if it's too personal."

"Well, my dad—my *real* dad—has cancer. It's terminal."

"Oh, Natalia. I'm so sorry to hear that. Please do whatever you need to do and take as much time as you need. Is he in New Orleans, like your mom?"

"He is, and I'm packing so I can head there now," she said.

While Shelly knew a lot about her, she had no idea that Natalia was the illegitimate, one-sided-love child of a married Italian man. She'd always referred to her stepfather as her dad for simplicity. She'd have to clear that up later.

"Please be careful, and let me know if you need anything," Shelly said. "We'll call your cell if anything urgent comes up."

Natalia arrived later than she planned, but early enough to see in the graying light that not much had changed since her last visit eight months ago. The white two-story house had seen better days, but it was well-built, having endured Mother Nature's hurricanes and floods since the fifties. A fresh coat of paint wouldn't hurt. But the house wouldn't seem so worn if not for the string of old cars badly in need of repairs parked in the driveway and on the street. Rust, missing tires, dents. All relics of her stepfather and a reflection of his country upbringing. This was perfectly acceptable in his narrow mind.

Though conflicting, the yard offered some saving grace. Her mother recently had planted periwinkles, marigolds, and zinnias. Vibrant and showy, shades of blues, yellows, and oranges were a welcome distraction from the surrounding jumble.

She was halfway up the black, rusted iron stairs, struggling with her suitcase, when her stepfather called her name.

"Hey," she called back as she turned to see him standing on the crooked concrete walkway. His eyes begged the question, "What are you doing here?" He folded his arms as he stared up at her.

She was sure her mother hadn't said a word about Joe or why she was visiting on a weekday.

"I . . . I needed a break from work," she called over her shoulder. When she reached the porch, she dropped her suitcase and pressed the doorbell, its plastic, dingy cover cracked.

Her mother flung the door open. In her excitement she rushed past the screen door, bringing along a strong whiff of that evening's dinner—it smelled like fried catfish, yams, green beans, and cornbread—along with the booms of a gospel choir. The bass reverberated off the large windows and dark wood floors.

On any given day, the house was full of people, most of whom did not live there. Cousins. Aunts. Uncles. Siblings. Grandbabies. Former inmates. They were hungry folks, always looking for a good home-cooked meal and a comfortable spot on a couch after they'd gorged themselves. They knew exactly where to find both. They also knew to bring their own adult beverages, 40s in paper bags waiting in gleaming cars with rims or disguised in 7-Eleven Big Gulp cups if they were bold enough to bring them inside.

They made their way into the kitchen, where her mother simply seemed to belong. Having everything she needed—a small television that stayed tuned to Fox News or the 700 Club, comfortable chairs surrounding a large, white, worn country table, and, of course, food.

Her stepdad detoured down the hall and disappeared—his usual mode of action. The extent of their communication had ended when Natalia walked through the front door.

She watched her mother maneuver around the kitchen—back and forth from the stove, to the sink, to the fridge, and back to the stove. She was still tall and graceful with beautiful amber skin, big brown eyes, and high cheekbones. Natalia could see why her dad had fallen so hard for her. She'd only wished her mother had felt the same way.

But she could also see the sadness in her mother's stance. The slight downward tilt of her head. The slump in her shoulders. The distracted way she moved about the kitchen, clattering pots and pans, shifting them from one place to another unnecessarily, it seemed.

"I'm happy to see you, but you know, you really shouldn't have come, honey," her mother said matter-of-factly.

How could her mom possibly understand how she felt? Her only concern was her dad. She had to see him—hold his hand, touch his face, tell him she loved him—before it was too late.

"Well, I'm going to see him while I'm here. What are you cooking?" she asked, hoping to change the conversation.

"What do you think his wife and children will say when they see you?" her mother whispered. "And do you think you just gonna drive up to his fancy house?"

She hadn't thought that through. She figured she'd come up with a way. "I don't know. I'll just say we used to work together or something." She grabbed dishes and silverware to set the table.

"Natalia, you look just like him!" her mother said, her voice still hushed. "How many times do I have to tell you this?"

"That could just be coincidence. He's not the only person in the world with gray eyes. And I'm not sure any of this matters now. He's dying. Don't you think he'd want to see me?"

The question was a plea—a cry for justification. She could see her mother mulling it over.

"I'm sure he would want nothing more than to see how beautiful and smart you turned out to be," her mother said, smiling wistfully. She was quiet for a while, holding a wooden spoon in midair.

"I was just thinking about the day you were born," her mother said. "At raggedy Charity Hospital." Natalia could see her mother had transported herself back in time twenty-eight years ago. The bittersweet memory brought tears to both of their eyes.

Natalia could picture it so easily. Massive, tall, and jutting into the sky, Charity was a shabby state-run hospital. Though the structure had begun to lean ever so slightly to the north, everyone was told it was still safe. And even if it wasn't, if you were poor and black, you had no other options. Besides, with a constant influx of patients, the doctors were known to be the best.

Natalia laughed softly. "Yeah, Grandma used to say, 'If you ever get shot or stabbed, make sure they take you to Charity.' I don't know why she thought I might end up shot. I always thought she was psychic and had a glimpse into my future."

"Well, the doctors are more than capable. They get their share of experience."

"What was it like having a baby there?" Natalia had heard snippets of her birth story over the years, but she got the feeling her mother didn't like rewinding her memory that far back. Or maybe the day was torn between happiness and sadness.

Her mother finished a bite of her cookie before she closed her eyes and began. "The bed was very hard and narrow. I guess they didn't want us to be too comfortable or we wouldn't be able to push those babies out fast enough. They needed to make room for other deliveries. There were at least twenty other beds in that room—it was so loud and so crowded. I wondered if white women had their babies that way, like cattle herded into a pen. It was nothin' but black women in there, you know.

"One minute the nurse was checking on me, and I was just fine. I didn't think I was ready to deliver yet, but she said I was very close. I kept waiting for the pains to start and the contractions to grip me when all of a sudden, I felt water gushing beneath me and the urge to push.

"I yelled after that nurse, 'My baby's coming!' I was trying to sit up when one of the doctors came by my bed. He looked like I'd just told him the sky was orange. I thought maybe he didn't hear me, so I told him again. He walked down to the foot of my bed, lifted the sheet, and said: 'Well, I'll be damned.'"

Natalia laughed softly as she imagined the look on the doctor's face.

"I delivered you without a single pain. The doctors and nurses couldn't believe it. Said they'd never seen anything like it. I watched them clean you up while the doctor was writing on his clipboard. He looked down at you when they were all done and said, 'This baby looks mighty white.' I asked him to repeat what he said, but he just ignored me.

"When I held you in my arms, of course I noticed how light your skin was right away. That doctor was right. I checked your ears, and they were just as pale as the rest of you. You barely had any hair. Just a layer of thin, smooth strands. And when you opened your eyes, I gasped. I was shocked. I assumed my genes would be dominant. I couldn't believe how much you looked like Joe—and how little you looked like me. He came to the hospital right away, by the way, and he held you for such a long time. I can still see the look on his face. Nothing but love—pure love."

"Why didn't you stay with him?" Natalia asked. She pictured the three of them, a happy family in that hospital room.

"I tried for a couple of years at least. He was such good a man—except for the married part. Such a provider."

Natalia cringed when her mother said "married." Her mother didn't notice and continued, lost in her reverie.

"He loved you so much. You had everything a toddler could ever want. Socks trimmed in lace and ruffles. Satin hair bands. Rattles and stuffed animals. A swing. A rocking horse that you were deathly afraid of. His love for you suspended me in this imaginary world, this illusion of a life. But I knew it could only be temporary. I—we—were living in the shadows of his real life. Back in those days, mixed couples were frowned upon. I didn't see how we could be together. Plus, I wanted more than that. I wanted a soft, silvery love. I wanted to feel those tingles. I wanted a smile spreading across my lips whenever I thought of that person."

"And you found that with James?" Natalia asked, incredulous. A man who harbored hate in his heart and jealousy in his joints but claimed to be a Christian. A man who ridiculed her when, at the age of twelve, she announced she wanted to go to college. "You think you belong in the white house?" he'd sneered. A man who pitted her half-sister and half-brother against her, creating a hateful divide based on skin tone. He'd led the rest of the family to believe Natalia thought she was better than they were because she was a "redbone."

"I met James at a house party. He had this country accent and smelled of musky cologne. His hands were calloused—the hands of a working man. There was just somethin' about him. My heart was beating a thousand miles a minute as we talked. I started spending more time with him and less time with Joe. I felt like I could be all his and he could be all mine. We could be in public without condemnation or stares.

"But what changed everything was when he invited me to go to church with him. I hadn't thought about church or God since I was a child. I remember I was biting my nails in his car on our way there.

"Every time I thought I had a man figured out, he sprung somethin' on me. First a wife. Then God. Yet when I walked through the doors of that small church, I felt like I could breathe easier. That choir sang like their lives depended on those notes. By the end of the sermon, I was standing at that altar with tears streaming down my face. When we left, I felt like a new woman. I was born again and felt I couldn't live a life of sin no more. I knew I had to tell Joe."

Natalia didn't want to hear the rest of this story. She didn't want the details of how her mother had crushed her father's heart and severed his connection to his own child. She'd heard this part of the story and knew her dad had pleaded with her mother for the three of them to move to Mexico.

"Well, you know the rest," her mother said, her eyes weary with the weight of these decisions and their consequences.

"Cancún, Cozumel . . . but we couldn't just run away. Living on a beach wasn't going to make us happy. I couldn't let him leave his wife and kids. I couldn't be responsible for that."

"Momma, you just didn't love him the way he loved you," Natalia said accusingly.

"I knew he would get over me. But losing you—that was more than he could bear."

Natalia imagined her father's sadness. His gray eyes muted, flat caverns of steel.

"Why did you let James control your life like that? Why did you let him decide there was no place for Joe in *my* life?"

Her mother's face turned two shades darker as she bowed her head and folded her arms. When she looked back up at Natalia, her eyes were two tunnels of wisdom: full of the benefit of hindsight.

"I didn't know that the real reason he didn't want Joe around was because he was jealous. He thought Joe and me would continue to have some kind of relationship. When I got pregnant with your sister, he said he just wanted us to have our own lives— and to let Joe go on with his. I was in this strange place."

"Did you ever tell Joe this? Or did we just disappear?"

"Oh no. I told him. At the time you were almost three years old. I remember it so clearly. You were wearing a red poufy dress and your curls were springing out of two ponytails. You were walking with your arms kind of stretched out." Her mother demonstrated, prancing carefully around the kitchen on her tiptoes.

Natalia smiled sadly as she braced herself for the painful ending. She shifted her weight in the wooden chair and took a sip of her room-temperature milk.

"I figured it would be easier if I did it in a public place. He was so happy to see you. It hurt me to look at him. To see how much he missed you. He scooped you up and spun you around, then held you tightly, kissing the top of your head. Then he noticed my stomach. I was three or four months along. So, I told him we had to move on. Live our own separate lives. I told him James would raise you. Apparently, James had already gone by the store, and that didn't go over well."

"James went there and didn't tell you?" So much for being open and having a trusting relationship.

"Oh, Joe was angry. I'd never seen him that upset before. His face was red, veins were popping out of his neck. He couldn't understand how I could just take you away from him. He didn't care about me at that point. It was all about you. When I pulled you away from him . . ." Her mother paused as she searched for the words. "I—I pulled you away from him, and he grabbed me as I was walking away. Turned me around real rough. And he whispered in my ear—real harsh, 'You know damned well this is wrong. But I'll let your God deal with you.' His words have haunted me all these years."

Natalia's stomach lurched involuntarily. "It was wrong. You were wrong. James was wrong. You were all wrong." Natalia's jaw was tight. "You were all wrong."

Chapter 6

The sounds and smells of Saturday morning filled the house: blaring cartoons, clanging pots and pans, sizzling bacon, and brewing coffee.

Natalia wasn't surprised to find her mother standing at the stove. With its dingy white linoleum floors, white metal cabinets, and once-ruby-now-salmon countertops, the kitchen was mostly as it had been originally in the fifties. The oven door whined as her mother opened it, grabbed her oven mitt, and pulled out a cookie sheet of baked biscuits.

"You need help?" Natalia asked.

"Oh, no. You know I'm used to this," her mother answered as she poured grits into a boiling pot of water. "You want some?"

"Nah, I think I'll just have some bacon, eggs, and toast."

"You need some meat on your bones, child," her mother reminded her, as if she were anorexic.

"Ma, I'm a healthy weight!" she exclaimed. "A hundred and thirty-five pounds, to be exact!"

"Well, you just look so thin. I think you work out too much, and you don't eat enough. You need to eat some of these grits."

Natalia laughed for the first time in three days. "Fine, if it'll make you happy, I'll have some grits!" She kissed her mother's cheek and gave her a quick hug.

She was in the middle of her second bite when her mother asked what she was going to do. Her two nieces and nephew had planted themselves at the kids' table in the corner and were quickly shoveling food in their mouths to get back to their cartoons. Her stepdad had already gone into the auto mechanic shop to pick up extra hours.

"What am I going to do about what?" She noticed a large area behind her mother's chair where the paint was peeling off the wall. The chair had rubbed it away after so many years, the surface beneath it smooth and drab.

"Seeing Joe." Her mother peered over her eyeglasses. "What are you trying to prove? It's too late."

"I'm not trying to prove anything. I just have this feeling that he wants to see me—that he's thinking about me. And I have just as much right to be at his funeral as his other children. But I want to see him while he's *alive*."

"But have you thought about what they'll think when they see you? What will you say? What will you tell his wife?" She took a bite of her scrambled eggs.

Natalia hadn't thought beyond seeing him. She needed to get to that moment—one that she thought would be the most important of her life. Nothing else would matter after that.

"You don't realize how much you resemble him. They will know that you're related—your eyes, your hair, your skin. You're the spitting image of him—just a darker version."

Natalia wasn't sure she agreed. After all, people often said she looked like her mother.

"If they know about you, it will change how they see Joe," her mother continued. "Sometimes, you have to do what's best for the majority—not for yourself."

"I think they'll have to accept that he was human, just like the rest of us," Natalia responded as she examined her nails.

Her mother shook her head, and Natalia knew what that meant. "You're as stubborn as he was. I think you should pray about it and ask the Lord to guide you."

Natalia dug her fork into the grits on her plate. They were already cold and stiff. She finished them anyway, then washed the dishes and retreated to her room. She decided to call Pamela. Her best friend would know what to do.

"Hey girl," she said.

"Heeey! You doing okay? I was wondering when you were going to call!"

"Not really. I'm so confused, stressed, sad. I'm everything right now. I need your advice." She explained her dilemma, talking quickly. "I'm just really torn. Something is telling me I should go see him at his home, but my mom is so against it."

"Well, there could be a lot of drama if you go," Pamela said quietly.

"I guess so. Would you go?"

"Hmmmm, I don't know. I'm trying to put myself in your shoes, and it's hard. I mean, you're sad because he's going to die soon, but you would be even sadder if you never even had a chance to meet him. You've always been on the outskirts of his life. You've always been on this perimeter. You want to be let in somehow, but you don't want to force your way. You'd rather be welcomed or asked to come in."

Pamela had always had the gift of empathy and knowing exactly what to say. Sometimes Natalia wasn't sure how Pamela related to her crazy life. She'd grown up in a loving and normal family, one quite similar to the Huxtables from TV, with a few minor revisions. Her mother was a doctor and her dad was a lawyer. Her brother was quite a specimen and ended up getting drafted into the NFL. Her older sister, who could have easily been a model, was finishing her last year of medical school. Pamela, who always followed her own path, taught fifth graders during the day and pursued her singing career at night and on the weekends. She was on the verge of getting a break as a backup singer for an up-and-coming R&B group. Her brother knew somebody who knew somebody.

Natalia had spent a good part of her teen years hanging out in their comfortable home. She and Pamela had been roommates in college and moved to Houston after graduating.

"You're exactly right. I don't want to barge in and create a scene. Maybe I'll just go to the visitation and figure out some other way to get to know who he was."

"I think you should go to his home first. What do you have to lose?" Pamela's raspy voice was deep with conviction. "Hell, I'll go with you. They'll either cuss us out and make us leave or invite us inside. Do you want me to come down there and go with you?"

"Oh, you don't have to do that."

"Well, I wouldn't mind," she said. "I can take a couple of days off next week and drive down tomorrow morning."

"My stomach is in knots," Natalia said as they drove up I-10 toward Metairie with Q93.3 on the radio.

"Don't worry. You'll either be able to see him, or we'll get our asses kicked," Pamela giggled.

Natalia thought back to when she and Pamela first met. They had both just started junior high and were stuck with Mr. Mahafeny for science. Rumors proclaimed him to be a pervert. In fact, he bore an uncanny resemblance to a man who had exposed himself to Natalia one day when she was walking home from school in the fifth grade. Terrified, she'd practically run home, looking over her shoulder every two seconds. She never told a soul until she met Pamela. When Mr. Mahafeny introduced himself to the class, she and Pamela glanced at each other. Pamela's expression said it all: *He seems like a real weirdo.* Natalia couldn't resist smiling, then laughing. They were joined at the hip after that.

"Okay, turn left here," Natalia said as they entered his neighborhood.

They drove below an arc of magnificent oak trees with twinkles of sunlight and blue sky peeking through the clusters of leaves. Shamrock-green lawns led to layers of flowers and hedges and expansive porches—some wraparound—and two-story brick and stucco mansions.

"Dang, it's nice over here. You didn't tell me he had money like this."

"Girl, like I would know. Okay, turn right here," she instructed, following the GPS. "This is their street. The address is 30."

Pamela guided her Honda Accord slowly up the street as they approached a two-story stucco home with clay roof tiles. A large, carpet-like lawn led to a front porch that extended along the width of the house. The double, dark wood doors looked heavy and ominous.

"Very nice house," Pamela said as she parked in front.

"Yeah, very," Natalia said, sitting still as a statue. She inhaled deeply and turned to Pamela. "I don't think I can do this. It feels so intrusive. My God—he's probably asleep." Seeing fear skitter across Pamela's eyes, she added, "You don't seem so sure either."

As she began wringing her hands, Pamela gasped.

"What is it?" She followed Pamela's gaze toward the house. A man was outside on the porch looking at them.

"Oh my God. What should we do?"

Before Pamela could answer or put the key back in the ignition to drive off, he barged off the porch and marched up until he was standing at the window staring at Natalia.

With her chest constricted and panic taking over, Natalia stared back at him wide-eyed. He was probably twenty years older than she was. Dark brown hair, dark brown eyes. About six feet tall with a slender build.

"Shit. Girl—what do you want me to do? Should we leave?" Pamela asked.

His rap on the window brought Natalia back to their imminent danger.

"Do you want me to put the window down?" Pamela asked.

"Oh God, help me. I'll just get out." She felt like she was in a slow-motion movie scene as she pulled on the door handle. Rising to her feet, she held on to the top of the open door for support. She felt her knees go weak, like her joints were collapsing. Stepping back, the man looked at her, from her hair and face all the way down to her feet.

"I know who you are." He spat out the words as if he had a mouth full of flies.

"You do?" She was incredulous, trying to brush off his clear disdain and hoping that he had her mixed up with some other person.

"Yes. Natalia." He said her name as though she had given Joe this terminal disease. As if it were all her fault.

Several seconds of uncomfortable silence followed. Her heart racing, she whispered, her voice trembling, "You know about me?"

"What do you think you're doing here?" he snarled, ignoring her question.

Ninety degrees of humid heat surrounded them. But when a hot breeze rustled the trees, she felt a chill.

46

"I . . . my mother told me about—that he's . . . he's dying. I would really like to meet him." She released the words as though they were a plea. A cry for help.

"That's not going to happen." He shook his head.

Squinting at him and feeling anger rise up to replace her fear, she asked, "I'm sorry, but who are you?"

"It's really not your business, but I'm his son."

"Why are you so angry?"

He laughed then. A haughty but fake chuckle. "Did you think you could just walk into my parents' home like this? That you could just introduce yourself and destroy my mother in the process? If my father wanted her to know about you and your whore of a mother, he would have told her. If he wanted my sister and brother to know about you, he would have told them."

She wasn't sure how to respond. So much information and so dismissive at the same time. Did he just call her mother a whore?

When Pamela opened her car door, they both turned in surprise. "Look, she just wants to meet him while he's still alive," she said over the top of the car. "She's not trying to cause any trouble. Wouldn't you want to meet your real father if you had never met him?"

"It's not happening." He spoke the words as if Pamela were a three-year-old who lacked understanding. Then, flicking his eyes back to Natalia, his lips downturned, he said, "You need to go back to your own little life. As far as we're concerned, you don't exist."

"Can you believe this motherfucker?" Pamela asked, speaking to the air around her as she made a 360-degree turn.

Natalia knew where things would head soon if she didn't get Pamela back in the car. "Okay, let's just go." She turned and stepped behind the car door.

"We don't *have* to go anywhere," Pamela said, looking at Joe's son with venom in her eyes. She was still standing on the driver's side. "Why would you deny her this? You're either a major asshole or a racist son of a bitch."

"Oh, damn," Natalia muttered.

"Or, maybe I'm both," he replied. As he turned to walk away, he tossed his final words over his right shoulder. "Stay the hell away from here."

"You'll be sorry, asshole," Pamela yelled as she thrust herself back in the driver's seat and slammed the door.

Natalia lowered back into the passenger seat. As she reached for the handle to close the door, she saw a woman dressed in white, standing in the window, staring at her. Their eyes locked for several seconds before Pamela sped off, the tires squealing in protest. A feeling of déjà vu rushed over her, replacing her anger with fear.

Chapter 7

Rosa stood near the window of their living room staring through the sheer white curtains that separated heavy gold-toned draperies on either side. She watched a small blue car speed away. She tried to get a glimpse of the passengers, but the windows were tinted and the afternoon sun beamed down like a spotlight. Joe Jr. stomped back toward the front doors, swinging the left side open with so much force it slammed against the wall.

"What was that all about?" she asked.

"Nothing, Mom. Nothing you need to be worried about." He stormed down the hallway through the kitchen and slammed the back door.

Before Rosa could make it to the kitchen, the stale, sweet smell of cigarette smoke infiltrated her nose as it traveled from the patio through the partially open kitchen window. She opened the patio door and shut it softly behind her. The sun bounced on the faded blue surface of the pool—yet another decaying relic of their lives—as a hot breeze wafted around, stirring leaves of the hundred-year-old oak tree and rattling the wax myrtle bushes that lined the cedar fence.

Trouble and torment had a way of taking thoughts hostage. She observed her son from the corner of her eyes as he rubbed his balding head.

"Who was that? Why were they here? What did they want?" A panic she couldn't explain crawled over her.

"I don't know. They were lost—two black girls definitely in the wrong neighborhood. I tried to redirect them." He took a long drag on his cigarette.

"One of them looked familiar," Rosa said as she dug through her many memories.

"All of those black girls sort of look alike. Just varying shades of brown and black." He took another drag before leaning forward to snuff out the cigarette on the concrete patio. "You've seen one, you've seen them all."

"Don't lie to me," she said, her arms folded. "I know when you're lying."

"Mom, why would I know two black girls? Just get back to your cooking. Everything's fine. They know where they need to go now."

Chapter 8

Natalia clenched her jaw. She was sitting on the back porch, rocking vigorously in an old wooden chair. The floorboards creaked beneath her as she pushed her feet and body back and forth. She could not believe the venom, the callousness that emanated from Joe's son—her half-brother. She tried to steady her breathing, but it continued to come rapidly, her heart pumping like a fist.

Who did he think he was? Did he think he could tell her where to go and where not to go? What to do and not to do?

She and Pamela had agreed she would do whatever the hell she wanted to. He would never decide her fate or her future. But they wondered if the entire family was as hateful as he was.

When her phone rang, she jumped. Where was the damned thing? She dug through her purse, which she'd thrown on the floor.

"Hello," she said, not recognizing the number.

"Natalia?" It was a deep male voice.

"Yes—who is this?"

"Natalia, this is David—Dr. Duplessis. Is this a good time?" His voice was smooth and deep as still waters. She forgot she'd written her number on his notepad.

She sat completely still on the edge of the rocking chair. "Uh, yes, yes of course."

"I'll FaceTime you, then?"

"Uh, of course."

A few seconds later she was looking at his face, his chest, and what appeared to be his office. She could see a bookshelf mostly filled with books but also stacks of papers and folders.

"I wanted to check on you, see how you were doing. Are you still in New Orleans?"

"Yes, I'm still here. But I'm not okay at all." She sighed as she leaned back against the chair.

"What's going on?" he asked, leaning closer in, his eyes soft and concerned.

As she explained the chaotic encounter with Joe Jr., she watched Dr. Duplessis nodding and listening closely. She wondered if he was really paying attention or if, as a doctor, he'd grown accustomed to pretense—automatic nodding of the head and sporadic "mm-hmms" while his mind was elsewhere.

"I just can't believe how hateful he was. How on earth could I be related to someone like that? And what does that say about Joe or the rest of the family, for that matter?"

"It doesn't surprise me," Dr. Duplessis said, leaning back and folding his arms. Natalia watched his biceps protrude and his veins bulge. "He questioned everything when I was treating Joe in a way that showed he doubted my abilities. The way he looked at me, out of the corner of his eye. Plus, he would interrupt me all the time. It got to the point where I asked him if he would prefer a different doctor. I wasn't going to stand there and let him disrespect me."

"And what did he say?" Natalia didn't blink for several seconds.

"He said, 'Well, they say you're the best.' And, I said, 'Then I need you to trust me. If you interrupt me again, you can find another doctor.' He kept his mouth shut after that. But I know he didn't like the idea of a black doctor treating his dad. I knew his type when I met him. He didn't want to shake my hand." His eyes were now dark as coals, anger simmering behind them.

"What an asshole." Natalia shook her head.

"Yeah, but I deal with that from time to time. You'd be surprised. We've come far but not far enough. I gotta keep it together in here, though. I've been trained to do that. The problem is, I didn't grow up that way, so it's extremely hard. A constant battle." He bit his bottom lip as if to tamp down the words that wanted to sprint out. He picked up a pen with his left hand and tapped it against his desk.

Natalia noticed he wasn't wearing a ring. She also wondered what he meant about "growing up that way."

"But enough about that. I could go on and on about the plight of black men in America, but that's not why I called you." He smiled, and a dimple appeared in his right cheek and lights glimmered in his eyes. She smiled in return, feeling her face warm and hoping her cheeks weren't as red as they felt.

"I just wanted to make sure you were doing okay, considering the circumstances. I haven't heard anything from the Russos, so I think it's just still a matter of time." He looked down and blinked rapidly. "Do you think you'll go to his wake or funeral?"

"After today, I think I should," she said.

He nodded gravely.

"Well, I'm here for you if you need anything," he said. "I mean it."

Natalia blushed again, thanked him, and said goodbye. She couldn't pinpoint exactly what she was feeling as she held her phone against her chest, but there was something promising and exciting about him. He wasn't like a lot of the men she'd wasted her time with.

Yes, there was something about Dr. Duplessis—a connection she couldn't explain, colorful threads intertwining to form a fabric of trust. She didn't have many men just calling to check on her, expressing concern about her well-being. But maybe that was just his nature, part of a doctor's duty. He was intriguing, caring, and quite good-looking, which meant he probably had a harem full of beauties and a couple of kids. A single black doctor with no kids. What were the chances? But she couldn't deny what she felt as they talked and looked into each other's eyes—as if the two of them had been enclosed by a cozy cocoon pulsating with a life of its own. At some point, they would emerge transformed, but into what, she couldn't be sure.

The sun was in its highest position in the sky, beaming its rays across the city and directly onto Natalia's face as she sat with her mother on the front porch swing, being nosy neighbors. People watching was so underrated.

I'm not sure how much longer I should stay, she thought. I need to get back to work. She despised this feeling; sitting around waiting for someone to die was more than morbid. She was an evil villain in a poorly constructed play as she selfishly felt the nudge of her real life expecting her back. She kept her phone close by, hoping for an update any minute. Dr. Duplessis had said he would call if he heard anything, which she immediately understood to mean when Joe was gone for good.

The phone rang, and she picked up right away. When she saw Dr. Duplessis's face, she knew.

"I'm so sorry, Natalia," he said. Catarine had called him just a few minutes earlier. "I wanted you to know right away."

Her body and mind were numb as if imbued with Novocain. She could only nod in response.

The next day, her mother handed her a newspaper clipping. "Here, I thought you might want to keep this." It was Joe's obituary from *The Times-Picayune*.

RUSSO

Joel Theo Russo at his home on Monday, August 12, at 12:30 P.M. Son of the late Thomas J. and Greta Landry Russo. Beloved husband of Rosa Aucoin Russo. Father of Joel L. Russo Jr., Catarine A. and John M. Russo. Grandfather of Elena and Gabriela Russo. Age 68. A native of New Orleans and a resident of Metairie, LA, for the past 45 years.

Relatives and friends of the family, also employees of J&J's Supermarket, are invited to attend the funeral mass from the Metairie Funeral Home of Lamana-Panno-Fallo, 1717 Veterans Memorial Blvd. at Bonnabel Blvd., on Wednesday, August 14, at 11:00 A.M. Followed by Interment in Greenwood Cemetery. Visitation on Tuesday evening from 6:00 P.M. until 10:00 P.M. and again on Wednesday morning after 9:00 A.M.

Now she knew five new things about her real dad: his parents' names, his children's names, his grandchildren's names, how long he had lived in New Orleans, and where he had worked. But this information was just a tease—crumbs dropped into an empty stomach. She was ravenous for more. She realized that she wanted to know everything. By knowing him, she couldn't help feeling, she might also know herself.

Chapter 9

Rosa sat in a conference room at Lamana, Panno and Fallo Funeral Home as she and Catarine waited patiently for Joe Jr. and John to return. She knew she'd lost a lot of weight, but she felt even more diminutive and weak in the oversize leather chair. She could barely maneuver it toward the glossy, cherry-wood table.

"Mom, can I get you something to drink? Water? Tea?" Catarine walked toward a tray set on a credenza in the back of the room stocked with bottled water, teas, and sodas. She grabbed a Diet Coke and cracked it open, the pop piercing the eerie silence in the room.

Rosa shook her head from left to right.

"How are you holding up?" Catarine placed her soda on a coaster on the table, sat down next to her mother, and began to rub her back.

"I don't know, honey. It's like I'm living in a fog right now. Like I'm floating away."

"I know. We can't believe he's gone. He just seemed so full of life. Then all of a sudden."

Rosa blinked rapidly. Her tears were infinite and perpetual, ready to fall at any moment.

"I keep—I keep thinking about something. It's nagging at me."

Before she could continue, Joe Jr. and John entered the room with the funeral director. She attempted to stand to greet them, but they motioned for her to stay seated. They were ready to discuss Joe's funeral—a wake, mass, and committal. Rosa let Joe Jr. take charge as usual. She simply didn't have the strength. Their words hovered above her like soft fuzz blown from dandelions. She didn't catch any of them.

With her hands clasped in her lap, she stared beyond the floor-to-ceiling window at a lake in the distance. A chill traveled through her body, raising goose bumps on her skin. She shuddered. For several days, she had been disturbed by Joe's final words.

Though his speech was slurred, she knew he had been trying to tell her something as he bolted upright like a suddenly revved motor. His eyes were wide and tormented when he flopped back like a rag doll. Storm tossed, she thought, as she perched above him. She sensed whatever he was trying to say was something deep and dark.

Since his death, she'd been trying to string together the words and decipher the meaning. She'd heard labored, barely audible breaths infused with sound, but not much enunciation.

"Saaaweee."

"Tell huuuuu sawreeee. Leee. Naaaaa. Naaaatteeee."

He was apologizing for something. But what?

"Wuuuv. Aaaways. Leeeees. Wuuuv."

"Saaaweee."

His doctor had said that patients sometimes hallucinated in their final weeks and hours, and the words could have meant nothing. But Rosa thought otherwise.

With their children around her, she had held both of his hands in hers, squeezing them tightly as if she could transfer strength into his frail body and somehow prevent the inevitable. She listened in horror to his final, rattling breaths. His eyes opened, bright like fireflies, staring in wonder at something only he could see. He didn't fight. He didn't struggle. When he closed them, a faint smile spread across his lips. Joe was gone.

The finality of this last gesture sent a shiver down her spine. She released Joe's hands and laid her head on his chest. Nothing. No heartbeat. No blood circulating. No laborious up-and-down inhaling and exhaling like the swell of ocean waters. Only stillness and complete silence broken by their children's cries. She kissed his face over and over while his body was still warm. Had he risen above his body to look down at them?

The four of them walked back to the parking lot of the funeral home, thinking of Joe.

Joe Jr. held open the car door and held Rosa's arm as she gingerly placed herself in the passenger seat.

"What do you think Joe was trying to say?" she asked after he'd started the car. There had been a vehemence behind Joe's words not previously associated with any other words he'd tried to utter. He'd used all of his strength to force them out. After that, he hadn't said anything else. She'd hoped he would offer some clarity, but she knew he couldn't.

"I'm not sure," he muttered, adding, "I think the doctor was right. He was just confused. I bet it was brought on by the meds."

"Well, I don't think it was," Rosa said. "I know he was trying to tell us something. He was apologizing for something. I think he was saying other people's names."

Years of insecurity and suspicion began to resurface. She thought she knew Joe. All of the years they'd spent together. Eating dinners. Sharing a bed. Laughing. Crying. What did it all mean? She only knew what Joe wanted her to know. Maybe she'd never been exposed to the deepest chamber of his heart, where something was hidden, undisturbed for years.

"Well, I don't know about that," Joe Jr. said. He sounded like he wanted to create doubt in his mother's mind, but Rosa thought he must know that Joe was deeply remorseful.

She stared out the car window for the rest of the ride—a blur of life passing her by—as she rewound Joe's words over and over again.

Then something was revealed in her mind, like the hinge of a clam had opened, not to reveal a pearl but rather its dark, pasty lining and mushy, spoiled organs. One night she had been cooking dinner when their phone rang. Her hands covered in ground beef grease, she'd yelled for Joe to answer. All that week, someone had been calling and hanging up whenever she said hello. "Probably just some teenagers making prank calls," Joe had said when she complained about it and threatened to unplug the phone.

She watched him pick up the receiver and say "Russo residence" in his I'm-messing-around playful way. Then his face fell. She watched him leave the room and walk down the hallway toward his study. When he didn't return for several minutes, she became concerned. He was facing the window and speaking in a hushed tone when she opened the door. Before she could ask if something was wrong, she heard him say, "You can't call here."

"Joe, what's going on?" she'd asked.

"I have to go. We'll talk later." He pressed the Off button of the receiver.

"It's nothing," he said dismissively.

"Who was that?" It was more of a demand than a question.

"I told you, it's nothing. Nothing you need to be concerned about."

But she had been concerned. And now she had a feeling that conversation—whoever he'd been talking to that day—had something to do with his final words. The feeling clung to her like cobwebs—abandoned and dusty, beckoning to be removed.

Chapter 10

Planning Joe's funeral was the one of the most torturous experiences of Rosa's life—second only to watching him take his last breath. Death was not the end. It was the beginning of grief and difficult decisions. What would he wear? Who would be his pallbearers? Which photos did they want to include in the program?

The photos. This would be the most painful part of it all. Printed proof that he had been here—that he did exist. That they'd enjoyed a good life together.

She retrieved several boxes from the hallway closet, carrying them one by one to the old oak coffee table in the den. The weight of each and the back-and-forth trips left her heart racing and her breathing shallow as she sat on the edge of the couch to catch her breath. She'd been tasked with summing up Joe's life in just ten images.

She lifted the lid of the first box—purple with red roses splattered all over it—full of photos tucked in neat stacks of Walgreen's photo envelopes. These would be recent as she hadn't created new albums in several years. She placed the lid back on the box and pushed it aside.

The next box, pink with black-and-white stripes, was the one she was looking for. It reflected their early years in numerically ordered albums arranged chronologically: 1970s. 1980s. 1990s.

She pulled out the 1970s. A faded blue album with gold trim on the cover and spine. Joe in his uniform—a serious look on his face, his eyes somber and steady. Their wedding photo—Joe with his arms around her then-slender waist, she with her arms around his neck. Both of them looking at the camera, their young smiles shiny and new and full of promise.

The memory of their wedding was strong as steel, its sharp edges stabbing her as she closed her eyes and thought back to that day. She walked down the aisle past hundreds of their friends and family toward Joe, her arm looped into her father's. She could still see him standing at the foot of the altar—eyes sparkling, dimples punctuating, foot tapping. The poignancy of the moment ingrained in her memory. A mural of three painted angels on the wall floated above them amid soft blue clouds on the cathedral ceiling. Two flames flickered on tall white candles sitting in gold, embellished candelabras on the other side of Joe.

Her ten bridesmaids at her side in floral A-line dresses. Joe and his groomsmen in black suits. Joe sliding a solitaire diamond ring on her finger. Joe lifting her veil and sealing their vows with a soft kiss that whispered the beginning of their new life. The breaking of a glass into tiny pieces to signify their many years together.

At the reception just steps away at Old Ursuline Convent, their guests were greeted by an abundance of flowers—red and white roses and pink calla lilies—and white ribbons strewn from the ceiling. Flickering white candles and polished silver sat on damask tablecloths.

She held Joe's hand tightly as they entered and were formally introduced, and they headed toward the center of the room for their first dance. The parquet floor was a cushion of springs, each step lifting her higher to a place where she was light and weightless. Their guests doused them with colorful paper confetti and candy-covered almonds—a sea of brick reds, royal blues, poppy pinks, and seafoam greens landed at their feet. Joe had held her close and whispered in her ear, "I'm so happy and so blessed."

Soon their bridal party took part in the festivities with a coordinated rendition of "C'è la luna mezzo mare" that left her and Joe holding their stomachs and drying their eyes, their laughter loud and boisterous. Joy bubbled up inside her, rushing out like a flooding brook. She was suffocating in a happiness that washed away all her past pains.

Ten courses of food eaten on Wedgewood china followed: prosciutto, olives, and pickled sweet peppers, Italian wedding soup, pastas, breads, fruits, salads, cheeses, seafood, pastries, candies, and their four-tiered cannoli cream wedding cake. Bottles of wine and champagne seemed to be everywhere—practically part of the décor.

They clapped, laughed, and danced the tarantella for what seemed like hours—linking their arms and moving in circles as they whirled and twirled across the floor. Their steps, light and swift, moving in time to the clanging tambourines.

The wine and liquor took effect as their guests became louder and rowdier. At one point, Rosa thought they were drowning out the band.

How many times had they raised their wineglasses to toast: "*Evviva gli sposi!*"— "long live the newlyweds"?

They had thanked each of their guests for their gifts—envelopes of money and cards that overflowed from their boosta box.

She left the memory and found herself back in the present. She was off and imbalanced, like a heavy weight tipping a scale. It wasn't just Joe's death weighing on her. She replayed his last words repeatedly as she pictured his distraught eyes. They say your entire life passes before you just before you die, but Joe seemed to pause at one of those moments. A flashback that jolted and distressed him to his core.

She couldn't shake the unsettling feeling she'd had when that young black woman showed up at her house the other day. Her gut told her there was a connection to her and Joe. Why else would she show up unannounced? And why was Joe Jr. so angry after she left? Why did he seem to despise the woman's race? She flipped through the photo albums more quickly, subconsciously expecting to see the young woman's face and a confirmation of her imagination—or something that would dispel her mounting fears.

She continued turning the pages: Catarine's confirmation—dressed in all white, her hair long, dark, and curly. Joe holding Joe Jr., John, and Catarine when they were born—a proud father whose tenderness shone through the curve of his arms, the slight smile, the verge of tears.

"You okay in here?" Joe Jr. peeked his head through the doorway.

The old sofa was threadbare in some areas, and the coffee table, with its chips and stains, needed to be sanded and restained. But it had been her parents', and Rosa liked knowing that some of the wear and tear came from them—their propped-up feet, their coffee cups, their moves from one home to the next. Filled with other belongings her parents had owned, this was Rosa's favorite room. Her mother's pendulum clock—gilded and Gustavian with gold leaves framing the face—hung on a wall above what had been her beloved balloon armchair. Her father's collection of handguns—Colts, Remingtons, and Smith & Wessons—filled a case in the corner. Her mother's Italian side table with its inlay of geometric patterns. The room was a flashback—a memory vault that stirred her emotions and soothed her soul.

Walking into the den was like stepping back in time. She thought she could feel her parents' presence. Which is why when Joe wanted to get the chair and tables restored, she'd vehemently opposed it.

"You know, you don't have to do this. I can take care of it," Joe Jr. continued when she didn't respond. He was standing in the open archway, his lips pressed together in a squiggly line.

His façade never seemed to come clean, Rosa thought. What lay beneath it? As a child, he had been a mama's boy. But as he entered his teen years, he drifted away from her and closer to Joe. An established bond held together by secrets she would probably never know. Hushed conversations at night that she didn't bother to discern. Fishing trips that lasted entire weekends. Joe Jr. taking on more and more responsibility at their grocery store. The chain had served them well over the years. Rosa never wanted for anything. Precious pearls. Flawless diamonds. Even a fur coat that she would never wear in New Orleans's typically tepid weather.

"I can handle it. I want to go back in time and relive our life. Sometimes I can't distinguish my dreams from reality." She was looking at a photo of Joe she didn't recall ever seeing before. His eyes, normally bright and full of life, seemed sad and empty as he stared at nothing.

Joe Jr. walked over and sat down next to her on the couch, the springs creaking in protest.

"How old was he then?" he asked, peering at the photo, his head nearly touching Rosa's.

"If I had to guess, I would say he was in his late thirties. Doesn't he look sad to you here?"

"I bet he was just tired or thinking through something," Joe said, adding quickly, "He was probably in one of his contemplative moods."

Rosa didn't believe him. She saw the flicker of recognition, the gears clicking into place when he looked at the photo. He knew more than he let on. She thought back again to the young black woman who'd showed up at their house. His reaction to her had been similar—a thin veil covering the truth on the other side. He was hiding something. Rosa narrowed her eyes. She just needed to find out what.

Chapter 11

A white butterfly fluttered above the perfectly trimmed hedges of Lamana, Panno and Fallo Funeral Home. With its tall columns, wraparound porch, and rocking chairs, the two-story brick building looked more like a home where people lived—not one where they lay lifeless in caskets.

Natalia stood nervously—alone—staring at the white butterfly. She held her hands tightly for several minutes, willing herself to calmness, before she walked inside. She'd taken extra care while getting ready to try to blend in: scant makeup, her hair pulled back into a bun, a simple black sheath dress, sunglasses.

She paused at the entrance, taking in the expansive foyer. Crema beige marble floors, a large chandelier, and heavy cream-colored drapes. A white world, she thought as she listened to classical music emanating from four discreet speakers in the ceiling. A loud discussion from a group of people standing in a circle to her right nearly drowned out the instrumental playlist. Her eyes darted around to the faces she could see—a younger woman in her late thirties with long curly hair, a man also in his thirties with dark hair, the profile of Joe's hateful son, an elderly woman she knew she'd seen before. Joe's family, talking to a couple who must have known him. But the woman—where had she seen her before? Her eyes widened as the memories came to her. The hospital. Joe's house, as she'd stared emphatically at her.

She froze, her feet cemented to the shiny floor, looking for a way out. She could feel her heart thumping hard against her chest, her body trapped in a wave of fear that made her lips tremble and her legs feel like water. The thought of Joe's son spotting her gave her the courage to move. She'd come this far; she couldn't turn back now. He wouldn't dare cause a scene, as he wanted to keep her a secret, something that didn't exist—not expose her and break his mother's heart in the process.

She tiptoed awkwardly across the loud floor, hoping she wouldn't attract attention or produce stares as she headed toward a large room just past the foyer. She moved like a burglar, furtive but fast. Near the mahogany doors that led to the entrance, the open pages of a guest book lay next to a large arrangement of flowers on a long table. She hesitated as she debated whether to sign it. No one would know who she was if they saw her name, she reasoned. Her hand shaking, she picked up the black pen and scribbled her name across a blank line below several others who were already inside or had come and gone. *I do exist*, she thought, as she gingerly placed the pen back on the table.

She expected to find a crowd, but only five people sat quietly in brown pews. Dispersed across the room, they too had come alone. She glanced at them as she walked toward Joe's casket—closed, with a massive arrangement of white flowers spread across the top. A nearly life-size crucifix loomed against a paneled wall behind it. As she got closer, she could see a large photo of Joe framed in gold sitting on an easel. Dear God, this was a long walk. She sped up, her eyes focused on the photo.

He was smiling brightly. Perfectly straight teeth aligned like a picket fence and white as the tips of a French manicure. A mass of dark, wavy hair. A prominent nose. Olive skin. The gray eyes— exactly like her own. Joe in his younger days. He was quite handsome. She began reaching for the picture but felt something stop her midway—a light brush of air that lifted the flowers' leaves and shifted their petals ever so slightly. She turned, half expecting to see someone. A chill ran down her spine as her gaze connected with Rosa, who was staring at her from the doorway at the back of the room, her eyes hard and inquisitive.

Natalia turned around quickly as she backed away from the picture, afraid her legs would give out. She collapsed into the first pew, slouching and continuing to stare at the photo. She studied Joe's smiling face, archiving every feature. The dimple on his right cheek. The thick eyebrows. The empty piercing in his left ear. The angles of his jawline. The three lines across his forehead. She sank lower into the pew, her hands shaking, palms beginning to sweat. What would she say if Joe's wife approached her? Should she lie or tell her the truth?

When someone touched her right shoulder, she was sure she'd screamed, but perhaps it was more of a muffled gasp. She looked up to see Dr. Duplessis.

"Sorry," he mouthed, his hands raised in surrender. "I didn't mean to scare you," he whispered. He made a movement with his arm and nodded toward the space on her left, asking permission to sit next to her. She nodded quickly. She hadn't realized until that moment how badly she needed someone. She smiled at him, a sense of protection and security enveloping her. He took her hand and squeezed it, a reassurance that helped steady her heartbeat and reset her mind.

As the room filled with people who had known Joe, Natalia searched for the woman she presumed to be his wife in the gathering crowd and among those now seated in the pews. She spotted her in the back, talking with a family of four as she dabbed a crumpled tissue into the corners of eyes. She squeezed Dr. Duplessis's hand and nodded toward the left exit—the middle aisle and doors would lead them right to Joe's wife. As they walked down the aisle, Natalia stayed close by David's side like a shadow, stealthy and precise as she tried to leave undetected.

"Dr. Duplessis," she heard a woman's voice say. She stopped when he did, a panicked statue, as he turned to respond. She remained hidden behind him.

"Oh, my. We didn't expect to see you here," the woman continued, her voice getting closer. "How nice of you to come." The woman was breathless now as she reached up to hug him.

As the woman was buried in his embrace, Natalia rushed through the doors that led into the lobby. She felt like prey running from its predator as her instincts and adrenaline kept her legs moving. Maneuvering in and out of the crowd, she put on her sunglasses, hoping to become less conspicuous. Several other people were hiding their grief behind their lenses, and she thought this was a perfect disguise.

As she exited through the double doors of the funeral home, a warm, sticky night greeted her with a chorus of cicadas' urgent cries. With the sun long gone, a full moon reflected its light on cars, a pond, and the windows of the funeral home. She walked toward the parking lot, where she waited anxiously for Dr. Duplessis to join her.

She watched a stream of people head into the building, their heads hung low, their shoulders carrying the weight of grief. Finally, one of the double doors swung open, and Dr. Duplessis emerged, his eyes scanning the parking lot. Natalia waved to catch his attention, and relaxed her shoulders, relieved to see him alone. He rushed toward her, his long strides covering the distance within the seconds.

"That was a close call," he said, almost as breathless as she felt.

"That was Joe's wife, right? It had to be. She didn't see me? What did she say?"

"Yes, her name is Rosa. If she did, she didn't ask. She seemed very out of it—confused, sad, distraught."

"I'm not sure what would have happened if you hadn't shown up. I think I was just going to make a beeline with my head down. Thank God it got crowded."

David nodded his head in agreement as he stared at her, his eyes slightly narrowed.

"Are you okay? How are you holding up?" He touched her arm lightly.

"I think so. I've calmed down at least. I think I now know what it feels like to have a heart attack. You were my knight in shining armor." She smiled.

"Glad I could be of service, madam." He bowed.

"So do you always attend your patients' funerals—or visitations?" He'd really made a special effort, considering the distance from Houston. They walked toward a garden away from the parking lot. The sweet smell of yellow primrose drifted along, a faint breeze taking the scent for a slow ride.

"I try to. Though it's quite difficult. Sometimes it's a sad reminder that we can only do so much. Medicine has its limits. I sometimes think, what could I have done differently? Sometimes we miss things. Test results aren't always accurate. False negatives and false positives. In Joe's case, there was nothing we could have done. But I also think that ten years from now, twenty years from now, someone like Joe shows up with a malignant stage-four brain tumor, and he could live."

Natalia could see the light of his dream off in the distance as he looked beyond her.

"So, you're saying modern medicine will truly be modern? More like miracle medicine?" She smiled.

"Something like that," he said with a nod. "Just think about the history of medicine and how far we've come. It pains me tremendously to lose patients. Especially when they have so much life ahead of them. Children. Babies. Teenagers."

As the doctor set his jaw and furrowed his brow, Natalia noticed his high cheekbones, the slope of his nose, the shape of his full lips. Almost the opposite of Tyler. More rugged and strong than pretty boy.

"I know this must be very hard for you," he said. "I never knew my father either. I believe I am the product of a one-night stand."

"Seriously?" she asked, eyes wide, mouth agape.

"Very." He went on to reveal that his mother was only sixteen years old, a runaway practically, when she became pregnant. Having lived on the streets, she was ashamed to admit that she wasn't sure who his real father was. But she somehow managed to meet a good man, who raised him like his own.

"Only my closest friends know that about me," he said. "Everyone believes that my stepfather is also my biological father."

"Well, I won't tell a soul, Doctor," Natalia said.

His smile made her feel like sunshine. She couldn't explain why she was so comfortable with this man when she hardly knew him. Why it was so easy to talk with him, so natural to be in his presence. Maybe he was this way with most people—his bedside manner. Maybe it was just the grief creating a connection. She couldn't be sure, but she didn't want him to leave her alone.

He must have sensed as much. "Would you like to grab something to eat?"

"I would, actually. I don't think I've eaten all day, now that I think about it."

"What are you in the mood for? I know New Orleans is known for its food."

"Well, I'm not that familiar with this area, but I think there's a string of restaurants about five minutes from here on the lake if we want to head that way. I'll pull up Maps so we don't get lost over here."

"Sounds like a plan. I'll follow you."

She nodded in agreement, and they walked back to the parking lot, where he opened her car door and closed it after she sat down. She chose a marina grill a few miles away.

"This is lovely," she remarked as they approached a quaint Creole cottage. The interior was exactly what she'd expected: white linen tablecloths, white chairs on a stone floor, open French doors, white curtains moving slightly in the breeze, the yellow glow of candles sprinkled across the room. She could see Lake Pontchartrain just beyond a wall of windows. It was like they'd stepped into a dimly lit, magical oasis.

They chose a corner table with a view of the marina where tethered boats bounced beneath a navy-blue sky. The soft hum of indistinguishable conversations floated across the room. This was a place for calm, peaceful discussions.

She was staring at him, watching the flicker of the candlelight dancing in his eyes, when their waiter arrived with menus and water with no ice.

"I'm so glad you're here with me tonight. My mother didn't want me to go to the funeral, so I agreed I would just go to his visitation."

"You're not going to the funeral?" he asked, surprised.

"I don't know. I'm kind of torn. I don't want to cause any trouble or disrupt his family's life. What do you think I should do? Would you go?" She'd formed a new habit: self-doubt. No decision felt right to her anymore.

"I think it depends on why you would or wouldn't. Do you want to know your family—his other children?"

"I'm not sure. I wanted to know him. I've always wanted to know him. Part of me wanted to meet his kids so they could tell me what he was like. But I realize why they probably wouldn't be thrilled to meet me or know that Joe had an illegitimate child—and a black one at that. I think his wife is on to me, though. I

75

think she has some idea or is wondering why I keep showing up." She explained how she'd seen her at the hospital the day she and the doctor met. "She would be devastated if she knew for sure. I would if I was married and years later, I found out something like that. It's the ultimate betrayal."

"What if she already knows for sure?" he asked.

"You think she might?" She hadn't thought that Joe's wife might have an inkling of what he'd been up to for that brief period of his life—if he ever actually stopped. But perhaps there were signs in the marriage, and if she read them correctly, she might have known. Surely a man couldn't cheat on his wife for more than a year without her having any idea. What was she doing or thinking when Joe was seeing her mother?

"She may have known that he wasn't faithful, but a child . . . that's another story," she said.

"It's certainly not your fault things turned out this way. I wish you could have met him before he was diagnosed, when he was full of life."

"What was he like?" She would relish any bit of information she could get.

"Well, by the time Joe came to us, he wasn't the man he used to be. I could see that he had been strong and solid. He'd lost a lot of weight and his skin was already changing. But something about his eyes—they drew you in; they made you take him seriously and look at him more closely."

She nodded somberly. "My mother thinks my eyes will give everything away if I go."

"I think she's right, Natalia." He said her name with such concern and care. "The first time I saw you, I thought you were absolutely beautiful—as I'm sure any man would."

She felt her face flush and looked down at the black napkin in her lap.

"But there was something else I couldn't put my finger on. I had this feeling that I'd seen you before or that I knew you from some other place. When you said you were Joe's daughter, it all made sense. Well, it made more sense.

"But back to your question. I know you want to know the Joe from thirty years ago—or even the child that he once was. It's not enough to look at a photo of him, is it?"

"It's really not," she said as she ran her finger up and down her glass.

"If you want to go to his funeral, I'll go with you," he offered. "But you have to think about what could happen. You already had a close call tonight."

"Would you go? If you were in my shoes?"

He looked out the window as he considered her question. She watched him closely, admiring his thoughtfulness—and his profile. A full minute later, he said, "I would avoid any drama. You paid your respects tonight. I think if you want to know who Joe was, maybe reach out to one of his children."

She reminded him of the horrible encounter she'd had with Joe's son.

"He sounds pretty angry—at you, at your mom, at your dad for dying. Angry with the world. Maybe you shouldn't take it personally."

"It was kind of hard not to, but you're right. Considering the timing and how he was feeling, I'm sure I'm the last person on earth he wanted to see. I just wanted to see Joe so badly. I actually considered pushing his son down and running past him into the house."

He laughed at that notion. A hearty sound that came from his abdomen and drew her in toward him like a rip current. She joined him, thinking how ridiculous the story sounded as she told it—and how comfortable and natural it was being with him. She felt like she was surrounded by rainbows. There was no beginning or end—just a perfect, long moment full of highs and no lows.

"I'm picturing you doing that, sorry." His chest was still heaving.

"I guess that would have been pretty ridiculous. Of course, Pamela cussed him out, and we sped off like we'd committed a crime."

Shaking his head, Dr. Duplessis said, "Maybe he'll come to his senses one day. After his grief. After his anger. And he'll realize you're blood. I bet your dad would want them to know you and for you to know them. He just couldn't bear to tell them."

"That part makes me bitter. When I think that he could have said something all these years. I know I shouldn't judge him. But that was cowardly and selfish."

"The ramifications were just too great," he said, looking into her eyes.

They talked until the restaurant closed. Until someone flipped a switch, and bright lights suddenly illuminating the room broke the spell.

After she explained every detail she could recall about the visitation to her mother and after she listened to her adamantly discourage her from going to Joe's funeral, Natalia put on mismatched pajamas, hung her black dress up in the closet, brushed her teeth, and washed her face. Then she called Pamela, who'd gone back to Houston after the debacle at Joe's house.

"Hey girl," she answered expectantly. "I've been waiting for you to call."

"Hey," Natalia said, her voice dry as parched sand.

"What's wrong?"

Natalia explained the details of the wake for the second time that night, exhaustion seeping through, her voice becoming lower and weaker. "This is just so wrong," she said. "I couldn't even grieve for him for fear of his wife approaching me as I sat there."

"Well, at least you had the good doctor next to you." Pamela laughed softly.

Natalia chuckled. Only Pamela could pull a laugh from the dark abyss that surrounded her.

"I wasn't going to go to the funeral, but now I'm just angry," she said. "The more I think about it, the angrier I get. I'm tired of being the secret."

"Well, it sounds like you may not be. What if her racist son told her?"

"He wouldn't. He's too ashamed, too embarrassed to have a black relative. I think he's in denial. He thinks if he doesn't say anything, then I don't exist."

Natalia knew it wouldn't take much for Pamela to join in her protest.

"To hell with him. To hell with all of them. I'm coming back and we're going. Let me get my black dress out right now. When is the damned funeral?"

"In two days. At eleven a.m.," Natalia replied numbly.

"I'll be there tomorrow. Be ready."

Chapter 12

The sun rose big and bright, its rays darting and stretching out like the arms and legs of a dancer. Some people awoke, showered, dressed, and went to work. Those without jobs— mostly older men from the neat neighborhood of Hollygrove— sat on corners with equally broke friends and talked politics, cars, women, and sports as they began their morning drinking routine. Children ate breakfast at kitchen countertops before running to bus stops, where they waited for the yellow vehicles to crawl up their streets. It was just another predictable day for them. One they didn't need to plan for or anticipate.

For more than three hundred others, the day dawned with altered routines and sadness at their sides. They donned black clothes and drove to a decades-old funeral home to pay their final respects to Joe. Of the three hundred, only three of them really knew him: Joe Jr., his best friend Dan, and Rosa. Had his mother been alive, she would have been the fourth.

This procession of people—mostly whites but a handful of blacks—gathered in the chapel for the blessing.

Rosa watched everything go by in a haze. Joe's casket covered with a pall—the white covering representing hope, resurrection, and the equality of all people before God. A blue cross in the middle. Did Joe know all of these people?

"In the name of the Father, the Son, and the Holy Spirit," the priest said. Seven others stood with him, their long white robes spotless and flowing with every movement.

"Amen," they all uttered.

Circling Joe's casket, the priest chanted scriptures about the Holy Spirit and sprinkled holy water with an aspergillum. One sprinkle, two sprinkles. Dip the metal receptacle back into the pitcher. Three, four, five sprinkles. Another dip. Six, seven, eight, nine, ten. Another circling. This time with incense. The clanging of the chalice accompanied by the smell of incense, its smoke rising up with their prayers.

As they proceeded into the sanctuary, they began to sing the Song of Farewell. When she briefly caught Joe Jr.'s eyes—he and John were two of eight pallbearers—he raised his chin an inch before looking back down.

The chords of the organ and the voices of a mass choir flooded the room as they attempted to overcome the grief that permeated the air. The resonance of their voices rose and reverberated. Rosa, sitting in the front row, head bowed and wearing a black hat with a thin veil to shield her face, tried to focus on the instruments, the voices. Anything to take her mind off Joe's casket, which was so close to her, she could almost touch it.

She was vaguely aware of the organ, the virgin Mary staring out from the pulpit, the flower arrangements—a blur of reds, blues, yellows, and greens—spread from one end of the altar to the other.

Hymns. Followed by the reading of several psalms.

"Our life doesn't end in death," the priest was saying. "God will give you rest."

We will be reunited, she thought, staring up at Jesus on the cross and clinging now to every word the priest said.

"Eternal rest, grant unto Joe, oh Lord. May his soul now rest in peace."

She stared at the folded U.S. flag on a table near Joe's casket, a triangle of blue covered with white stars. Yes, Joe was a veteran. How long had he served his country? She couldn't remember now.

A flame flickered on a Paschal candle. Christ is our light, Rosa thought as she watched the flame jitter on the dark wick. In darkness there is light. In despair there is hope. In death there is new life. But where would she find this new life? Could it ever be better than the one she'd shared with Joe?

She thought it strange, rather bizarre, that Joe wasn't sitting at her side. Instead, Catarine held her hand, squeezing it periodically, as if reminding Rosa to breathe.

Person after person plodded to the pulpit, stood behind the podium, and spoke highly of Joe. Veterans. Employees. And, finally, their family. A true friend. A great father. They praised his generosity. They spoke of his ability to make anyone laugh—or at least smile. They told story after story of how Joe worked hard all of his life. How he loved to fish and hunt. How he lived for his family.

The summation of an entire life in just one hour.

Joe Jr. had refused to speak. Something wasn't right with him, and she would have to figure that out later. But John rose, followed by Catarine. Rosa watched and wondered how they maintained their composure.

Communion. A closing song. A final kiss on Joe's cheek—cool and hard as a gemstone. Then sitting patiently, watching others trek slowly past Joe's casket to pay their respects. As she fiddled with the strap of her purse, her body rocking slightly side to side, she glanced up to see two women who stood out not just because one was holding the other's hand, practically pulling her along, but because in a sea of mostly white friends and family, they were black. She squinted as she tried to get a better look. She was almost certain one of those women was the girl with the gray eyes. When Joe Jr. also looked their way, he moved to the edge of his seat as if debating whether he should remain seated or stand. She knew something was amiss.

The women stopped when they reached his casket. But only one of them reached out to touch him for a brief moment, her arm extending slowly, fingers shaking as tears streamed down her cheeks.

From the corner of her eye, Rosa watched them continue down the other aisle, where they disappeared near the back of the church. She noticed Joe Jr. was watching them as well and gritting his teeth.

Soon, he rejoined the pallbearers. Before she knew it, they had come back to take Joe away. They folded and unfolded the flag, and within seconds it was draped over Joe's casket.

She followed behind them as they walked down the aisle and out of the funeral home. Each step took her closer to the cemetery, where they would place him above the ground in a vault, as was customary and necessary in New Orleans—a city built on a swamp that would reject caskets in its soft, muddy soil and send them floating away during a heavy rain.

She didn't notice the sun greeting them with open arms as they filed out of the church. She couldn't remember any of the words of sympathy. Her mind was on the two women—her curiosity growing from a spark to a flame that she needed to extinguish.

As she followed her children to their car, she saw a third person who also stood out because of his coffee-colored skin—Dr. Duplessis—talking to the two mysterious women as they stood near their parked car.

"Dr. Duplessis!" she yelled. She tried again, but they were too far away. She walked as quickly as she could toward them but tripped and fell. Joe Jr. grabbed her arms, pulling her back up, and she dusted the dirt off her knees. A trickle of blood seeped through her flesh-toned stockings.

"What are you doing?" he hissed.

"I'm going to say hello to Dr. Duplessis—and find out who those women are," she said as she yanked her arms away.

"Mom, this isn't the time or the place to do that. We need to bury Dad."

"Dr. Duplessis," she yelled again, waving her arms frantically as Joe Jr. tried to stand in front of her to block her view.

This time, Dr. Duplessis turned to look her way, and so did other people leaving the funeral home, their expressions confused and concerned. She watched him exchange final words with the two women, who then climbed into their car—the gray-eyed one running around to hop into the passenger seat. Dr. Duplessis continued walking toward his own vehicle.

Rosa attempted to run—a semitrot that resembled the hobble of an injured animal—as she tried to catch up with the car before they peeled out of the parking lot. She was out of breath before she could reach them and she leaned against a car, her lungs unable to fill completely with air. She watched in dismay as Dr. Duplessis drove off behind them.

Her anger rose from simmering to boiling as she glared at Joe Jr. He was at her side, holding her elbow and leading her back to their car.

"What in God's name is wrong with you? Why did you do that?" she said.

"Do what?"

"Don't play dumb with me. You know damned well that I was trying to get to Dr. Duplessis and those women, and you intentionally got in my way. I know you know something, and I'm going to find out what if it's the last thing I do."

"Mom, people are watching us. Please, let's just focus on Dad."

"Shut up!" she yelled. "Just shut up!"

Joe Jr. threw his arms up in the air and walked away. "You'll only hurt yourself," he mumbled. But Rosa was too busy trying to ignore a painful truth that began to emerge as she marched toward the car. A blurred image began to take shape and she didn't like the picture she was seeing—its sharp edges slicing her life into jagged pieces.

Chapter 13

Natalia was in the passenger seat of Pamela's car, her heart rate outpacing the speedometer as they sped through the parking lot of the funeral home toward Veterans Memorial Boulevard. She closed her eyes, leaned her head back, and sank down into the seat.

"You okay?" Pamela asked softly as she changed lanes and tapped the brakes to slow down.

"That was crazy. I can't keep doing this."

"But aren't you glad you went? You would have regretted it if you hadn't."

"It just feels so wrong. Having to sneak in and practically hide in the back—like we're some kind of criminals. I mean, I knew we'd stand out just because we're black, but I didn't think they'd notice or pay much attention to us."

"Girl, they were in the front row! How would they not? We agreed that we would walk up there, but you changed your mind, remember?"

"I don't know what came over me. I sat there hearing all those things about him—his time in the navy, his sense of humor, how he helped homeless people. He was really a good person." Her voice cracked and she cleared her throat. "I felt so left out. I should have been in the front row with the rest of his family, but instead I was in the back."

"Like Jim Crow at a damned funeral," Pamela said, shaking her head.

Natalia shoved Pamela's arm and smiled sadly. "It's just humiliating. Like I'm not good enough to be included. Like they're better than me."

"Well, they're not, so don't even think that way."

"I think his wife knows, and if she doesn't, she's very suspicious. We've crossed paths too many times now."

"The truth will have to come out at some point. It's just a matter of time."

Unsettling feelings have a way of worming their way into tiny spaces—the far corners of a mind where vacancy abounds.

Three weeks had passed since Joe died, and yet Natalia couldn't shake the sensation that something ominous was about to happen. Something more life-changing than Joe's death.

She had gone back to work. A job that was more of a passion—designing rooms in homes she probably would never live in. Coming up with ideas and sketches that solved challenges for clients who didn't have the inspiration to do it on their own. She loved creating beautiful spaces that conveyed feelings and moods when you entered them. Colors and décor decisions that induced calm, excitement, happiness, motivation. People didn't realize the power of a room.

And she'd signed up to volunteer at the American Cancer Society.

Her mind was a chamber of grief and fear. Her grief clung to her even as she found joy in small moments: a child's laughter, a jog around Buffalo Bayou Park, a home-cooked meal—a welcome gift from her neighbors. The gay couple that lived above her for the past year had also become good friends. Mike and Paul not only were fun but also loved decorating as much as she did.

But she hadn't returned any phone calls. Pamela. Her mom. Dr. Duplessis.

The emptiness she felt was profound. She thought it might be contagious, and she didn't want to expose anyone else to it. This feeling kept her from returning phone calls, from seeking the company of others. But today she had the strength to give something other than sorrow as she scanned an email from the American Cancer Society: orientation for new volunteers was today at noon. She could find interest in someone other than herself and her own feelings. It might even be a distraction.

She drove to the building just a couple of miles away from her office. It was a short building, a grid of amber-tinted windows covering the front, reflecting the sky and an American flag that flew from a pole nearby. As she walked beneath the green awning, she noticed a small garden filled with blush-pink rosebushes.

"Good afternoon!" a middle-aged woman with large, dark brown eyes greeted her. "How may I help you?"

"Hi. I'm here for the orientation for new volunteers."

"Fantastic! We're so happy to have you. Let me show you to the room. It's just down the hall here." The woman motioned with her right hand.

They click-clacked down the hallway, their heels creating a chorus on the tile floors. Natalia glanced at a photo collage of survivors, their smiling faces beaming with joy. All races, all ages. Men. Women. Children.

"We love adding to that wall," the woman remarked. "Here we are. Our coordinator will be right with you."

A row of white tables with black chairs tucked neatly beneath them filled most of the space. A projector screen hung from the far-right wall. She glanced out at the tinted view of the parking lot.

"Sometimes we only have a couple of people. We should have one other person joining you."

Natalia nodded and checked her watch as the woman walked away. She'd arrived ten minutes early and decided to check her email while she waited.

She heard a cough as someone entered the room. His legs were long and thin beneath a pair of khaki linen pants. He was bald and frail, but he looked like Tyler. She looked away, assuming that in her fragile state she was seeing things.

Why was she conjuring up images of old boyfriends? Finding attractive men to date had never been hard. The problem was, she tired of them so quickly. Definitely by the six-month slump—the point in the relationship when everything felt mundane. When boredom seeped in and excitement checked out. The point when it seemed there was nothing new to say or learn about each other and she began to detest the routine. She equated the freedom she felt after a breakup with the initial bliss she felt at the start of her relationships. That realm of possibilities where excitement sat on the cusp and the thrill of the unknown beckoned enticingly.

She recalled a conversation she'd had with Pamela. "Girl, you are unrealistic and idealistic," Pamela had said.

"I just want the sparks to last—not die out within a couple of months," Natalia replied. "I can never shake the nagging questions, you know? Could there be someone better out there? Is this the best I can do? Will he be faithful and honest? Will he be a great dad?"

She knew she'd have to get past this if she ever wanted to get married, have kids, take family vacations. Do the things society says you're supposed to do. She just hadn't met anyone she felt was her soul mate, someone she was meant to be with, until she'd met Tyler.

He had been her love at first sight. They'd met when she was a graduate interior design student at UCLA. After earning her BA in art history, she'd realized there wasn't much she could do with it. "Starving artist" took on a whole new meaning. When she was accepted into UCLA's program, she gladly moved from the Crescent City to the City of Angels.

She'd been a student there for all of two weeks when she awoke on a bright, sunny day in April, threw on a red-and-white sundress, and pulled her hair into a puffy ponytail. She was walking on campus, balancing a pile of books in her arms that she was returning to the library, when she saw him sitting at a table in one of the courtyards, turning to look at her, eyebrows slightly raised. They'd seen each other at the same time, and she couldn't hold back the smile that spread across her face.

He had to have been the most handsome man she'd ever laid eyes on. Caramel skin. Dark, curly hair.

Her nerves got the best of her, and she continued walking. But when she looked back, he was still watching her. And before she knew it, he appeared at her side, offering to carry her books.

This was a moment she had memorized and replayed often. His eyes admiring, drawing her in. His smile wanting and sincere. His smell arousing and inviting. His touch. The jolt from his hands as they brushed against hers when he took the books.

Five years. That's how long it had been since she'd last seen him.

She turned slightly as the man entered the room. It sure looked like . . . Her eyes grew wider as he came close.

"Oh, my God! Tyler?" she whispered.

When he smiled, she had her answer. "I thought it was you. I'd recognize you from any angle, from anywhere." His voice was deep and smooth. She pushed her chair back and rushed to hug him. "You look lovely as ever." He smiled as they released each other. He stepped back and held her at arm's length, admiring her from head to toe.

She was sure her face was fire red as she blushed and turned to face the window. Her stomach was doing somersaults. How was it possible that after all these years, he could make her feel like a giddy girl? But that girl retreated as confusion coursed through her brain. She wanted to deny what appeared to be Tyler's truth. His face gaunt. His hair shed. His body weak and visibly broken down.

"You work here?" She glanced at a badge hanging from a lanyard around his neck. She rested her hands on the sides of his arms and looked into his eyes. "Are you . . . You have . . ." She paused, unable to bring herself to say the word. "How on earth is that possible? You're so young. Please tell me you're going to be all right."

He glanced at the floor before nodding toward the tables and chairs. She walked ahead of him and sat on the edge of her chair as he lowered himself next to her and leaned back. Her heart began racing as she listened to him explain how he—at only thirty-four—had cancer.

"I have bad genes," he said with a light chuckle. "I inherited a pretty rare condition: familial adenomatous polyposis. Both of my parents were carriers, and I'm the lucky recipient."

Natalia's face was rigid as a brick as she disregarded his efforts to inject humor into his story. Cancer was an enemy—a killer that ruined people's lives and encased their loved ones with grief.

"I had hundreds of polyps in my colon. Apparently they'd been growing for years, and I didn't realize it, of course. I was so exhausted all the time and couldn't figure out why. Last year, I was mowing my lawn and passed out. Next thing I knew, I was in a hospital bed. They ran all of these tests and noticed that my iron was incredibly low. I'd been losing blood through my digestive tract.

"They ran a bunch of other tests and found the cancer in my colon. I had surgery to remove the polyps. One was huge, the size of a grapefruit. Now I'm finishing my final rounds of chemo to keep the cancer from coming back—hopefully. I'm fortunate that it didn't spread to my liver or lymph nodes. I started working here a couple of days a week now that I'm regaining my strength and the medical bills are piling up."

She didn't realize she was crying until Tyler wiped her tears away with the back of his hand. She couldn't speak as she absorbed Tyler's story. She felt it raising the hairs on her arms, seeping into her skin, and mixing into her blood before it settled heavily in her heart. For the longest time, neither of them spoke.

"I'm so glad they caught it in time," she said finally. She thought back to when she last saw him. They'd spent a long and tearful night together—their last—before she helped him load up a U-Haul to move to Chicago.

He'd held her close and tried to say all of the right things, but she knew it was over when he said, "I'm sure you'll find someone else. Someone who deserves you." She couldn't say the words, but she didn't want anyone else. She only wanted him. Couldn't he see that? She loved him. Couldn't he feel that? Perhaps it was an imbalanced relationship all along, and she was the one with all of the feelings while he held back, reserving his for someone else—the woman he married.

"So you want to volunteer with us?" he asked.

"Yes I . . . I decided to volunteer—doing something more with my life than just work—though I love my job," she added quickly.

"Well, we're glad to have you." His eyes twinkled. "What made you choose this cause?"

Natalia glanced out the window, then at the muted carpet tiles on the floor.

"Well, you know that I never knew my dad," she said finally. "He died recently from brain cancer. It was a rare form that spread very quickly."

She could see a wave of concern settle on Tyler's face and knew he could relate entirely too well.

"I'm so sorry," he said, squeezing her hand.

"No, *I'm* sorry," she managed. "You have your own worries."

"I'm going to be fine," he tried to assure her. "I'm pretty tired and weak, but that's my new normal. I think I'm getting used to it. My treatments are almost over, though. Just three more weeks."

She couldn't believe she was sitting so close to him. So many questions popped into her head. What had he been doing these last five years? Did she ever cross his mind? Where was he living now? Was he still married? She couldn't see his ring finger. And yet, she couldn't bring herself to ask him. His weakness rattled her heart and crushed her spirit. She just wanted to help put him back together.

"Back to you and your dad," he said. "Did you get to meet him before he . . . ?"

She shook her head. "It's been about three weeks now. I'm coming around. I think I'm most saddened by the fact that I'll never know him. I think I thought we had time—that at some point in my life, we would meet, and he would become the dad I never had. But I would probably feel even worse if I had known him. Does that make sense? I don't know exactly who I'm grieving for or what type of person he was. It's all crazy and confusing." She shook her head as if it would reset her brain.

"That's completely understandable, you know," he said. "Did you go to his funeral?"

She nodded and inhaled deeply before recounting the experience. She decided not to tell him about the drama with Joe's son.

"Wow, that's crazy," he said. "But it could have been worse—a real scene."

She agreed. "I'm glad I went, but essentially, my life is the same as it was before—just emptier."

Tyler nodded as if he understood.

"So, how do you get to your appointments? Are you able to drive?" she asked.

"I drive myself and hang out at the hospital every Tuesday until the immediate side effects wear off."

"You don't have family here—or your wife?" She paused before "wife," the word feeling shaky and odd as she said it. She hoped her bitterness didn't seep out. He did leave her to marry that hussy. Or maybe he never felt as strongly for Natalia as Natalia felt for him. Maybe his heart belonged to the wife all along, and she just hadn't known that.

"She left me. About three months after I found out I had cancer. She wrote me a letter saying she wasn't happy anymore, and she was in love with someone else. She was going to tell me months before, but she just couldn't continue living a lie." He raised his hands and curved his index and middle fingers around "lie." when he said it. "Turns out this someone else had been in the picture all along. Even worse, he's actually the father of the child I thought was mine."

"What? She led you to believe the child was yours all along?"

He nodded.

"That's crushing. I'm so sorry, Tyler." She rubbed his left arm, then slid her hand down to hold his—and that's when she felt the ring, cold and hard.

She couldn't help thinking he should have married her. She would have never done that to him. The thought of having his child would have kept her soaring. Waking up with him every morning—seeing his caramel skin and sleepy eyes. She wanted to tell him he'd made the wrong choice, but she kept her mouth shut. She was certain he already knew it, and he'd clearly suffered enough.

"That's almost unbearable—and unbelievable. Why can't people keep their vows? Does your son or daughter know?"

"It's a girl. We haven't told her yet. I'm not sure if we will. She's only three years old. I don't think she'd understand. And I've raised her like she's my own. I'm not ready to just let her go and not be part of her life. She's one of the few people I still love."

This was beginning to be quite the dose of depression. She had to turn the conversation around before she spiraled down with him.

"This too shall pass," she said. "You just need time. Time to heal. Time to create a new life. I know you've been through a lot—more than anyone I know—but you have to be strong. You'll get through this."

He nodded, but she sensed he didn't believe that was possible.

"Do you think she ever loved you? How could anyone do that to another person? She could have at least been by your side until you completely recovered."

"Well, once Sheila realized I was going to live, she felt like she could leave. She didn't need to be by my side. My forthcoming clean bill of health was her ticket out," he said. "I'm sure she's going to file for divorce soon."

"And how do you feel about that?"

"I guess I don't blame her. I probably could have been a better husband—less selfish, more giving and attentive."

"No one is perfect, Tyler. I'm sure she could have been a better wife, too, if she's honest with herself." *Of course, I would have been an even better wife if you'd chosen me.* "You know you broke my heart, don't you." It was more of a statement than a question. She hadn't intended to say this, but the thought rushed out of her head. "Sorry. I shouldn't have said that."

"Did I?" he asked, surprised.

Now that the topic was on the table, they had to address it. "Yes. You did." She looked him in the eyes. "I'll never forget the first time I saw you. The first time we saw each other. Do you remember?"

"It was like I was looking into your soul," he said. He stepped back in time with her to that day—his eyes dancing with recollection. "I can still see your smile."

"So, you thought we were soul mates?"

"I don't know," he said slowly. "I had been seeing Sheila before you and I met. We had history and you were so young. I didn't think you really knew what you wanted."

She thought about their age difference—five years—which seemed insignificant now. "I always thought it was so clear because of how I felt. You were my love at first sight. You were the first man I'd been with that I never tired of. After you left, I was always trying to find another you."

They were both quiet as they stared out the window. Looking out, but not really seeing anything. Maybe she'd said too much.

"So much of life is about timing," he finally said. "You know, I was hoping I would get you pregnant so that would seal the deal. We would have to be together and the decision would be made."

The conversation was beginning to feel heavier and heavier, and Natalia wasn't sure she could bear the weight of it anymore. All of the "what ifs" she'd dreamed about were starting to resurface. What if he had chosen her? What if they'd had children? She knew she might have easily gotten pregnant since she'd made no effort not to. No birth control pills. No condoms. They had been reckless. But she never did.

"Why don't we get out of here?" she said. "I'll drive, and we can come back and get your car, if you feel up to it. You can tell me all about the volunteer opportunities I came to hear about and get me all signed up."

"Good idea," he said, winking. "I could use some fresh air. And we could use some volunteers."

As they approached her car, Natalia noticed Tyler was winded, taking short, shallow breaths.

"You sure you're okay?"

"Yep. Normal side effects. Don't worry. I won't pass out on you." He opened her door.

She was still making payments on the loan for her Nissan Altima. When she turned the key in the ignition, a commercial for teeth whitening blasted through the speakers.

"Whoa! Sorry about that. I like my music kind of loud," she laughed.

"So what are you in the mood for?"

"Let's grab a bite to eat. Something light—I still try to eat healthy and work out. Mainly so I can have dessert."

"Whatever you're doing, it's working."

"Well, thank you, sir," she said. "You decide. I wasn't sure if you were in the mood for food or if you just wanted to sit on a park bench somewhere."

"I don't live here. I drive down from Galveston but am in the process of moving."

"Um, okay." She paused and then said, "I know a couple of lunch spots in the design district."

When they arrived at the restaurant—a soup, salad, and smoothie spot—Tyler grabbed the door for her and tilted his head toward the entrance. She obeyed and walked inside.

They grabbed a booth and ordered grilled chicken salads. Then they spent the next two hours catching up on the last five years of their lives.

Natalia talked about her job at D&D Group. She loved the creative side but sometimes felt like she was missing something. Like she needed to give back to the community. Do more for others. Hence their fortuitous meeting at the American Cancer Society.

Her duplex. She loved her place. It truly felt like home.

He talked about his interest in politics, teaching, and law. His passion for children. His wife, their marriage. How they'd struggled financially. He'd lost two jobs at two companies. Sheila had been the breadwinner even when he was employed.

Natalia felt her skin prickle when he said this. The ability of a man to keep a job, or find one very quickly after losing one, was very important to her. She began to realize that maybe she'd created an image of him that may not have been accurate.

Yet despite his financial problems and his possible inability to keep a job, she still felt so at ease with him. Sitting in the booth, they picked up right where they'd left off. Everything about him and their conversation felt so natural. When she looked into his eyes, she could see everything he wasn't saying. It was a type of extrasensory perception she still had with him.

"You loved me, didn't you?" She saw it in his eyes as they stared in silence—the wistfulness, the admiration, the remorse. She felt it in her heart. There was no need for words, but she had to ask. She had to confirm what she knew to be true.

"I did," he said. "And I never stopped." The words spilling out like lava, warming her soul.

Chapter 14

A cold draft traveled through the two-story home, leaving it chilly and pronouncing its emptiness. Dust settled on once shiny wood surfaces. Spiders spun their webs in dark corners. And the stale air—stuffy with the smell of old furniture, books, and lard—settled into crevices.

The silence reverberated against the walls as Rosa sat on the edge of their—her—bed and stared at the walk-in closet. The door was open, revealing shelves of grays, blacks, browns, and blues on Joe's side, and whites, pinks, purples, oranges, and reds on hers. She knew at some point she would have to get rid of his belongings—at least some of them. The rows of color-coordinated pants and shirts. His custom size-thirteen EEE shoes. His collection of Borsalino fedoras. His Rolex.

She found the strength to walk to his side of the closet as she grazed her hand across his blazers and moved along to his shirts. A crushing sensation enveloped her as she thought of him. She wanted so badly to smell him, touch him, hear his voice. And question him.

When she fell to the floor, she found herself on her knees, praying to God and asking for strength. She wasn't sure what she was even living for anymore. Her children were moving on with their lives. Their spouses. Their kids—her grandkids. She loved them, but they weren't Joe. Would they even miss her if she was gone? For a moment, she craved her own death. That would end this misery and bring her to Joe's side.

She was paying a price for her own longevity. A solitary confinement of sorts. Loneliness dug deep into her core. Silence punctuated the pain. She was watching her life from a distance. Seeing a past she could no longer live. She had become almost robotic as she went through her mundane daily routines. Sleeping alone. Cooking alone. Eating meals alone. Watching TV on the couch alone.

A screeching sound escaped from her throat and filled the oblivion of her world. Again and again she screamed as she began to grab bags, baskets, and shoes, throwing them with as much force as she could muster until her aching hands reminded her of their limits. Pale, wrinkle, and covered with age spots, her hands didn't seem to belong to her. Her fingers, knobby and arthritic, had taken on a claw-like appearance. When did she become this old?

Squeezing and wringing her hands together, stuck on the floor, wondering how she would get back up, she found herself staring at a small black leather duffel bag. As she reached for it, she didn't think she'd ever seen it before, though it was quite worn. The leather was smooth and supple and she rubbed her hands across it. The sound of the zipper pierced through the silence as she slid the pull tab along.

On top was a white T-shirt, which she smelled, searching for Joe's intoxicating scent—fresh cedar and bergamot that reminded her of walking through an enchanted forest. She didn't find it. Instead the shirt smelled of old leather, earthy with a hint of musk. She tossed the shirt onto the floor, followed by a pair of jeans, socks, and underwear. A matching toiletry bag filled with all of the necessary items needed for an overnight stay: a tooth-brush and toothpaste, soap, deodorant, Q-tips, a travel-sized container of lotion.

An old magazine. *Essence.* She read the 1990s cover: "Whitney Opens Up." She recognized Whitney Houston with perfectly styled hair smiling back at her. She studied her plum lipstick, smooth brown skin, dangling earrings, and sheer black top. She began flipping through the pages. "When Men Cheat." "Reclaiming Our Culture." Why would Joe have a woman's magazine in his bag? One for black women at that?

Her heartbeat began to accelerate, and a feeling of uneasiness seeped through her blood as she continued tossing items out of the bag. A brown leather belt. A pack of peanuts. A pair of oxfords. Then, a small black velvet box. She'd almost missed it because the interior lining of the bag was a dark gray. She retrieved the box carefully, as if it were a ticking bomb or bubble that might burst.

Her fingers trembled as she opened it and saw a sparkling diamond ring set in gold with baguette diamonds on each side. It was at least a carat. She pulled the ring from the satiny slit. Not just a ring, she realized, but an engagement ring.

She felt like Cinderella as she slid it on the ring finger of her right hand, thinking surely it would fit, only to discover that it wouldn't go past her knuckle. It was far too tiny to have been purchased for her, even before arthritis destroyed her joints. To be certain, she tried to slide it on her left-hand ring finger. No luck.

She could hear her heart beating, echoing in her head like a marching band gone mad. Her breathing was heavy and labored through her mouth—as if her nostrils were too small and her lungs constricted.

She brushed aside all of the irrational thoughts. Maybe this wasn't his bag? But these were clearly his clothes. Maybe he had been holding this ring for someone else? But surely, that person would have asked for its return after all these years. A sad realization clawed its way into her thinking.

If this ring wasn't meant for me, then who could Joe possibly have intended to give it to? She imagined the face of the girl with the gray eyes, and the impact of the realization hit her like a punch in the gut, her organs twisting and turning as she swallowed the urge to regurgitate her breakfast.

Another woman. A woman who was more than just a mistress. A woman who was also the mother of the girl with the gray eyes. A woman he must have loved.

If he bought this ring but never gave it to its intended recipient, why on earth didn't he return it and get his money back?

Because he still had hope.

Rosa listened to the gurgling water rising from the hot tub in their backyard as she dug vigorously into the soil of a flower bed. Some of the weeds came out without a fight, their roots wiggling in the breeze as she tossed them into a black plastic bag, but others had to be wrested from the ground. At one time in her life, she could have yanked them out, but now she needed the assistance of her trowel.

Prepping their yard for winter was a task she'd done for many years. She envisioned a landscape of colors as she glanced at her collection of perennials waiting to be planted: blue asters, white clematis, and purple echinacea. She was thinking she would have fresh-cut flowers for their—her—kitchen once they spread and bloomed. *My* kitchen, she thought. *Mine*, not ours anymore. She was considering where she would plant the poppy seeds when she heard the creaking sound of the iron gate.

"Hi, Mom," Catarine called.

"Oh, hi honey," Rosa replied. "How are you?"

"So-so. How are you?"

"I'm hanging in here still. Tackling this garden has been a good distraction."

"You ready for a break? I brought lunch from Fausto's—Caesar salads, manicotti, and eggplant parmigiana." Catarine held up a brown paper bag as if she'd won a prize.

"That sounds delicious." Rosa removed her gloves and joined Catarine at the patio table.

"I'm glad to see you being active, Ma—getting back into your gardening." Catarine scanned the yard as she unloaded the brown paper bag. "I see we have a lot of overgrown bushes and weeds. I think you could use some help."

"Well, I know you're busy. You have your own life." Rosa removed the lid from her salad.

"I'm not too busy for you, Ma. I know you miss Dad, and this has to be even harder for you being here alone now."

Rosa blinked back tears at the thought of Joe—and the black bag.

"Honey, do you think your dad ever cheated on me?" she blurted out.

She watched Catarine toss the question around in her head, open her mouth and then close it, before saying, "I think Dad was flirtatious—you know how charming he was. But I don't think he acted on any of it."

Rosa told her about the black bag, releasing the discovery like a gushing oil well.

"Hmm." Catarine's face contorted as she considered the bag and its contents. "Are you absolutely sure it was his bag?"

Rosa tilted her head, pursed her lips, and inhaled deeply. She thought Catarine would be more logical than this. "Of course it was his bag. All of the clothes were his size. The shoes were definitely his. But the bag was like a time capsule. The magazine date says it all. He must have forgotten about it, because he didn't touch it for years. And that ring! I don't know what to make of it. I've been racking my brain trying to remember the late 1980s or early 1990s. There was a period when he was traveling a lot for work."

She was trying desperately to recall those years, but it was like trying to see the bottom of a muddy lake. She thought again of the girl—a young woman, really. She had to be in her twenties.

"Let's say he did have an affair," Catarine said. "I think a lot of men do, right? But he stayed with you. He loved *you*."

"If he had an affair, our marriage was a lie. I lived with wool over my eyes all these years," Rosa concluded. "And to think that the woman was probably black."

"Black?" Catarine raised her eyebrows.

"There was a magazine in the bag. *Essence*. It's for black women." Not to mention, the girl with the gray eyes was mixed—a mulatto.

"Oh. I've never even heard of it."

"Well, why would you? I hadn't either, but when I flipped through the pages, it was definitely for black women."

"Was there an address on it, like was it someone's subscription?"

Rosa could feel her face lighting up at the thought. In her angst and haste, she hadn't examined it that closely. "Let's go find out." She slammed her fork on the table and shoved her chair back, nearly losing her balance as she stood. They rushed into the house, through the kitchen, past the den, and down the hall to the master bedroom. Rosa hadn't had this much energy in months.

Breathing heavily when she reached the closet, she pulled out the black bag. She had practically buried it in a corner beneath a pile of sheets. Out of sight, out of mind. But every time she walked into the closet, she glanced at that corner and thought about the bag. She thought about when she watched TV, when she prepared her meals, when she showered, when she did almost anything. Always, always, that diamond engagement ring was sparkling in her mind.

As Rosa bent over to pick up the bag, Catarine gently placed her arms on her mother's shoulders and pulled her back.

"I'll get it for you," she offered. She grabbed the handle of the bag, walked into the bedroom, and placed it on the bed. She unzipped it quickly and began searching for the magazine. Holding it flat against her chest, she asked, "Do you want to look, or do you want me to?"

Rosa snatched the magazine from Catarine, flipped it over, and inhaled in disbelief.

They both stared at a name and an address: Lisa Foster, 4100 N. Rampart, New Orleans, LA 70117.

Rosa's chest heaved as she struggled to breathe. Her face felt drained of blood, and her hands trembled as she held on to the magazine.

"Here, Mom, why don't you sit down," Catarine said as she pulled the magazine, with some effort, from her mother's hands and escorted her to a wingback chair in the sitting area of the room.

"It's true. It's true. I can't believe it's true," Rosa said. "I knew it. I knew it all along, but I didn't want to believe it. Lisa fucking Foster."

"Mom!" Catarine exclaimed. "I know you're upset, but this was a long time ago. Many, many years ago. Whatever happened, it must have been over when he put this bag away. It seems like he never touched it again."

"I need to find this Lisa," Rosa said. "I need to know exactly what happened. What is the address on that damned magazine?"

"Um, I doubt that she lives at this address anymore," Catarine sighed as she read the address to her mom. "I mean, she may not even be alive."

"You never know. We've lived here for more than thirty years." Rosa's voice was flat. "Will you take me there, to that address? I at least want to see where Joe was apparently spending his time when he claimed to be working."

His love child might also be there, she thought, as she bit her bottom lip and dug her fingers into the sides of the chair. She had a few things she wanted to say to the love child.

Chapter 15

The paintings on Natalia's living-room walls captured the beauty of the world. She'd always wanted to travel, but without the money to do so, she tried to bring the world to herself instead. Some of the paintings she'd done herself over the years in her spare time. Others she'd picked up at art shows or thrift stores. She'd found her collection of the Seven Wonders of the Ancient World at garage and estate sales. The colors created a soothing space for her—shades of blue from the sky and Mediterranean Sea, beige sands, and white columns.

Her own drawings included architectural buildings, beaches, and sketches, and were mixed among the Wonders. She was still refining her techniques but thought if she could see some of these wonders in person, she could better re-create them. The closest she'd come to seeing anything amazing was a mission trip to Haiti she'd taken as a teenager with her church's youth group. She had marveled at the vibrant colors of small boxy homes stair-stepping up mountain slopes, the height of the palm trees, and the turquoise waters of the Atlantic, but what she remembered most were the children's faces—their bright eyes and ready smiles despite the poverty that surrounded them. That's when she began sketching.

She was staring at a sketch of a young girl she'd met there—Esther—when her phone rang. She didn't recognize the number on her caller id, but she picked it up anyway.

"Hello?"

"Well, hello stranger." It was the deep, recognizable voice of Dr. Duplessis.

"Hello, Doctor." She smiled.

"Now, I told you, you can call me David," he said lightly. "How are you?"

Three words she'd heard a million times, but never with such sincerity. The words enunciated in such a way that each could stand on its own. He really wanted to know.

She was glad he didn't ask why she hadn't returned his call two weeks earlier. She wasn't sure herself whether she was avoiding him, if she was just afraid, or if she was too focused on Tyler.

"I'm better. If I were to go through the stages of grief, I would say I'm at acceptance. I feel like everything happened so quickly. One minute I'm living my life, thinking I'll have a chance to meet my dad one day, and the next minute he's gone. I think I liked having that hope—you know, it gave me something to hold on to. And I'd created all of these images of him and imagined what it would be like to meet him for the first time. When I was a kid, I would see men in random places—grocery stores, the mall—and wonder if they were my dad. Crazy, right?" She was talking too much and too fast, and suddenly she was worried, wondering what David was thinking.

"Not crazy at all."

"How are *you*?" she asked.

"Pretty good. Keeping busy at work as usual—and thinking about you."

The words arrested her mind. Piqued her curiosity. Made her lips spread into a hopeful curve.

"What exactly have you been thinking?"

"Hoping you're okay. Wondering if you need anything and how I might be able to help you," he explained.

"Well, that's very nice of you. I do think I'm coming around."

"Have you thought any further about reaching out to one of his other children?" he asked.

"No. I think I'm too afraid. I don't even know how or if we would relate to each other. I mean, they're white after all, and were raised completely differently. What if they're all racist?" she asked, half joking.

"Yeah, members of the KKK?" he went along.

She laughed—though she thought it was certainly possible they believed their race really was superior, their white privilege eclipsing the truth. "I need to give it more thought. It's a matter of how badly I want to know the Joe that used to be. Would I completely tarnish his name and their image of him?"

"You never know. The other siblings might be happy to meet and get to know you. As far as I can tell, you seem pretty cool."

"Thanks. You're not so bad yourself."

"That's good to hear," he laughed.

They moved from the topic of Joe and his children to David's hobbies: basketball, cooking, camping, and listening to music. Then on to her hobbies: painting, running, and anything artsy—plays, museums, dance performances.

"So, what are you doing this weekend? I have a hookup and can get tickets to Alvin Ailey. I'd like to take you."

"I'd love to go," she said quickly. She thought about holding David's hand again, feeling his warm skin, but stopped herself before she went further.

"I'll take you to dinner first," he said. "Am I allowed to know where you live, so I can pick you up?"

"I suppose I can give you my address," she laughed.

The weekend couldn't arrive fast enough. After dealing with a difficult client all week—a woman with an unlimited budget who seemed to not like anything (Natalia preferred parameters, people who knew their limits)—she needed a break. She couldn't believe how excited she was about her date with David. The problem was, she realized she had no idea what she should wear. She dialed Pamela's and begged her to go shopping.

"Girl, you know you never have to ask me twice to go shopping," Pamela replied. "I'll pick you up in an hour."

"It's ridiculous. I can't believe how excited I am."

"Maybe you're excited because Tyler's broke ass can't take you anywhere," she said matter-of-factly.

Natalia had told her about their chance encounter. "Now, you know that's not fair. He's fighting for his life! You just don't like him."

"I sure in the hell don't. I don't like what he did to you. I know he's trying to live, but didn't you say he was going to make it?" Pamela didn't wait for Natalia's response. "He's going to be just fine. You need to let him be. Maybe he should beg his wife to take him back."

"Well, they're not actually divorced yet."

"Either way, he's just not the one, and I don't know why you ever thought he was. Now, Dr. Duplessis—he sounds like a fresh start."

"But you know, I kind of think maybe my dad somehow led me back to Tyler. What are the chances that I would have run into him? If my dad hadn't had cancer, I don't think I would have chosen it as a cause to support."

"Well, what are the chances you would have met an attractive doctor who's never been married and doesn't have kids? Maybe Joe—or God—led you to him. Satan led you to Tyler."

Natalia couldn't help but laugh. "You're crazy! So, back to me and my date with David. I need something to wear. We're going to Alvin Ailey, but we're having dinner first."

"Ooh, now that's what I'm talkin' about! Most definitely a dress. I'll be there soon. Bye!"

They were in Express, sliding hangers across the bars as music blared from overhead speakers.

"This would look fabulous on you!" Pamela held up a royal-blue and black dress with a ruffled bottom.

"That's pretty cute. Let's find a few more just in case it doesn't fit right."

After Natalia had tried on three more dresses, Pamela convinced her that the black and blue one was the way to go. They checked out a couple of other stores for accessories and shoes, then decided to grab a bite to eat.

As they approached the fiesta food court, Natalia stopped abruptly. Tyler was sitting at a table with a woman and his daughter, or rather, his wife's daughter. Pamela followed her eyes and froze. It seemed like an eternity before Pamela grabbed her arm and led her out of the area, but not before Tyler noticed Natalia standing there. His eyes turned into saucers, his lips slightly open.

Dazed, she let Pamela lead her away toward the stores and back into the throngs of the mall. People rushing by, pushing babies in strollers, shifting shopping bags from one hand to another.

"So, was that his wife and kid?" Pamela was staring intently at Natalia.

"Yes. They looked pretty cozy sitting over there."

Natalia's heart was still racing when she felt Tyler place his arm at the small of her back. Her spine tingled at his touch. As she turned to face him, everything else became a blur—except him. His blue baseball cap, pecan-colored skin, white T-shirt, and the apology in his eyes.

"Hey. It's not what you think," he said calmly.

"So, what is it?" Pamela asked in a nasty tone, jolting Natalia back to the fact that they were in a mall.

"Hey, Pamela!" Tyler said as if they were old friends. Pamela turned her lips downward in response. "I'm sorry—can you give us a minute?"

Pamela looked at Natalia, who nodded, and she stomped off to a nearby bench.

"It's not at *all* what you think," he said.

"So, you two are at least still friends, I see?" Natalia hoped she was disguising her jealousy.

"Yes—just friends. I think she may want to work things out, but I don't know."

Natalia was astounded. She thought they'd reconnected. That they had rekindled whatever they'd had six years ago. They'd been texting each other regularly. He had insinuated that he wanted to see her again. That there was still hope for them.

"It's a long story. I can't get into right now, but I promise I'll explain when we have more time."

Natalia watched him walk back toward the food court. She was still stunned when Pamela pulled her arm and dragged her away. She tried to erase the image of them sitting, laughing, the little girl staring up at him, then leaning her head against his arm. Love was all around them. A happy family.

But the trio stayed with her like her own shadow.

Wrestling with her shopping bags, Natalia slammed her front door with the back of her foot. Still simmering from the glimpse of Tyler and his family, she realized she didn't know him anymore. Years had passed, and they were completely different people. She needed to let the past go and focus on her future. She needed to focus on David.

She tossed her bags on her bed and decided a long bath would do her good. She still had three hours before he picked her up. The thought of it made her begin to second-guess her decision to give him her address, which she had a rule never to give out on the first date. But this was technically their second date, and the thought of him knocking on her front door, opening the passenger door of his car for her, and driving her around was far too appealing. She wanted to stare at his profile, study every angle of his face, his neck, his hands on the steering wheel. She wanted to breathe in his scent.

She took her time applying makeup, layering conditioner on her hair as she tamed it, and choosing from her new accessories.

When her doorbell rang, she'd been watching TV for over an hour. *On time*, she thought as she walked to the door, her heels clicking against the wood floors.

"You look stunning." He smiled as he handed her a bouquet of white calla lilies, lavender daisies, and green poms.

Well, this is a first, she thought and felt herself blushing. "Thank you. And you look very dapper." He did. Black shoes, black slacks, and a black-, white-, and blue-striped button-down shirt. He was clean-shaven and smelled of citrus and spice, a warm yet formal fragrance full of something familiar—bergamot maybe. Or was it sandalwood? She wanted to bury her face in his neck. "Are we actually color coordinated?" she giggled. She'd have to thank Pamela later.

"Yes, yes—I'm glad you got my message," he laughed.

"Come on in. I'll put these beauties in a vase." She turned around as she inhaled the fragrant smells.

"I finally get to see some of your artwork," he said as he stepped into her living room and toward her art wall—a burst of colors, patterns, acrylic paintings, and watercolors.

"Yes," she called from the kitchen. "You should be able to easily tell which ones are mine and which ones were purchased!"

She placed the flowers in the center of her dining table and joined him. Standing side by side, they played a guessing game as he correctly identified all of her pieces.

"Well, they are all signed. You're definitely talented. And look at your place," he said admiringly, sweeping his arm around the room. It's eclectic and cool."

"That could be partly by accident and not design." She smiled, thinking of her secondhand purchases and garage sale finds.

"I know it's by design. You'll have to help me with my place. It's more sterile than an operating room. Now that I think about it, everything is basically black and white."

"Typical bachelor pad," she said, shaking her head.

"Also, it looks like maybe we need to plan a trip to Greece, Turkey, Egypt . . . in the future?" He gestured toward the Seven Wonders.

He's already thinking long-term. She smiled. His words were like a halo hanging above her, a ring of light filtering down, illuminating her heart. But she didn't want to get her hopes up. It was certainly too early to tell.

"You know, I wanted to be an architect when I was much younger. I would sketch and design buildings. But when I got to college and realized I would have to take a bunch of math courses, I had to figure out something else. So now I just admire the buildings and cool architecture."

"Instead, you paint and sketch lifelike portraits. Look at her eyes." He squinted, studying the sketch of the smiling girl.

"Thank you." She felt herself blushing again. She told him about her missionary trip and about Esther, the Haitian girl who had so little but who was still so happy.

"Hey, we better get going," he said, looking at his watch.

Just as she'd imagined, he opened the car door for her and she slid into the passenger seat of his sports car. She wasn't sure what kind of vehicle it was, just that it seemed high-end with its black leather seats and shiny silver paint.

"So, I hope you're hungry," he said.

"I'm starving actually!" she exclaimed. "But don't worry. I'll maintain my manners."

"Good, I was kind of concerned about that—your manners. Glad I don't have to school you on that," he laughed. "I'm taking you to my favorite seafood restaurant," he continued. "They have the best fish in town."

"Any desserts?" She raised her eyebrows.

"Yes, award winning." He smiled.

Being with David was like stepping into a fairy tale. He held her hand throughout the night: as they walked into the restaurant, when they left, as they made their way to the concert hall, and when they strolled back to the car. During the concert, he wrapped his arm protectively around her shoulders. They sat close to each other, their legs touching.

She was in awe during the performance. Brown, muscular, elegant bodies jumping and moving gracefully across the stage. The beautiful colors of their costumes coinciding with the time periods. The music flooding the room, taking them to faraway places where anything was possible.

She felt warm and light as they emerged from the hall into the cool night, David holding her hand. A full moon illuminated everything around them—intricate iron rails along the staircase outside the theater, small puddles from yesterday's downpour—giving the night a dreamlike appearance.

They approached his car and then stood facing each other. His arm encircled her waist and he leaned down and kissed her softly. Her face was upturned and slightly angled, lips completely ready and accepting. As he drew her in closer, she wrapped her arms around his neck, wanting more.

They pulled away to take a breath. Her nose brushed against his neck and she inhaled his cologne. She wanted to taste him, but knew she needed to take things slowly. Wasn't that her problem all along—moving too fast and tiring too quickly as a result?

They had no need for words when he released her. She breathed in deeply, feeling like she was in a field of roses as she floated into the passenger seat.

Chapter 16

Catarine made a sharp turn on St. Claude, throwing her mother's body sharply against the passenger door. Rosa continued to bark directions at her daughter, who simply wasn't driving fast enough.

"Mom, I'm seeing a side of you I never knew existed," Catarine marveled. "Were you this feisty when you were younger?"

"I was never a pushover, if that's what you think," Rosa said. "I know you're probably thinking I was naïve and how could I not have known? I've thought about that myself. Your dad—he was pretty sneaky about this." She refused to use the word "affair," as that would give the relationship more meaning. But she knew that's exactly what it was. There was a ring, after all. And a child. "Slow down," Rosa demanded, looking at the GPS on her phone. "You need to turn left here."

After a couple of blocks, they approached a double shotgun house with small patches of unedged grass, pale-yellow peeling paint, and mismatched front doors, one black with a screen and the other white. Concrete steps framed by iron rails led to two small porches with miscellaneous items: a bench, potted plants, a rocking chair, a baby doll's stroller. The home looked much like the others on the street, old but solid and well lived in.

"She can't possibly still live here, Mom," Catarine reminded her as she peered over her sunglasses at the house.

Rosa inhaled deeply before she opened the car door and walked toward the side of the house with the black door.

"Mom!" Catarine yelled. "What are you doing?" She hopped out of the car and reached her mother just as she was approaching the steps.

"You never know," Rosa said, her eyes dark and narrow.

"You said you just wanted to *see* the house," Catarine pleaded as she pulled on Rosa's arm.

Without thinking twice, Rosa yanked her arm away and charged up the stairs. Wringing her hands, Catarine followed and watched as her mother pushed her crooked finger on the doorbell button, which triggered the barking of a dog.

"I wonder what kind of dog they have," Catarine asked in as casual a tone as possible. "Maybe a pit bull or a Rottweiler."

Rosa stared straight ahead as if she didn't hear her.

"You know, we probably shouldn't even be in this neighborhood," Catarine said as she looked up and down the street. She clicked the car remote to lock the doors.

When the front door burst open, the dog—a black and brown German shepherd—lunged at them. A teenager with mocha-colored skin and a hi-top fade grabbed its collar, pulling it back. "Yeah?" he asked, rubbing his eyes, looking from one to the other.

"Do you know a Lisa Foster? Does she still live here?" Rosa's voice was clear and strong.

"Nah, I don't, why?" he asked suspiciously.

"I need to talk with her," Rosa said. "She lived here—I guess before you and your family moved in."

"I don't know." He shrugged his shoulders, seemingly bored with Rosa's line of questioning.

"Well, is your mother here?" she asked.

He partially shut the front door. "Ma!" he yelled. They could hear traces of words, his voice deep as he tried to whisper: "white ladies," "looking for," "no idea."

"Yes, may I help you?" A middle-aged bronze-colored woman appeared from the kitchen.

"Are you Lisa Foster?" Rosa asked.

"No," the woman said, her brows furrowed. "She doesn't live here anymore."

"Do you know her?"

The woman squinted as if she were thinking through an algebra problem. Then she shook her head. "Sorry, I can't help you."

"You don't know who lived here before you?"

Now the woman was looking at Rosa as if she had six eyeballs.

"Mom, let's go. She doesn't know," Catarine said emphatically as she backed away, hoping her mother would follow.

"I don't know her. Sorry."

"No problem. Thank you," Catarine said over her shoulder as they walked down the stairs.

The car ride back was tense as Catarine endured her mother's rants and tears. She tried to console her, but Rosa seemed to be crumbling, rocking back and forth on a fast pendulum of anxiety and despair.

For Rosa, the car was filled with an invisible, suffocating cotton. She stared at the people in the cars passing by. She wondered whether the woman had been telling the truth. Now that the moment had passed, she thought about what she would have done if she had come face to face with Lisa Foster. She didn't know. But she was going to make sure that she would find out more about Joe's mystery woman.

Chapter 17

Fervent feelings have a way of magnifying everything—every moment, every memory, every expectation.

The more time Natalia spent with David, the more clarity she found as a veil lifted and revealed the truth of her relationship with Tyler. Like the view through a camera lens coming into focus, those days she'd had with Tyler became more of exactly what they had been and not what she'd imagined them to be. He had never brought her flowers. He had never called her baby. He had never talked of a real future with her.

But. (There was always a "but" with Tyler.) They were young. And now things could be different. Perhaps her comparisons of him to David weren't fair. So, when Tyler called to apologize again for the mall scene and asked to meet her in person to explain, she relented.

They decided to get drinks after work at a bar near her duplex. He was already there when she rushed in five minutes late.

"Hey, you," he said as he hugged her tightly. She was surprised at his strength.

"Hey yourself," she said, smiling.

"You look so artsy and cool," he said, commenting on her wardrobe—white slacks, a pink sleeveless blouse, and gold jewelry.

"I had a meeting with a client, so I had to dress up a bit."

They grabbed a booth directly across from the bar and began the dance of small talk—how was her client meeting, fine; how was his day, good; had she been here before, yes, she lived nearby; how's the food, pretty good.

"I usually go with one of their salads—the crab cake one is the best," she recommended.

They placed their orders as she realized this was turning into dinner.

"So, Mr. Davis, I guess we have some catching up to do again?"

"We do. First, let me just say, that was not what you thought. We're being cordial for our child."

"Your child?" Her face contorted at the misnomer. She needed to tamp down the crazy person that was raring to come out.

"Well, yes. I'm the only dad she's ever known. I love her like she's my own."

"I can certainly understand that," she said, though she really couldn't. She'd never created a bond with a child or paid much attention to babies.

The waitress plopped down their drinks, two waters with a lemon in each. "You sure you don't want a glass of wine or one of our mixed drinks?" she urged.

"No, thank you. We're good," Tyler responded.

"Ooookay," she said, as if they would regret it. They must have looked like they were having an intense conversation.

Natalia studied Tyler as he explained the problems in his marriage and the pain he'd suffered. She'd heard some of this already, but she listened anyway. *That's it*, she thought. That's what's changed. He carries the disheveled look of heartbreak: slightly wrinkled clothes, sad eyes, and an aura of disappointment and defeat. He was no longer the carefree, smooth-skinned, athletic young man she once knew. Fine lines were making their mark around his eyes. He was thinner. He even seemed to move in slow motion as he placed his glass back on the table. Of course, that was also side effects of the chemo. He needed a wave of happiness to wash all of this away. She felt an immense amount of sorrow for him. When her eyes began to tear up, he stopped talking.

"Sorry, I'm just—you've been through so much," she sighed.

"No, *I'm* sorry. I shouldn't be dwelling on these things with you. I should be enjoying your company, enjoying just looking at you."

She could see admiration in his eyes, and she couldn't deny that despite all of the baggage he carried, she still felt drawn to him. She couldn't ignore the feeling that she wanted to help him—relieve him of his load, even if for only a little while. But she also couldn't ignore a feeling that she needed to be cautious. It was as if Tyler was surrounded by a ring of flames. The closer she got, the more she could feel the heat. She didn't want to be burned again.

They finished their meals and decided to window-shop as they strolled through the district, walking at Tyler's slow pace. Windows full of expensive home décor from fur rugs and hand-blown glassware to leather ottomans and luxurious bedding enticed passersby to come in and browse the full selections.

A subtle breeze stirred the tubes of a wind chime, and the melodic and calming sounds resonated across and down the street. Magnolia trees rustled while flowers in planters on each corner danced. A couple of performers filled the streets with their voices and instruments—a woman and man singing a capella, joined by a harmonica.

"I can't believe how much some of these things cost." Natalia shook her head, looking through the window of a home décor boutique. "We have so many clients who have no problem with these prices. They spend thousands on rugs, lamps, artwork. Meanwhile, I'm thinking, 'I could refurnish my entire apartment for the cost of one of these purchases!'"

They were approaching the window of a lighting store when Tyler reached for her hand. She tensed up, her fingers becoming rigid as wood.

"What's wrong?" he asked.

How could she explain the turmoil in her head? If only he'd chosen her to begin with. Instead, he'd gone off and ruined their love. And now she was falling for someone else.

"I don't know. Things just feel off to me." She folded her arms.

"Let's sit down." He motioned to a nearby empty bench in the courtyard of a small office complex.

"You're dealing with so much," she began as they sat, "and you're still legally married. You have a child now. You're recovering from cancer. I don't know how you're managing, and I don't know where I fit. The fact is, I don't think I fit anywhere in your picture. I want to—my heart wants to, but I don't see how. Not to mention . . . I've met someone else."

There. She'd said it. She and David were spending more and more time together. Working out. Lunch. Dinner. Movies. Art museums. She anticipated his calls and couldn't stop smiling when she thought of him. By their sixth date, she felt like she'd known him all her life. She was already helping him redesign his home, a home she might live in someday. Once torn between the two, she was tilting and falling hard for David. She would close her eyes and relax just listening to the sound of his voice.

Yes, Tyler had tried to spend time with her. She'd ignored his calls and the messages he'd left for a couple of weeks, still stung by the mall episode and the sobering reality of his life. David would always win out when it came to her time. She was somewhat saddened to completely let Tyler go—not that he was actually hers to release—but she knew the time had come for a real commitment to David.

"You met someone?" Tyler raised his eyebrows.

"Yes. I don't want to get into details, but I just don't see how you and I could work. I'll always care for you. I know you know that."

He was staring incredulously at her. "I don't want to lose you again, Natalia."

Strong words, she thought. Words she wished he'd uttered six years ago.

"I know things seem complicated right now, but they'll change. My health is turning around—"

"This has nothing to do with your health," she said defensively.

"I know, I know. I can tell you're concerned. I see the pity in your eyes. Are you just hanging around because you feel sorry for me?"

"Of course not! You know how much I care for you," she said. "It's just—how do I explain this?" She turned to face him but couldn't speak when she saw the pain in his eyes. She felt uncertainty shaking the solidity of her decision. Her thoughts turned into mush. She didn't do well with confusion. Second-guessing her decisions was now second nature to her.

"I know what you're thinking," he said. "I know I should have chosen you. Believe me, I thought of you often. I felt even worse about it, because my wife had no idea. I felt like I was cheating on her mentally. Really, I was. I wondered what you were doing with your life. If you'd gotten married. If you had kids. What you looked like. I thought about your smile. I almost looked you up and called you one day." He turned to face her, taking her hands into his. "I regret not choosing you. It was one of the biggest mistakes of my life. But we have a second chance now. I feel like I've been transported back in time. Nothing has changed. My attraction for you. My feelings for you. It's like we're picking up where we left off."

"But we're not," Natalia responded, pulling her hands away and folding her arms. "So much *has* changed. If it were just you and me, that would be one thing. But it's not. You have a divorce to get through. That will be incredibly difficult. I know you still care for her, too, or you wouldn't have married her. You have a child now. You have to figure out a whole new life—possibly a new career even."

He'd mentioned wanting to go back to school and becoming the lawyer he thought he was meant to be.

"Everything has been derailed, I know. I'm trying to get it all back on track now," he pleaded.

"Oh, Tyler. I don't know what to say. I've thought about you, too. I've loved you and hated you at the same time. I just don't know that my future is in my past anymore."

"You don't think it's a sign—serendipity—that we ran into each other again?"

Of course she had thought about that. She'd thought Joe had led her back to Tyler. But Pamela had been right: he'd also led her to David. She shrugged her shoulders and shook her head.

"So, where does this leave us?" he asked.

"I don't know," she sighed.

He rested his head in his hands, elbows on his legs. Natalia rubbed his back and they sat in silence.

The conflicting nature of emotions could take their toll on a person. Wearing them down. Wearing them out. Like being shaken instead of gently stirred. Each day brought about varying outcomes. One day, things are going one way. The next, they're going another.

When Natalia was back in the solitude of her bedroom, with the darkness dispelling some of her anxiety, she tried to reconcile the past and think more clearly about her future. The men weaving in and out of her life. The father she never had. His family. Her career. She wished she had a crystal ball. Her gut had normally served as her guide, but she couldn't trust it anymore. She knew she couldn't continue to follow her heart, because look where that had gotten her. She had wasted years pining over a love that may not have been true. She had to be smarter about her decisions. She couldn't let destiny dictate her path.

But she saw so many scenarios before her. So many ways things could play out. She could only hope for happiness. A fulfilling career. A relationship with a family that, at the moment, seemingly wanted nothing to do with her. And true love. She closed her eyes and prayed.

Autumn – October

"The wound is the place where the light enters you."

—Rumi

Chapter 18

It was the fourth of October, and Natalia was keenly aware that she needed to pay several bills, including her rent. A procrastinator by nature, she seldom took care of them on the first of the month. *No use putting it off any longer,* she thought, as she trudged over to a tray that was tucked away on a bookshelf in her dining area. She grabbed a short stack of envelopes she'd tossed inside and realized she hadn't checked her mailbox in several days. Begrudgingly, she opened her front door, walked down the stairs, and used a tiny key to open the small metal door of the mail compartment. Envelopes and flyers were wedged inside. Maybe it had been more like several weeks.

She marched back up the stairs, added the pile to her stack, and decided she could use a cup of Community Coffee. Even though she no longer lived in New Orleans, she was still stuck on its food and some of its beverages. She flipped through an interior design magazine on her kitchen counter while she waited for the coffee to finish brewing. The aroma wafted across the kitchen and into the living room as she listened to the bubbling and gurgling of the pot. When it stopped, she poured a cup into her favorite mug—an oversize one-of-a-kind piece of handspun porcelain streaked with brown, tan, and black. She added half-and-half and three teaspoons of sugar, stirred, then sat down at her kitchen table to sort through her financial life.

Discover. Express. Macy's. *I need to stop using these credit cards*, she thought. Junk mail. Junk mail. More junk mail. Then, at the bottom, a thick, official-looking envelope from:

MACCINI & MACCINI
909 POYDRAS, #800
NEW ORLEANS, LA 70139

She slid her thumb across the seal. Surely it wasn't a collections agency. She wasn't *that* far behind with her bills.

IN THE MATTER OF THE ESTATE OF JOEL L. RUSSO
CASE NUMBER J00034268

NOTICE TO HEIRS

THE STATE OF LOUISIANA

PROBATE COURT OF ORLEANS PARISH

To the heirs and devisees of the above-named Estate:

This is formal Notice that Joel L. Russo, the decedent, died on August 12 of this year, and you have or may have an interest in Joel L. Russo's Estate.

Dan Maccini has been appointed as the administrator of the Estate.

All documents, pleading and information relating to the Estate are on file in the Orleans Parish Civil District Court under case number J00034268.

The assets of the Estate of Joel L. Russo will be distributed 30 days following the date of this Notice. We request your attendance at a hearing within this timeframe. Please call our office for details.

All recipients of this Notice are hereby informed that each is entitled to information regarding the administration of the decedent's Estate.
In the event any heir or devisee has a question or issue relating to this Estate including the distribution of assets, payments of expenses or other administration matters, the heir or devisee may petition the Court in Orleans Parish.

Dan Maccini, Administrator of the Estate

Dan Maccini

After reading the letter twice, she called her mom.

"Good morning," Lisa answered.

"Hey, Ma. You are not going to believe this." Natalia paced frantically around her living room, her slippers flopping against the floor. Before her mom could respond, she continued, "I just received this letter in the mail—well, it's probably been in my mailbox for several days. . . ." She walked back to the table to grab the letter. "Yes, it's dated October twelfth, but I think it's basically saying that . . . that I'm in Joe's will and that I need to schedule an appointment at this lawyer's office in a couple of weeks."

She waited several beats, and when her mother didn't respond, she asked, "Did you hear me?"

"I don't know what to say. Are you telling me Joe actually named you in his will?"

"I guess. I mean that's what it sounds like, right? He had an estate? That sounds pretty grand."

"Well, he did the right thing in the end, then," her mom said softly. "He did the right thing."

"Do you think they'll all be there? His family—wife and kids?" Her voice was shaky and her feet unsteady. She sat on her couch and began rocking back and forth.

"I have no idea," her mom said. "You could call the lawyer that sent you the letter and find out."

"Good idea. But would that seem suspicious?"

"I don't think so. They would be able to tell you how that type of thing works. We never had no estates in our family, so I couldn't even guess."

"I'll call them first thing Monday morning. Love you."

"Love you too, baby."

Natalia held the letter and reread it several times, unable to do much of anything for the next hour but ponder what it could

135

mean. Not only financially but emotionally. What would his family say? She assumed they would also attend this hearing. She imagined their anger would swell since presumably they couldn't all already know about her. She was sure his son hadn't spoken a word about her existence. If they knew about her, she imagined they would have tried to contact her by now. This could get very ugly. She twirled and pulled at her hair as she pictured the venom, the turned-down mouths, the up-and-down looks: not only an illegitimate child, but a *black* one?

Chapter 19

Enthused by the arrival of fall, cooler temperatures, and no humidity—she loved the changing colors, the crunching sound of dead leaves beneath her feet—Rosa thought some fresh air might do her good. She would rake the leaves fallen from their red oak, pull weeds, and plant a few perennials in the front yard.

She craved the feeling of the cool soil between her fingers as she showered, dressed, and brushed her hair. She noticed more of it in the brush but decided not to dwell on it. She would head to Home Depot to purchase her wish list: purple petunias, blue bachelor buttons, pink Knock Out roses, irises, purple foxglove, and probably pink snapdragons.

She picked up her purse and was looking for her keys when the phone rang. "Hello?" she said hesitantly. In the weeks following Joe's death, she'd received phone calls every day from family members and friends who wanted to make sure she was okay. Her neighbors left casseroles at her door. She also received cards daily in the mail. But after a few weeks, silence. The phone stopped ringing. The casseroles stopped showing up on her porch.

"Hello, Rosa?" a deep male voice asked.

"Yes?"

"This is Dan."

"Oh yes, hello, Dan. How are you?" She could picture him in his plush office, legs propped up on his oversize, cherry-finished desk. She'd always found him a bit cocky, but he and Joe had been friends since high school.

"I'm good, good. I know this is probably still too soon. But I, uh, wanted to see if I could come by to meet with you to discuss Joe's will?"

Silence.

"Or, you're welcome to come by our office. I just thought it might be easier for you if I visited with you at your home."

"Is it something we can discuss over the phone?" she asked, not in the mood for company, and certainly not a legal discussion. She knew it was coming, but she was hoping she had more time before they dissected and distributed Joe's finances—their finances.

"Well, I think it would be better if we met in person. I need to review some paperwork with you and explain some things now that we've completed succession."

She wanted to get to her gardening, not discuss financial matters with a lawyer. She knew Joe had more than provided for her with his life insurance policy and an annuity. In addition, she knew he would do right by their children.

"Okay, why don't you come by?" she relented.

"What time would be good for you?"

"How about one o'clock?"

"You bet. I'll see you then."

Rosa stared at her complexion as she dabbed at her freshly washed face with a hand towel. She'd hoped the cool water would deflate the bags beneath her eyes. Like the ground emerging after a thick fog, the woman staring back at her was suddenly visible in a new light—and she was almost unrecognizable.

I've let myself go. She wondered what Joe would think about her appearance. It was like she was seeing herself for the first time. *When did I begin to look this way?* She reached for a tube of red lipstick—a wand of hope—as she slid it across her thin lips. *I look like a clown,* she thought as she pulled out a Kleenex to wipe it off. *Maybe just some blush will do.*

A hard knock at her bedroom door jolted her back into reality.

"Ma!" It was Joe Jr.

"Yes, son?"

"Dan is here." She listened to his footsteps as he walked away.

She was happy to see that Dan already had a glass of water and was seated on their living-room sofa, papers stacked on their mahogany coffee table. She was glad she didn't have to deal with treating him like a guest.

"Hello, Rosa." He stood and hugged her warmly, a gesture seeping with sympathy.

"Hello, Dan," she said before lowering herself into a burgundy side chair at the end of the coffee table.

"I'm here to walk through Joe's will and several documents—life insurance, annuities, transfer of assets, savings accounts." He began separating the papers into stacks.

"Were there any surprises in Joe's will?" Rosa asked. "Anything unexpected we should know about?"

She followed Dan's gaze to Joe Jr., who was sitting in an armchair at the opposite end of the coffee table. She noticed the almost imperceptible movement of his head.

"Junior, is there something we—I—should know?" she asked accusingly. Though she'd assumed Joe had stopped seeing Lisa, she couldn't shake the doubts and haunting questions that followed her around: What if he'd started seeing her again, years later? What if he had a new mistress? What if he cared enough about another woman to leave her money? And, if he did, would she be authorized to know about it? And what about the girl with the gray eyes?

"No, not that I know of," he said with a hard stare at Dan.

"What's done in the dark will be brought to the light," Rosa warned, and she scooted forward in her chair and waited for Dan to explain the fan of documents that lay before them.

"Well, there is one thing—well, not 'thing'—just someone you don't know about. But let me start from the beginning, and we'll get to that later."

"Dan, can we step outside for a few minutes?" Joe Jr. asked.

"That won't be necessary," Rosa said sternly. "Whatever you want to discuss with Dan, you can do right here in front of me."

Joe Jr. sighed heavily. "Never mind."

After explaining the terms of Joe's life insurance policy, annuities, and real estate, Dan took a deep breath and retrieved a final piece of paper. He placed it on top of the others in his lap. He took a sip of water and cleared his throat before he began.

"Joe also set up a trust arrangement." He paused. "For a Natalia Foster." He raised his eyebrows as he glanced from Rosa to Joe Jr.

"You've got to be kidding me!" Joe Jr. jumped up from his chair, his fists balled up, knuckles protruding.

Rosa sat calmly, hands folded in her lap, eyes focused on the paper in Dan's hands. She realized then that Joe Jr. knew about the affair. He'd probably known all along.

"She's the beneficiary of a separate life insurance policy that was purchased when she was born," Dan continued. "But the trust will be disbursed over the next ten years in a specific amount each month. Joe felt like this money was rightfully hers as she was growing up." Watching Rosa, he added quickly, "None of this is public record."

She could feel her cheeks redden, heat spreading unevenly down her neck like thick crude oil. She couldn't decide where to direct the anger and pain brewing in the pit of her stomach—a toxic and infectious waste gurgling and tearing away at her insides.

"I'm sorry, Dan, but would you like to explain to us who Natalia Foster is?" Rosa said. "Or maybe Joe Jr. would like to explain?" Someone needed to say it. She needed to hear the words to make them so. She still had a tiny seed of doubt—a plea for denial—that maybe all of this was in her imagination.

"Joe wanted to tell you," Dan said, looking at Rosa. "He said he was going to."

She couldn't explain what came over her as she lunged toward Dan with the strength of an ox, pushed him toward the back of the couch, grabbed the papers in his lap, and tore them to pieces. A loud guttural sound filled the room—morbid and long in its duration—as Rosa threw the torn pieces at Joe Jr.

"What kind of son are you?" she spat. "Get out of my house. Get out! Both of you!"

"Mom, what did you want me to do? Betray Dad's trust?" Joe Jr. tried to hug her.

Dan grabbed his briefcase and walked swiftly toward the door, letting himself out. Joe Jr. gave up trying to calm his mother and followed close behind as Rosa beat her fists against his back.

As he crossed the threshold, she grabbed a metal candelabra from the entry table, aiming at his back. *Damn it,* she thought when she missed. She left it on the porch where it landed and slammed the door as hard as she could.

They will all pay for this. I will get my revenge.

Chapter 20

Pamela joined Natalia for the five-hour drive to New Orleans that would help determine her destiny.

As they sped up I-10, Pamela turned the tuner to find a radio station. She passed Stevie Wonder's "Part-Time Lover" and quickly turned back.

"This used to be my jam!" she mused, singing along. Natalia couldn't help but join her, both making up lyrics they weren't sure about.

"Listen to Luther in the background! Oooh! I love his voice! I loved him actually," Pamela said. "I need a man who can sing."

Natalia laughed. "You are so crazy. Maybe you can get Kevin some voice lessons?"

Kevin was Pamela's long-term beau—long-term by Natalia's standards. They were nine months into the relationship, so who knew where it would go.

"Chile, please. That's the last thing on his mind right now."

"But you like him? I mean, y'all should be damn near in love at this point."

"I do. He's cool—makes me laugh, we have a lot of fun together. Our conversation is effortless. He doesn't have any baggage—like some people," she chided.

Natalia rolled her eyes. "Well, give it some time. You don't know what skeletons might be in his closet."

"So, are you nervous about this will deal?"

"Of course I am. His whole family may be there." She'd called Dan Maccini's office, and his assistant had explained the family could be there, but more than likely they would not. Based on his calendar, it looked like he was planning to meet with her privately.

"You're sure you don't want me to go to the meeting with you?"

"I'm sure. I think his son might actually attack you if he saw you again. Hell, he probably would attack me. Lord help me."

Pamela looked up at the ceiling of the car. "Yes, Lord, please help my friend. I don't want her to die, especially over a will she had nothing to do with."

"You are nuts."

"I know, I know. So, let's say he left you a bunch of money. What are you going to do?"

"I don't know. I can't imagine having a bunch of money. I'm not gonna lie. I was surprised at the size of his house. My mom never said anything about his finances. I know he hooked her up and bought her all kinds of things, but I assumed that's what all married men do for their mistresses."

"His family is going to go crazy when they find out about you." Pamela tapped her fingers together one by one.

"Don't remind me. I hope they have security guards in there. I bet they're used to having all kinds of drama. I mean, you're talking about money or valuable things that are worth money, and you know how people feel about that."

Natalia had no idea what to expect when she arrived for the reading of Joe's will. She imagined they would convene in a dark office with paneled walls and shelves filled with books—Joe's family on one side, Natalia on the other.

Her mother had offered to join her, but she thought that would be too much for the family to handle. She also sensed her mother didn't want to be involved in this muddle, even though it had all started with her. She knew her mother felt bad for her, as if she were sending her off into a lion's den. "I'll be praying for you," she'd said last night.

Natalia decided she needed to look as innocent, inconspicuous, and respectable as possible. Wearing a pair of gray pants and a winter white sweater, she applied a light, rosy blush to her cheeks, a few layers of mascara, and pink lip gloss. With the help of conditioner and lots of gel, she smoothed her hair into a low bun at the nape of her neck.

She drove slowly up Poydras, hoping no one would blow their horn at her as she searched for the office building for Maccini & Maccini—a thirty-six-story skyscraper in New Orleans's business district. She found the postmodern building with its granite façade and bronze tinted glass. It was flanked by two bronze sculptures perched on six-foot bases—one of them a replica of Bernini's *David*, partially clothed, readying his slingshot and rock, and the other a man playing a string instrument. Several oak trees managed to thrive amid all the concrete and asphalt.

She followed the signs into the parking garage, which was conveniently located below the building. She checked her reflection in the car mirror and took a deep breath as she tried to slow down her heart rate. She thought her heart might escape from her body at any moment and looked down to see if the thumping was visible through her sweater. The palms of her hands were cold and clammy as she double-checked her purse to make sure she had the letter—proof that she was supposed to be there. Proof that she was Joe's daughter.

As she walked through the elegant main lobby and toward the elevators, the sound of her clicking heels echoed up toward the mirrored ceiling. Bright lights, like miniature suns, seemed to reflect off everything: granite floors, ceramic planters, glass tables.

She stepped onto the elevator and felt her chest constrict as the doors closed, squeezing her lungs and making it impossible to take a deep breath. She stepped off, looked to her left, then to her right, and saw suite 800. Walking delicately across the granite floor, she pulled the glass door open and was immediately greeted by a perky blond receptionist. A gold nameplate that read AMY BATISTE was set on top of a slightly elevated area of the desk. "Good morning!" she exclaimed. "How may I help you?"

"I have an appointment with Dan Maccini?" Her voice sounded tight and far away.

"Yes, he's expecting you—Natalia Foster?"

"Yes, I'm Natalia."

"Okay, honey, follow me. Can I get you some water?"

"Yes, that would be great," Natalia said, though her hands were trembling so badly she didn't think she'd be able to hold the bottle or glass.

Amy escorted her to a conference room just steps away from her desk. "Please, have a seat wherever you'd like. I'll be right back." Natalia decided to sit on the far side of the table so she could have a view of the entrance. Amy returned a few minutes later with a glass of water. "Mr. Maccini will be with you shortly."

Natalia took a few sips of water, hoping the cool liquid would awaken her vocal cords. She stared at three abstract paintings by the same artist on a wall at one end of the table. They appeared to be originals. She rubbed her hand across the glossy wood of the table. When the door opened, she jumped.

"Hello, Ms. Foster. I'm Dan." A man came through the door, extending his hand.

"Hello, Dan. Nice to meet you," she managed as she stood. She felt her hand swallowed up in his huge, firm grip.

Tall with a protruding belly, a mass of gray hair, and large ears, he looked ten years younger when he smiled at her, a parenthesis appearing on each of his full cheeks. Natalia's memory took her back to Joe's funeral and Dan's tearful words. He was one of Joe's best friends.

He sat directly to her left at the head of the table.

"Thank you for coming in today to meet with me. This won't take very long, but I need to walk you through a couple of documents and get your signature, and make sure you are who you say you are." He winked, then waved a hand over the stack of papers, as though confirming everything was in order. "Joe had some specific wishes he wanted me to carry out for him."

Her gaze darted from Dan to the door.

"You expecting anyone else?" he asked.

"I, well, I thought his family might also be here?"

"Ah, no, no. That's just TV—not the real world. It's much less exciting in real life," he laughed. "It's just me and you, kid. I met with his wife and eldest son yesterday."

Her shoulders immediately relaxed as she breathed a sigh of relief.

"It didn't go so well," he added, his forehead crinkling into three parallel lines.

"It didn't? Why not?"

"When I got to the part about you, that's when things fell apart."

"You told them about me?" Natalia's voice was two octaves higher than usual. She scooted forward as she waited for his response.

"I just read the terms, which I'm about to share with you. I didn't say exactly who you were, but Joe Jr. seemed to already know and Rosa, his wife, seemed to have an inkling. I was glad to get out of there."

Natalia's eyebrows rose sky high, and she opened her eyes wide enough to stretch her skin.

"Don't worry. I didn't tell them where you lived or give them any other information about you."

"I'm—I'm just surprised Joe wanted them to know." She shook her head.

Sounding more sympathetic, he said, "I think he always wanted them to know, but it wouldn't have done him any good since he couldn't be part of your life. Joe and I were very good friends—practically best friends. I knew him for many, many years. We played football together in high school, and we were in the navy together."

"Was he good at football?" she asked, intrigued.

"Actually, he was. He was a lineman; we both were," he said fondly. "Made us pretty popular with the ladies."

She smiled at the thought of a younger Joe playing football.

"I'm sorry you didn't know him—and that he didn't know you. You were easily his biggest regret. He's tried to make it up to you." He motioned at the documents before him.

Dan spent the next twenty minutes explaining the trust arrangement Joe had set up for Natalia when he was diagnosed. She was also the beneficiary of a separate life insurance policy he had purchased when she was born. They would need to transfer funds into her account; did she have a deposit slip with her?

She signed several documents before digging in her purse for her checkbook. As she tore out the slip, she felt something rip inside her. "I wish he'd left me a letter—words I could hold on to," she said as tears began to fall.

Again, he sounded kindly as he responded. "I see this all the time. You're not alone. I know that doesn't make it any better, but people are weak. They're afraid. I know he loved you, and he thought about you often. It broke his heart not to be able to raise you. He told me that himself. I wish he was sitting here right now. He would be so proud of the way you've turned out. I know he would be so proud." He leaned over and patted her shoulder before he stood.

She didn't want him to leave. He was a connection to Joe, someone who could tell her more about him. And what about his family? What would happen now that Rosa knew? *Wait, don't go*, she thought as he headed for the door. But the words were stuck beneath her grief and sadness.

Chapter 21

Natalia awoke late on a Saturday morning, sunlight squeezing between the cracks of the blinds of her bedroom window. Fan-shaped crimson leaves fluttered from the red maple in the courtyard and landed on the ground below.

Feeling light and extricated from all worldly concerns, she stretched and continued to lie in bed. The soft sateen sheets were smooth and cool against her skin. She wished David were lying next to her. Their desire for each other was intense, their connection strong. Sparkling with healing powers. He was the bow to her violin, pulling and producing yearning sounds.

But they were doing everything by the book. They were waiting. Waiting for the right time. Waiting to be certain they would be together indefinitely. Waiting to be sure their relationship was blessed by God. Waiting, it seemed, for marriage.

This would be a first for them both. Having also had a series of unsuccessful relationships—women who only wanted to be with him because he was a doctor or women who were selfish or women who couldn't be faithful—David was overly cautious. Caught in her own conundrum of feelings, Natalia didn't mind at first. But she was beginning to long for more. She wanted a deeper level of intimacy to keep her rooted, firmly planted at his side. She wanted her feelings for him to completely flood her heart and mind, drowning out any inkling of emotion for Tyler.

She found herself replaying the moments she shared with David as she thought about their time together last night. They'd gone to a movie that left her teary-eyed and longing to cling more closely to him.

He also seemed shaken when they talked about it. "You know, it just made me think about my own brothers. We were raised in the same house—mainly by my grandmother—no dad around. They could have been anything they wanted, but we all chose different paths." He furrowed his brow.

Natalia was quiet as she watched him think. She could look at his face for hours, studying his peanut-butter-brown skin, his dark eyes, his full lips, the dimple in his right cheek that surprised her when he smiled.

"Sometimes, I wish things could have been different. I wonder how we would have turned out if we'd had a dad—how my brothers would have turned out." One had gone to prison for 10 years; the other could have easily done the same but somehow managed to use his athletic talents. He'd played basketball, almost went pro, but was now coaching a high school team.

"I wonder the same thing. Would I be a different person if Joe had raised me with my mom? But even when two parents are around, there's no guarantee," Natalia said softly. "I'm probably better off growing up the way I did—knowing the struggles of life, wearing hand-me-downs and used clothes, missing field trips because they didn't have the money to pay for them."

"Yeah, I think we end up exactly where God wants us to be," he said, looking into her eyes.

She'd gotten past the initial process of picking him apart, looking for anything that could possibly be wrong with him. He acted arrogant at times, but she realized it was a façade, a mask to hide his insecurities. She knew it wasn't easy for him being a black professional in America. How many times had he been met with surprise when he revealed he was a doctor? How many times did white patients express discomfort upon meeting him? Does he know what he's doing? they wondered openly, like he didn't have feelings. "Hell, our own people doubt me," he'd told her once. But she was beginning to settle into their relationship.

She was heading out for a run when he called her.

"I was just thinking," he said, his voice gravelly with sleep. She imagined him lying in bed, his head propped up on layers of white, down-filled pillows. "We should cook dinner together tonight—at my place."

"Sounds like a science experiment." Natalia smiled as she imagined the two of them measuring out ingredients, adjusting the knobs of his chef's stove, smoke rising and racing toward the cabinets.

"Exactly," he laughed. "No, really—I was watching Food Network and got inspired. We can do this."

"We can certainly try," she grinned. "What's on the menu?"

"Whatever you like."

They decided she would drive over to his place first, then they'd head to the grocery store together.

She'd never thought a trip to the grocery store could feel so romantic—like walking on cotton candy clouds. She looped her arm through his as they strolled down the aisles, their heads tilting toward each other as they stood before a plethora of options. They chose different spices (cumin, coriander, and saffron), a quinoa color (white, red, or black), and feta based on the country of origin. They left with their paper bags, the sliding doors opening silently to release them into the evening.

As David dug into his pocket for his keys, they heard a woman's voice.

"David! David!"

They both turned to face a honey-colored woman with long straight hair, sleek and shiny like she'd just left the salon. She was wearing a short black dress, revealing long, toned legs.

"Hi, stranger. I thought that was you!" she said breathlessly before giving him a hug. But it wasn't any kind of hug, Natalia noticed. It was a "I haven't seen you in such a long time and I've missed you" kind of hug.

David stuttered when he introduced them. "Uh, B-Bianca, this is Natalia. Natalia—Bianca."

The woman seemed surprised by Natalia's presence, as if she hadn't noticed her standing there. "Oh, hi sweetie," she said dismissively before tossing her hair and turning her attention back to David.

Natalia felt barbed wire prickling her skin. She narrowed her eyes while watching the woman talk to David. She could perceive a thick bond of emotion connecting the two, drawing them together. Currents of chemistry rippled back and forth.

"So, uh, you're in town for the weekend?" David asked.

"I'm actually moving back," she said.

"Oh, really?" David seemed surprised. "How's your family?"

The woman spent several minutes talking about nearly every member of her sizable family.

Natalia cleared her throat and touched David's arm. How long was this conversation going to go on? This woman needed to shut the hell up and move along.

David got the hint. "Okay, well, it was good to see you," he said.

"You too," she said, and winked.

"Good to see you"? "You too"? Her curiosity antennas were on high alert, swaying frantically. David opened the trunk and they dropped their bags inside. As she got in the front seat, she wanted desperately to inquire about this woman. Her intuition told her she wasn't just some acquaintance of David's. But she didn't want to seem like the jealous type. Or, rather, she didn't want David to know she was the jealous type. She continued to simmer, tossing around possibilities as they drove back to his place. David didn't offer any answers to the questions she silently hurled at him. He seemed absorbed in his own thoughts.

Natalia realized a different David was sitting next to her in the car. She felt a loosening of their bond—a force yanking and breaking the middle, the crystal cracking along a seam. Walls began erecting themselves around her heart. She would mirror his behavior and retreat. She began packing away her feelings and pulling herself in toward safety.

David slammed on the brakes, and she lurched forward before her seat belt forced her back against the seat. He'd almost missed a stop sign. She stared at the red octagon, then back at David, taking the sign as a warning for herself.

As they approached his driveway, the sun disappeared, and dusk took its place, settling above them like a weight crushing and flattening the moment. The excitement of the evening dissipated like a fading rainbow, soft and subtle colors lost in the night.

There was something about that woman. A background story—and, it seemed, a current one. Natalia knew her curiosity would gnaw at her until she found out what it was.

Chapter 22

Rosa felt a fire raging inside her. She was so hot her skin took on a scarlet hue. She thought the heat was brought on by her anger, but when the sweating and chills began, followed by a severe headache and her body feeling like she'd been beaten with a crowbar, she knew she was sick. She was barely able to move as she called Catarine for help.

"Mom, you look terrible! Why didn't you call sooner? You know better," Catarine admonished.

Rosa lay in the bed like an unwieldy mound of dirt, her mouth dry. She hadn't eaten in two days. As she listened to Catarine in the kitchen—water running from the faucet, the creaking of the pantry door, the clanging of a pot on the iron grate of the stove—she thought she saw Joe standing before her. She blinked rapidly and reached her hand out to touch him. She was yelling his name and cursing him when she saw Catarine standing above her.

"Mom, you must have been dreaming," Catarine said. "Or hallucinating. Let me get your soup and crackers. I also made you some hot tea."

"I-I don't think I was dreaming," she said weakly. But Catarine had already disappeared back into the kitchen.

As she dozed in and out of fitful sleep the rest of the day, Rosa listened to the activities in her home. Catarine preparing another meal, watching Fox News, the volume too low for her to distinguish the erratic, quarrelsome voices. The doorbell; someone had come over. They were in the kitchen whisper-shouting as Rosa gathered her strength and walked to the doorway of her bedroom, holding on to the bed and dresser for support along the way.

"You've known this all along?" she heard Catarine gasp.

That was the trouble with secrets. Though relished initially, the keeper would soon begin to abhor them. Secrets had a way of begging for attention—other people's attention. They wanted to be free, to be seen and revealed. Living in the dark was no way to live. They craved light. Rosa had a feeling. Her intuition told her that for many years, Joe Jr. had felt the gnawing, the tugging. The struggle to keep his father's secrets in a vault.

She froze, her head tilted toward the kitchen entrance, ears straining to catch as many words as she could.

"Unfortunately, yes. You don't know how hard it was. To watch and not say anything. To not be able to stop it. Dad was into her. She had a *baby*." Joe Jr. spat the word out like it was poisonous.

"So, it's true." She heard the grating sounds of a kitchen chair against the floor tiles. Catarine needed to sit down.

"Well, at first I didn't think she was Dad's. I figured she was probably seeing other men—a woman like that. But then I saw the daughter when she came here before the funeral, and I knew." Joe Jr. made a gagging sound, as if he had a hair ball in his throat.

"What do you mean, a woman like that? You know Mom already knows there was another woman. She found an *Essence* magazine and this girl with Dad's eyes keeps showing up. You're saying she came here? Who came here? When?" Catarine was no longer whispering.

"That figures. She lost it when Dan was here – tore up those papers, started hitting me and yelling before she threw us out. She probably wondered at times when he was alive. Dad just had a thing for—" He stopped talking midsentence. Rosa heard him crack his knuckles.

"Who came here?" Catarine asked again.

"That—that girl. Dad's . . . Dad's . . ."

"Just say it! Damn it. Why are you holding all this in?"

"I don't want to talk about it. I promised Dad I never would."

"You can't be serious. You've already told me about the affair. It's already out. So you may as well tell me what you know about his child."

"Look, I will do whatever I need to do to protect Mom—and Dad's reputation. This is our family. Our pure blood. There is no room for a person with tainted blood. Don't worry: she will remain invisible forever. If she didn't get the message then, I'll make sure she gets it in the future."

Rosa could see two veins protrude from his forehead.

"Oh God," Catarine said. "Don't tell me you're back on that nonsense! What is your issue with black people? Or should I say any race that's not white? None of us think that way. Dad obviously didn't."

"I was seventeen when I started working part-time for Dad. I saw the way he looked at her whenever she came in the store. Before long, Dad was taking longer lunches and leaving earlier. It was like he was transforming right before my eyes. He had a new pep in his step, a wider smile, a new air about him, like he had everything he could possibly want in the world. He seemed genuinely happy. So at first, I didn't interfere. But, one day—it was a Friday and it was raining—Dad asked me to go to lunch with him. He said there was someone he wanted me to meet.

"We got in his pickup truck. That was when he had that Chevy. It was spotless inside and out. Not a speck of dust on the dash, not a piece of trash in the cup holder. I remember the rain drops gathering and running down the sides and Dad cussing, because he'd just gotten it washed. We got inside, and I just had this bad feeling. So I asked him if he wanted me to meet the black woman he'd been seeing. I thought he was gonna be surprised, but he didn't bat an eye. You know what he said?"

Rosa watched Joe Jr. balled his fists up into two tight knots.

"He said, 'That woman has a name. It's Lisa, and she loves me, and I love her.' I was so angry I wanted to jump out of the truck. I told him Mom loved him, too. I told him I couldn't understand why he would cheat on Mom, especially with a black woman. I was so torn. I felt like I was standing above a chasm, and if I didn't choose a side, it would swallow me up.

"Dad tried to have this conversation about how we're all people, and the color of our skin doesn't matter. It's just how God made us. It's what inside that truly counts. But we all know that's bullshit. I tried to warn him. Told him Mom would eventually find out, but he was just so confident about the whole damn thing. He basically said Mom wouldn't care anyway after twenty years of marriage. I think he felt like he was still committed because he was taking care of Mom so what difference did it make?

"He said people wear on you over time. The monotony of it all. The predictableness. He started complaining about their marriage and said Lisa never complained. The more he talked the angrier I got. We went back and forth, with no real agreement. No consensus. We were in this limbo for years."

"We went to that hole-in-the-wall, you know, the po'boy place. And she was standing at the door waiting. I could tell she felt like she was more important because Dad had introduced us. She talked about going to cosmetology school and how she wanted to travel and see the world. So I thought it would just be a temporary thing. And she just didn't seem like she was in love with Dad. She wasn't all giddy or awestruck around him. She seemed like . . ." He paused, and Rosa watched him trace an area of wood grain along the kitchen table. "She acted like she was on way her to something else."

"So you thought it would just end and that would be that?" Catarine asked.

"Yeah. I thought she would always want her freedom, that Dad was just a stop along the way. I thought it was just a fling. But a year later, she was pregnant. That just did it for me. I confronted Dad in the warehouse. I can still hear the hum of that compressor in my ear. Do you know what he said?"

"I don't think I want to know."

"He said he wanted another child. I couldn't believe it. I reminded him that he was married, and I asked him what he was going to do if Mom found out. He said Lisa would never tell."

"What in the world was he thinking?" Rosa noticed Catarine chewing on her thumbnail now.

"I felt like I was giving them permission, and it just gnawed on my conscience. I swore I wouldn't go near her or her bastard child." The rage had settled on to him, he said, covering every nook and cranny of his thoughts and decisions. He began to filter everything through this new rage he carried with him.

"How did Dad seem during all this?" Catarine asked.

"What do you mean?"

"Did he seem unstable? Was he happy? Do you think he was in love?"

"Yes—was he in love?" Rosa asked. She was standing fully in the middle of the doorway now. Arms straight by her side, fists balled up, mouth a thin line of torment.

Joe Jr's. eyes widened as his face and neck turned into a strawberry patch. "Mom, you were never supposed to know. Dad loved you. And it was a long time ago." He spoke quickly, the words running into each other.

Rosa narrowed her eyes into thin slits as if she were trying to focus on something in the near distance.

"It could have been someone else's child. I never saw that woman again after I found out," he said.

"You know damn well it's his child." Rosa paused as she tried to organize her thoughts. They were swirling ahead of her as if on a racetrack, each with its own lane. "You . . . met . . . this . . . woman?" Each word stood on its own, four pillars digging into the chambers of her heart. She walked toward him and pressed her hands into the kitchen table. She wanted to smash it into the floor. Her own son had also deceived her.

Joe Jr. stood and began backing up, as if he had encountered a wild boar. Catarine held her breath and watched the two of them.

"I can't believe you've known all these years!" Rosa yelled, her voice nasally from her sickness.

"Ma, I promised Dad . . . We shouldn't even be having this conversation."

"What did she look like?" Rosa demanded.

"I don't really remember, Ma. It was a long, long time ago."

"I'm sure you can remember something," Rosa prodded. "I need a description." A full minute passed as Rosa watched Joe Jr.'s besieged face, the twist and turns of his mouth, the bouncing of his eyes. "Just tell me," she yelled, banging on the table with her fists.

"She was . . . she was black, okay?" Joe Jr. hunched his shoulders.

"No shit! And when in the hell did his child come to my house?"

Joe Jr. was stuttering now. He was like a suspect in an interrogation room. Stuck. Fearful. Yearning to be free.

"Sh-she came here when . . . when Dad was home from the hospital. During his final days. Don't worry, I told her to stay the hell away from us."

"Get out of my house!" She spat the words at him. She couldn't stand the sight of her son right now. He was as repulsive as maggots on rotting meat. "Leave!" she yelled when he continued to stand as if his feet were stuck in cement.

He walked from the kitchen to the front door with his head down.

"I need to be alone," she said to Catarine.

"Mom," Catarine said, attempting to protest, but Rosa looked at her as if she were an accomplice. So Catarine reluctantly exited after Joe Jr., leaving Rosa alone.

She sat at the kitchen table, twisting and turning the ring she continued to wear on her left hand. How did Joe come home each night and climb into her bed after sleeping with another woman? How did he flash his smile at her without a hint of guilt in his eyes? How did he live all those years knowing he had another child? How did he live this whole other life? What if there were others?

You think you know someone, she thought. The years they spent together. Eating dinner. Sharing a bed. Laughing. Crying. Struggling through the intricacies of a relationship. *But you only know what they want you to know.*

Who the hell were you? Why wasn't I enough for you?

Joe. Joe Jr. They were both strangers to her. They'd kept a part of themselves hidden all these years. A whole other life. A whole other side to them. Who was this other woman? And who and where was this child?

Little by little, Rosa promised to herself, she would pull out all the pearls that formed Joe's precious strand of secrets. All she needed was a plan.

A private investigator. The thought popped into Rosa's head as she was watching *The Golden Girls* still nursing her lingering symptoms—a mild headache and runny nose. The four women were having a murder mystery weekend at a museum where Blanche was vying for a job as an assistant. Dorothy turned into Sherlock Holmes, of course, as she tried to help Blanche solve the case. Rosa wished she were more like Dorothy, with her confidence and strong will. But she often identified most with Rose: hopelessly naïve and spacey to a fault. She loved Sophia the most. With her Sicilian roots and beliefs in ancient customs, her brazenness and bluntness, she reminded Rosa of her own mother. It seemed those traits had skipped a generation, though, and were bestowed on her own children—especially Joe Jr.

The thought of her own son keeping Joe's secret all these years made her wonder why she'd ever had children. They were a joy when they were born, beautiful blessings that smelled of pure bliss. But then they waltzed out of her life without any consideration of the sacrifices she'd made, starting with her body and moving on to her time.

She'd had dreams she could have pursued. With her culinary skills, she could have been a chef at a five-star restaurant. Or a landscape architect on a design team, considering her passion for gardening and ability to layer flowers and plants. And not just any plants or flowers. She knew almost intuitively what should be planted and where it would bloom and thrive. But instead she'd devoted her life to her family. And now she was 70 years old, watching television alone, smoldering. Her fury was fresh, kindled daily by betrayal and the existence of two people she was unaware of until several weeks ago.

Which brought her back to her investigator idea. She rushed into Joe's office and began digging through his files. He'd used a private investigator before. Something to do with a customer who was threatening him. Of course, Joe had taken matters into his own hands with a PI instead of calling the police. She found the business card in Joe's Rolodex: Timothy Smith. Her fingers trembled as she pressed the numbers.

He answered the phone after the first ring: "This is Tim." His voice was deep and hushed as if he were at a movie.

"Tim, yes, hello. This is Rosa. Rosa Russo. You did some work for my husband some years ago." She hoped he would remember.

"Hello, Rosa. What can I do for you?" He didn't acknowledge whether he remembered Joe or not.

Rosa explained her predicament. "Can you find out where this woman lives if I have a past address?"

"If you have her full name, approximate age, and a past address—yes, I could probably track her down."

Rosa rushed into the bedroom closet to grab the magazine and recited everything on the address label.

"Any other details you have would be helpful." Tim waited.

"She also had a child who would be in her twenties now," Rosa said.

"That's good. Let me see what I can do. I'll get back to you soon."

A thrill circled her as she imagined finding and confronting this woman. It was like planning for a vacation where the destination was sure to be an adventure.

Chapter 23

Waiting for the weekend, but tepidly. That was Natalia's new mantra because weekends meant time with David. The week had been uneventful, and he'd seemingly returned to his senses.

On guard, she could feel needles protruding as she now approached their relationship with caution. She found herself searching for the right moment to casually bring up Bianca. She just hadn't found it yet.

Now that the stifling summer temperatures were retreating to make way for fall, they'd planned an early afternoon picnic. Natalia was making chicken salad, shredding pieces of the white meat into a bowl, when her phone rang. She slid the green button to the right and quickly tapped the speaker icon with her semi-clean pinky.

"Hey, girl," she said. "You're up early!" Pamela was not a morning person and detested the peppiness of early risers. She preferred the silence of the night when she could feel truly alone and focused.

"Yeah, I couldn't sleep," Pamela mumbled.

"That's unusual. What's wrong with you?" For as long as she'd known Pamela, sleeping had been one of her favorite pastimes. Even during her worst relationships and breakups, Pamela pulled the covers over her head and shut her eyes like a groundhog in hibernation.

"Well, it's not me. It's something . . . something I need to tell you."

That didn't sound good. Natalia stopped shredding the chicken, washed and dried her hands, picked up her phone, and switched off the speaker mode. She sat down at her kitchen table and took a deep breath before asking, "What's wrong?"

"Maybe I should come over there?"

"Um, sure—if you want."

"Yeah, I'll just come over."

Twenty minutes later, Natalia's chicken salad was on the second shelf of her refrigerator in a clear plastic container and Pamela was knocking at her door. They hugged each other briefly before Pamela tossed her miniature backpack on the entry console and headed for Natalia's couch. They plopped down on the worn cushions and faced each other, legs crossed, for several seconds in silence.

"Okay, girl. What's up? Are you pregnant? Is someone dying?" Natalia held her breath as she waited.

Pamela shook her head, closed her eyes briefly, and took a deep breath before beginning. "Well, I was having dinner last night with Kevin at that new African restaurant off Westheimer near the Galleria. He tried something on a skewer, but I had these pork chops that were good as hell. I wanted to pick up the damn bone and lick the seasoning off it, but the restaurant was too fancy for all that. Kevin would have been mortified." She huffed at the thought.

"Anyway, the restaurant is pretty dim, like ten-watt bulbs and lamps all over the place. So when we walked in, they sat us in a booth. We'd been there for maybe fifteen minutes—sipping our drinks and having an appetizer. Something called Bobotie, which was also good as hell. It was minced meat in a little bowl with a crust on the top of it." She cupped her hands to indicate the size. "I see this couple walk by out of the corner of my eyes, but I didn't really look at them, because, you know—that would have been rude since Kevin was in the middle of telling me about one of his crazy coworkers, and how he wouldn't be surprised if this guy showed up in a black trench coat with an Uzi."

Natalia tilted her head as she waited through Pamela's delaying tactics. She had a point, but she was taking her time getting to it. "Okay, the food sounds amazing. I'll try the restaurant—with David!"

"Um, no, you may *not* want to. Let me finish. So, we finish our meal and Kevin is paying the bill when I decide to go to the restroom. I walk in, take care of my business, walk out, and as I'm heading back to our table, I see David sitting in a booth with some woman. At first I didn't think it was him, and I kept walking. But then I backed up, because I'm like, it has to be him. I looked him dead in his eyes and said, 'David?' His eyes got so big! And the woman—she's looking me up and down like, 'Who is this bitch?' Like, 'Can we help you?'"

Natalia felt herself turning two shades lighter as the blood drained from her face. Since she couldn't speak, she continued looking at Pamela, waiting for an ending to this story that would make sense.

"So, I just shook my head and walked off. I heard David call my name, but I just kept walking. Of course, he gets up and follows me back to the booth and tells me it's not what I think. I told him he needed to explain that to you."

They looked at each other, two still statues, as Pamela gave her best friend time to process this new information.

"What did she look like?" Natalia asked. "Light skin, long straight hair?"

"Uh, yes," Pamela said, surprised. "She was cute. Not gorgeous or anything."

"Hmmm. I think I know exactly who she was. She's actually really pretty." Natalia frowned before recounting the run-in with the woman in black outside the grocery store. "You said this was a nice-ass restaurant, so they must have been on a date," Natalia said. "What the hell? We're supposed to be going on a picnic today."

"I'm sorry, girl. It definitely looked like a date, so I don't know what he's going to say, but I'm sure he's going to bring it up."

As if on cue, Natalia's phone rang. She hopped off the couch and jogged back to the kitchen where she'd left her phone on the table. David's face with his dimpled smile was on the screen.

She wasn't ready to have a conversation with him. Her body was ten degrees warmer, her heart rate was accelerated, and her jaw was clenched as she gritted her teeth. "I can't talk to him right now. All he's going to do is tell me some bullshit story about—oh, she's just an old friend of mine. Or, she just needed advice about something. Or, nothing happened."

"You should at least hear him out," Pamela advised.

"He's probably going to lie, though. I can't take that. I can't deal with that. I just don't want to talk to him right now." With her heart being compressed and misshapen from pain and disappointment, she wasn't sure when she'd be ready to talk to David.

Distraction was the only solution against the doldrums that began nipping at Natalia's heels. While she wanted to keep the blinds shut and lie on her couch like an invalid, Natalia let Pamela talk her into going to a movie—something new with Denzel Washington, she'd said. Natalia's ears perked up. Anything with Denzel was worth seeing. She matched Pamela's morning attire and threw on sweatpants, a T-shirt, and tennis shoes, and they headed to the early matinee at the AMC.

As Pamela drove, Natalia tried to focus on the world whizzing by instead of the internal scolding she was giving herself. She should have known better, she thought, as she leaned her head against the window and turned upward to watch low, thick clouds moving across an overcast sky.

A storm was coming.

Chapter 24

Memory is a slippery slope. One minute you're moving smoothly, passing through time, through tender moments that feel like they happened yesterday—images clear and sharp, feelings deep and true. The next minute you're bouncing, jostling, trying to piece together disconnected fragments that you're not sure ever happened at all. Memories obliterated like patches of rust on what was once smooth and shiny steel.

When Lisa's doorbell rang one cool evening in October, she wasn't prepared for the ride—or the woman—in front of her.

"Who is it?" she yelled as she peeked through the side shutters, trying to get a glimpse of this unannounced visitor.

When she didn't get a response, she unlocked the door, sliding the top lock to the left and turning the bottom knob to the right. A white woman—hair completely gray, eyes dark and worn, and loose skin beneath them—stood before her.

Jehovah's Witness, she thought as she looked above the woman's head at the leaves on the red oak tree that framed her home. The leaves had taken on varying hues of yellow and orange overnight, it seemed. Typically, she enjoyed letting these people into her home and debating the Bible—the Truth—with them. She was the queen of converting people to mainstream Christianity. Her stack of religious tracts was in the drawer of a nearby side table, along with several small New Testament Bibles. But not today, she thought wearily.

"I'm in the middle of cookin' dinner," she explained. "Can you come back tomorrow?"

The woman was silent as she stared long and hard at Lisa. "Are you Lisa Foster?" the woman asked pointedly.

"Well, I used to be." She stared down at the woman. "I have a different last name now. What is it?"

"Well, where should I begin?" The woman inhaled deeply. She held her purse tightly beneath her arm on the side of her compact body. Her gray coat was snug, buttoned from top to bottom. Her short gray hair fluttered lightly in the breeze.

Lisa was beginning to feel like a kid in the classroom being questioned by a teacher who already knew the answers. "How about you tell me who you are and why you're at my home?"

"I'm Rosa—Rosa Russo."

Lisa's mouth opened, then closed, then opened again. Her right hand involuntarily flew up, covering it.

"I'm Joe's *wife*. I'm sure you already knew about me way back when. You know, when you decided to have an affair with my husband. And, as I understand, you also had a child—his child. How could you?" She hissed the words, slamming her purse against the screen door.

Lisa jerked back, startled. Then her blood warmed. Rosa's fury triggered something in her, as though the rage were contagious. "How dare you just show up at my house like this?" She felt like a knight without its armor—a soldier without weapons on a front line she hadn't been trained to battle on. She'd never imagined meeting Rosa. Never thought that Rosa would find out.

Never thought she would revisit a guilt she thought she'd banished years ago. Her shame was fresh and exposed.

"You have an affair with my husband and have his child. What, was I supposed to call and schedule an appointment with you? How dare *you*?" Rosa threw the question back at her like a hot coal. Red splotches were popping up on Rosa's cheeks and neck and she was panting as if she'd just run a mile.

The woman had a right. "Look, I can understand that you're upset. I don't blame you. You should be. I would be too if I was in your shoes. But I don't owe you no explanation. You want to take your frustrations out on me? Joe was just as much to blame, you know."

"Well, Joe isn't here with us—with *me*—anymore, is he? So I'll never know his side of the story." Rosa folded her arms and stood stoically. She clearly wasn't going anywhere anytime soon.

"Look, I just—I just can't tell you the full story right now. My husband will be here any minute, and like I said, I'm in the middle of cookin' dinner."

"Oh, you have a husband of your own now, huh?"

Lisa looked into Rosa's eyes and could see the torment, the fury, the pain. "Okay, come in." She stepped back and watched Rosa pull the screen door open. She hoped James would work late tonight. "Have a seat. Can I get you something to drink— iced tea, water?"

"No, thank you. I came to hear your story, not for your hospitality." Rosa walked to the sofa Lisa motioned toward. Lisa watched Rosa study the room as she unbuttoned her coat; her eyes darted from the worn La-Z-Boy to the glass coffee table to the brass-, wood-, and silver-framed photos arranged neatly across a white mantel above a ruby brick fireplace. Photos of children. Several of Natalia, which was exactly where Rosa's eyes stopped and widened like two quarters.

"Are you okay?" Lisa asked when Rosa jumped up, nearly fell over on the coffee table, and walked toward the mantel. She held her breath as Rosa picked up a gold-framed photo of Natalia from her college graduation, her hair flat ironed beneath her black cap, her lips hot pink, her cheeks rosy with blush. She was beaming in the photo, proud of her accomplishment.

"So this is Joe's daughter. I knew it! The last time I saw her, I was certain."

Lisa's lips felt like a crusted-over wound, sealed and tightened with stitches, as Rosa grabbed another picture of Natalia. "You've seen her before?" The words tumbled out of Lisa's mouth as if she had just learned a new language. She felt fear creeping up her spine and the desire to push Rosa out the door. The woman's eyes were wild and vacant—the eyes of a crazy person. She could have sworn Rosa's pupils momentarily disappeared, then returned as they darted around.

"The hospital. I saw her at the hospital. Oh God. Oh my God. I felt chills when I saw her. She smiled at me. I remember—I can still see her face. Then she had the nerve to come to his wake and his funeral."

Lisa felt indignation rising inside her. Her desire to protect Natalia was a basic instinct she'd carried since her daughter was born. She knew her child had suffered enough, and she refused to let this woman inject more pain into her life. Her thoughts did an abrupt about-face.

"What do you mean, 'she had the nerve'? He was her father. Like it or not, she's his blood. She deserved to be there." She took two steps toward Rosa and grabbed the photos from her hands, then placed them against her chest. Why was she so angry now? She closed her eyes as she tried to put herself in Rosa's shoes. The woman was seething, her chest rising up and down, eyes narrowed. "Look, it's not Natalia's fault. If you want to be angry with me, that's fine. What I did was wrong. And I'm sorry. I really am. You were never supposed to know. I promised. I promised Joe that I would never mess up his life or ruin your marriage."

"You must have decided that *after* you had his child," Rosa growled.

"I know. It's probably impossible for you to understand how a woman could do such a thing. When I look back, I wonder too. I can't make excuses for what I did. I was young and desperate for someone to love me. For someone to help me. I grew up with nothing. No father. An unaffectionate mother. We—my brother and sister—we were burdens to her. She had no husband. No help. We struggled in every way you can imagine. But that's no excuse. I was living in sin. I met Joe before I met God. Before I turned my life over to Him and changed my ways."

Rosa's face rearranged itself. Her eyes softened, the hard lines around her mouth relented, her jaw went lax.

"When I became a Christian, I stopped living in sin. I asked God to forgive me. That was still a difficult time in my life, though, because I still had Natalia to think about. I still needed to do what was best for her. She's, she's . . ." Lisa paused as tears rolled down her cheeks. "I'm sorry. Natalia was just stuck in the middle of a mess I created. That Joe and I created. She's paid for this more than I have." She walked through the dining room to the bathroom to grab tissue from the toilet paper roll. When she returned, Rosa was standing near the mantel, where she was studying another picture of Natalia's smiling face. "I'm sorry, Rosa. I never meant to hurt you or your family. You have every right to be upset. I sure would be." As she said the words, she realized Rosa was eerily calm.

"Did Joe love you? Did he ask you to marry him?"

Lisa thought back to that time and place. They were in his truck, and he'd asked her to grab a box out of the glove compartment. She opened it. Stunned. She could see the diamond sparkling against the black velvet. Joe's pain when she'd said no. The look of surprise. Then the anger. And when she looked at Rosa, she could see her pain. She feigned surprise at the question.

"No," she lied. "Marriage? Of course not. I, we..." . . ." She faltered. "We didn't love each other." She had to reduce their relationship to a nothingness that would soothe and comfort this woman. *Lord forgive me*, she thought as she watched Rosa's shoulders drop, her face relax. That was all that had mattered to her. *As long as she views me as some mistress, some whore, she can hold on to her fairy tale.*

"Where is Natalia now?" Rosa asked.

"Why do you ask?" Lisa's shield was back up. What if this woman wanted to harm her child? She could be crazy, she thought, as she watched the eyes become placid, indecipherable pools filled with quiet tears. Rosa inhaled and exhaled slowly.

"I would like to meet her," she said, looking at Natalia's photo as if she were having a conversation with her instead of Lisa. "You're right. None of this is her fault. It's not her fault that Joe betrayed me, or that you . . ." She turned to face Lisa now. She fumbled with a silver cross that hung from a chain around her neck.

"I—I don't think that's a good idea." Lisa wanted things to go back to the way they were before. She thought about Rosa's racist son. She still vividly remembered the disdain he felt whenever she encountered him. She knew it wasn't just because she was the other woman. He despised the color of her skin, and he felt the same way about Natalia. "We don't need you or your family in our lives."

"How do you know that's what Natalia wants?" Rosa countered.

"How do you know that's what your kids want, especially your racist son?" Lisa leveled at her.

"My son isn't racist. He's just confused."

"Are you kidding me? He had a Confederate flag on the back of his truck," Lisa huffed.

"Well, he doesn't anymore," Rosa said as if that settled the matter.

This woman seemed to live her life behind a veil, one that she lifted from time to time, depending on what view or truth she wanted to see. Lisa's thoughts were interrupted when Rosa began coughing profusely, her eyes watering as if she were choking.

"Let me get you some water," she said as she rushed into the kitchen. She realized the chicken she'd put in the oven was completely dried out now. She grabbed an oven mitt, quickly pulled it out, and placed it on top of the stove. When she returned to the living room, Rosa was sitting on the sofa, flipping through a magazine. "Here you go," she said, handing her the glass of water. She continued standing as Rosa took a few sips. She wanted Rosa to leave and never come back. Rosa must have sensed her desire, as she abruptly placed the glass on the coffee table.

"Well, I guess I should get going," she said reluctantly as she stood.

Lisa felt her skin prickle as Rosa looked at her from head to toe, assessing her, judging her, wondering what Joe saw in her. But she felt she could have done the same thing. They were both older now. Changed.

"Goodbye. I got what I came here for," Rosa said mysteriously as she walked to the hall and slid out of the front door.

Lisa simply nodded. She hoped she'd never see Rosa again, but she had a feeling the woman would become a nuisance. She closed the front door and walked toward the kitchen to see what she could do to rescue the dinner she knew was ruined. On the way, she paused at the coffee table. The magazines were no longer in the fan shape she preferred, and the mail was now stacked in one pile. Why had Rosa been shuffling through the magazines and envelopes sitting there? She'd been looking for something. But what?

She would have to warn her child about this woman.

Chapter 25

PLEASE CALL ME. I CAN EXPLAIN.

Written in red ink, the words were sprawled across a yellow sticky note on her door when she returned. Pamela convinced her to go thrift-store shopping after the movie—another attempt to keep her mind preoccupied. Natalia studied David's handwriting as she squinted her eyes and leaned forward. Wretched letters with jagged edges. She yanked off the note and crumpled it in her hand.

As she dropped her bag of knickknacks on her kitchen table—a tarnished silver dove that she would polish and place on her nightstand and a hand-painted porcelain plate in shades of blue for her coffee table—she felt pain encroaching all around her.

She could only imagine what he had to say. "It's not what you think. She's just a friend of mine." Or, "It wasn't a date. She's my cousin." She couldn't bear the thought of hearing a lie. But she knew the truth could rip through her—an EF5 tornado that would leave massive destruction she couldn't repair.

I should have known better, she thought as she tossed the sticky note in the trash. A handsome doctor with no kids, no ex-wife, and no drama. Something had to be askew. There had to be at least one skeleton in his allegedly clean closet. It *was* too good to be true. Did she miss the signs? Like the time he was unreachable for a couple of days, claiming work was hectic. Or the time he was out of town for two weekends in one month supposedly at a medical conference, then a guy's trip. How had she become so trusting all of a sudden? She was far too familiar with this game, but she'd forgotten the rules. She'd forgotten the plays and let her defenses down.

Her thoughts were interrupted by a knock at the door. She tiptoed toward it, avoiding the creaky areas of the wood floors, closed one eye, and looked through the peephole. David.

She stood frozen for several seconds and jumped when he said, "Please open the door. I know you're there."

She looked around her place, wondering how he could possibly know. Had he talked with Pamela? Was he sitting outside in his car watching when she dropped her off? Who buzzed him into the building, anyway?

"Natalia. Can you please let me explain?"

The mind and heart were fickle with their oscillations. They battled each other—a tug-of-war with sanity on one side and madness on the other. It was not a fair fight. She melted at the sincerity of his voice and braced herself as she opened the door and leaned against the doorframe. He tried to hug her, his cologne coming toward her first and tickling her nose, but she recoiled and pushed him away.

"Just say what you have to say," she said flatly, folding her arms and blinking to hold back tears. She continued standing in the doorway, shifting her weight to her left foot.

"Can I come in? Can we sit down and talk?"

"I guess so. If you need that much time," she snapped.

He crossed the threshold and walked toward her couch. *The pillows need to be fluffed*, she thought, noticing the seams misaligned from the cushions, but she resisted the urge to shake and straighten them before they sat down.

He looked at her, his eyes soft and moist around the edges. His larynx bobbed up and down as he swallowed. "I haven't been completely honest with you," he began, then paused, looking around the room as if seeing it for the first time. Natalia's right eye began to twitch as she crossed her legs and shook her foot up and down. "Well, I haven't lied to you. I just haven't been forthcoming." He paused once again, licked his lips, and continued. "I was engaged a couple of years ago, but we called it off because she got a job offer in New York that she couldn't refuse. At the time, I was doing my residency here and wouldn't leave my grandmother. We agreed to stay together and tried long distance for a while, but we couldn't make it work. We were both too busy and couldn't find time to see each other. Of course, we grew apart. She met someone else and so did I—before you. I dated several people. I just wasn't ready to settle down. Because, well . . . because I still loved her."

Rage boiled inside Natalia's stomach as she waited for the point of his sad love story. What exactly was he saying? When he looked expectantly at her, she stared back, her eyes wide and her chin dipped, as if to say, "Carry on." If she opened her mouth, the acid she felt inside would spew, burning him alive.

"We went through a lot together—she helped put me through medical school. She was there for me when I thought I wasn't going to make it. She got pregnant, but . . ." He bit his bottom lip and closed his eyes. The kitchen clock ticked loudly, announcing each second. "When I thought I was going to be a dad, it changed everything. I saw her differently. So, I asked her to marry me before she moved to New York. She was ride or die. We had each other's backs. When we lost our baby—" He stopped as he searched for the right words. "We were both grieving and—and things changed."

David leaned forward, his hands clasped between his legs, and looked down at the floor before he continued. "After we ran into each other outside the grocery store, she called and said she really was moving back here. Her mom's health is pretty bad, her brothers live here, nieces and nephews. All of her family. Anyway, she's looking for another job now."

His words were like punches in her gut. Blow after blow. She took them silently until she thought she would vomit the acid that continued to brew in her belly—involuntary words filled with venom.

"I just need some time to think." He reached out to take her hand, which she swiftly yanked away.

So, he was putting her on a back burner while he decided who he would choose. "You need time to think? You need time to think about what? You just sat here and professed your love for some other woman. She just waltzes back into your life and now you're confused." She shook her hands in the air wildly, indicating the instability of his mind. "And you think I'm supposed to sit around waiting for you to decide?"

"I didn't say I still loved her, Natalia. I do care about her, but I—I don't know how I feel right now. Look, I'm just trying to be honest with you."

"Trying to be honest? Maybe you should have thought about that when we were dating. Like, maybe you could have told me you were engaged before. Told me you could have been a dad." She was yelling now. Anger and hurt carrying her words up and away from the depths of her pain. "I'm not going to just sit around waiting for *you* to decide who *you* want to be with." She jabbed her forefinger at his arm twice, reinforcing each time she said "you."

"Men. Y'all are just un-fucking-believable. I thought you cared about me. What about us?" Tears began pouring down her cheeks. Damn it. She hated crying, especially in front of people. She hated anyone seeing her vulnerability. Her pain laid open. She stood up and walked toward her balcony doors, slid one open, and inhaled as she looked down at the backyard. The red blooms of the crape myrtles were beginning to take on an orange hue, the original color draining and losing strength. In another month or so, the landscaper would prune the tree, leaving it vase-shaped and naked, its bark peeling, bare branches reaching up to the sky as if giving praise.

"Natalia, I'm sorry. I do care about you. I don't want to hurt you. But I don't want to hurt Bianca either. I just need time to think through everything."

"Yeah, you already said that," she said angrily. Bianca. Did he just say this other woman's name? She wanted to grab him, shake some sense into his head. "Just go, David. Go do your 'thinking.'" She held up two fingers, putting air quotes around the word. She doubted that would be the only thing he'd be doing. "Just don't expect me to be here waiting for you when you're done."

"Natalia, please. Can you try to understand?"

"Understand? Understand what? Just go, David. I need time to think, too. How do you think I feel? Just go!" She followed him toward the door and pushed him away when he tried to hug her goodbye.

"Bye for now," he said, his head hanging low.

She slammed the door as hard as she could behind him. The small mirror hanging on the entryway wall fell to the floor, shattering into sharp pieces.

Chapter 26

The plan made more sense when they first put it together. Rosa and Catarine would pay Natalia a surprise visit, giving her a taste of her own medicine. Thanks to the graduation photo perched on Lisa's mantel, she'd found the girl's full name: Natalia Elayna Foster. Her middle name was the same as Joe's mother's. That they'd had the audacity to connect her to his family in this way was beyond Rosa. Seemed like a tribute to their love and the potential longevity of it, she thought, wondering if Lisa had been telling the truth or not. Or a slap in his mother's face. She couldn't be sure.

She'd been hoping to find Natalia's address in the stack of mail on Lisa's coffee table when she'd stumbled upon another clue: a business card used as a bookmark tucked inside a magazine. She'd slid the card inside her coat pocket like a lucky coin: D&D Group—Natalia Foster—Assistant Designer—3000 Milam, Houston, TX 77006. Now she was getting ready to take a five-hour drive from New Orleans to Houston with Catarine.

Getting to this point hadn't been easy. Catarine was adamantly opposed to the idea and had begged her not to go. "What good will it do?" she'd asked.

Rosa had detested her child's naivety as she felt her own shrewdness, buried all these years, come to the surface, gasping and grateful for new life.

"What do you mean, 'what good will it do?' This child needs to know her place, and she needs to stay in it."

"What are you talking about? What do you mean?" Catarine's shoulders slumped forward.

"Just what I said. I don't need or want her coming around our family. She may look like Joe. She may have his blood. But she doesn't have ours, and I'll make sure she understands what that means. She needs to go on with her life and let us go on with ours."

"But she's not bothering us, Mom. She doesn't even live anywhere close to here."

"She had the nerve to go to your Dad's wake and funeral. She's even come to our house. She's a bold one who seems to think she can get away with anything. She seems to think she's important."

"Mom, she's Dad's child. What did you want her to do?"

Rosa tossed the dish towel she'd had in her hands at Catarine's face. She needed her to wake up and use her brain.

"Think, Catarine," she'd said. "She is not part of this family and has no right to be."

"She's still my half-sister—and Joe Jr.'s and John's. What about them?"

"I don't give a damn what either one of them has to say, especially not Joe Jr. I still can't believe he kept this from me all these years."

"How is it that you can forgive Dad but not forgive your own son? He was protecting Dad. What did you want him to do?"

She had a point. Joe Jr. didn't ask to be privy to his father's secret, sinful life. If she was honest with herself, now that the truth had come to light and the wool over her eyes had been removed, she'd had hunches throughout their marriage. Lisa probably wasn't the only one. But she hoped Joe hadn't fathered any more children. She hoped his deception hadn't spread any further. She didn't think she could go that far—dealing with another child.

She'd always noticed Joe's eyes lingered longer than they should have when attractive black women walked by. He'd even commented on their beauty before. But she never thought he'd act on his lust. Or, frankly, that they would have any interest in him. But Joe was charming and could make anyone laugh. He had those piercing eyes, those perfect white teeth, and that sincere smile that lured you in.

She had been far too trusting. When he said he was working late, she believed him. When he said he was out of town fishing, she believed him. She never called his supposed hotel room to make sure he was there. Besides, Joe was the one who always proactively checked in, probably with Lisa or whoever nearby listening to every word. What a fool she'd been. She'd rigidly focused on denial, quashing doubt with excuses.

"You can either come with me, or I will go by myself."

"Mom, you shouldn't be driving that far alone."

"Then I guess you're coming with me."

As they exited Pierce off I-45 toward Midtown, they found themselves thrown back in time. They drove down a street flanked with two-story, squatty brick buildings: small-town storefronts with wood-framed glass doors, large serif letters etched on glass, flat rooflines of varying heights, striped awnings interspersed with brightly colored ones—yellows, oranges, and greens. A mixture of businesses, restaurants, and boutiques. Parking meters stood at attention every twenty feet.

Rosa fiddled with her silver cross, which dangled from a thin chain. She felt a tugging, a leash around her neck, pulling her toward something. She wanted to rip it off; the chain dug into her throat. But she was helpless as she began coughing fitfully, struggling to catch her breath. She reached for a bottle of water in the cupholder and tried to take a sip, but the water drizzled down her chin and onto the front of her sweater, where it formed five irregular circles.

"Mom!" she could hear Catarine calling as she continued coughing. She leaned forward and grabbed her stomach, struggling to inhale. She finally caught her breath as Catarine pounded on her back with the palm of her hand. "Are you okay?"

Rosa cleared her throat as she nodded. "We're almost there," she said quietly, defeatedly. "It's just a few blocks up on the right."

Rosa knew she needed to reach this destination before she could continue to the next one. She needed to set the record straight. Despite Lisa. A fling. A blip in her marriage. Despite Natalia. An accident that needed to stay in the oblivion it had previously known. Lisa had probably tried to trap her husband, she thought, getting pregnant in an attempt to keep him, pull him away from his family and from herself—his true love. She knew their hearts were one. Their connection stronger than links of a titanium chain. That's why Joe had stayed. Because she was number one. She came before these mistakes. She knew that if Joe could have erased them, he would have. Plus, she was the one who was still there with him after them. He would have never left her side, and he never did. He might have bought that ring, but he had no intention of giving it to her. Lisa had said so. He had realized the error of his ways.

"Poor Dad," Catarine sighed. Rosa turned quickly to look at her, as if she'd been reading her mind.

"He's in a better place now," Rosa said. "We're the ones going through hell."

"Well, here we are at the gates." Catarine parallel parked after several attempts.

They walked through the double glass doors and were greeted by a young receptionist with almond-colored skin and dreadlocks. She sat at an unfinished wood desk in the middle of an airy room with high ceilings. The steel-gray concrete floors gleamed beneath an oversize gold pendant light. A burst of geometric colors covered the wall behind the receptionist—triangles of cobalt blues and eggplant purple, rectangles of mustard yellows and oranges, and squares of cherry red and black.

To their right, a wall of white floating shelves held trophies, plaques, books, plants, and framed photographs. To their left, a staircase with an iron rail led to an open area above where they could see workmen milling around and hear the bustling of phone conversations, footsteps, and the low hum of indecipherable music. Two pairs of gray upholstered chairs were positioned in front of a side window, small wooden tables between them. A long, lean black leather sofa was positioned in front of another window.

"Hello, how may I help you?" the receptionist asked, her voice clear and chirpy.

"We're here to see Natalia Foster," Rosa said calmly, her hands clasped tightly in front of her protruding stomach.

The woman typed on her computer, her manicured nails clicking against the keys. She studied the screen before looking up at them. "I'm sorry, she's with a client right now. Did you have an appointment?"

"No, we didn't," Catarine said quickly.

Rosa glared at her daughter before looking back at the receptionist. "Can we make an appointment? Or can we wait? Do you know when she'll be done?"

"She should be back in about thirty minutes. If you'd like to have a seat and wait"—she motioned toward the chairs and the couch behind them—"or I can take your information and have her give you a call."

"That won't be necessary. We'll wait." Rosa forced a smile across her face.

"This is a terrible idea," Catarine whispered as she plopped down hard into one of the chairs. Her cheeks were pink, her forehead damp with perspiration.

"You can go sit in the car," Rosa said, picking up a design magazine from the small table and flipping through it.

Catarine folded her arms and pouted for the next forty-five minutes.

A strong gust of wind rustled the leaves of the plants near the doors as they burst open. Two women entered. Natalia was one of them.

Chapter 27

Moping. *It's not a way to live*, she thought as she trudged through each day. She was in a deep rut. A crevice so bottomless, it made it difficult for her to concentrate, to breathe, to eat. A drab, dark place where things just didn't make any sense.

Whenever she thought of David, she felt the pain of vice grips tugging and twisting at her heart. Apprehension quickening her pulse. Thick smoke smothering her spirit. Everywhere she went, she was reminded of him.

The day after he confessed his feelings for Bianca, she was leaning against her car pumping gas when a couple holding hands walked into the convenience store. The woman smiled lovingly at her beau. Natalia had rolled her eyes, turned, and stared at the gallons and cents quickly adding up above the pump.

The day after that, she caught a whiff of David's cologne at the grocery store. She was reading the nutrition label on a box of cereal when the familiar scent wafted by as if on a magic carpet. She anxiously looked around, expecting to see him, only to find another, younger man hurriedly pushing his cart up the aisle, the wheels squealing and whining on the shiny tile floor.

The music at the dentist's office, a chill station playing meditative, ambient tracks full of flutes, violins, electric guitars, drums, pianos, and wind instruments. David thought it was good study music when he was in medical school, and he'd continued listening to it after he graduated. She took a liking to it, too, and used it as background music when she painted and even at work through her earbuds as she maneuvered designs on her oversized computer screen.

Wednesday had been a bear smothering her with its weight. She was having lunch with her boss when she saw a group of doctors in their scrubs sitting at a table nearby. She picked at a kale salad drowning in vinaigrette, tossing the almonds and tomatoes around in between the few bites she took. Her boss had asked what was wrong; she didn't seem to be her normal self, was she missing her dad? Natalia had shaken her head and mumbled that she didn't want to talk about it. She knew better than to bring too much of her personal life to work. Any sign of weakness, emotional turmoil, or drama could create doubt in her abilities, diminish her creativity, and postpone the promotion to senior designer she was working toward. She had to pull herself together.

Still, she wondered what he was doing. Where he was going. Was he cuddled up with this other woman every night, cozy in his king-sized bed? What did this other woman have that she didn't? Why was having history so important when it came to relationships? That investment of time, bliss, and sporadic doses of misery always seemed to eclipse the uncertainty of a new bond, what could be a temporary ticket to happiness. The potential promise was just too risky.

"I tried to be all tough," she'd told Pamela that night. "I was just so angry. But when he left, I broke down and cried. Really cried. Like snotty-nosed, dry heaving, hyperventilating crying."

"I know. You're hurting."

"I thought we were soul mates," Natalia said, beginning to sob all over again. "I can't believe I let myself get all caught up like this."

"Soul mates are bullshit," Pamela reminded her. "We could be with hundreds of different people if we had the chance to meet them. Hell, you thought Tyler was your soul mate. How can one person be our end-all be-all?"

She had a point.

"You just need to give it some time," Pamela continued. "He'll come to his senses."

"But that's not fair," Natalia whined. "Why should I let him decide? I should be the one deciding. Or we should be deciding together. Why should I be sitting around waiting for him like I'm just at his beck and call?"

"But, Natalia." Pamela said her name like Natalia was a two-year-old. "We've all been there before. He's confused, but he wants to make the right decision. I mean, look at you and Tyler. You thought it was a sign when you saw him this summer. But he's got all that baggage. This woman, whoever the hell she is—she probably has baggage, too. And David will see that. Or he'll realize that you're the one for him. Just give him some space and some time."

By Thursday, Natalia had reacquired the habit of biting her nails. She knew she was allowing bacteria to enter her mouth and make its way to her gut; her mother had warned her as a child that it could make her sick. But she couldn't stop. She was like a baby involuntarily putting its fingers in its mouth. When she ran out of nail on the forefinger of her left hand—she'd bitten it down to the quick—she started twirling and pulling on her coily hair, but it wasn't as satisfying as the nail biting. So she started on her left middle finger.

Friday finally arrived, bringing with it the anticipation of a weekend where she could wallow in misery alone without the interruptions of coworkers and clients. She felt a twinge of excitement as she meticulously dressed for the day, anticipating a meeting with a new client she'd brought to the team. It was a wealthy woman whose family owned several restaurants and hotels whom Natalia had met her at an art gallery several months ago. Because it was Natalia's lead, she would be heavily involved in the work—commercial design—which would be a first for her.

She tried to erase the memory of meeting the woman. David had been at her side, and the woman had approached them, commenting on what an attractive couple they were. The conversation detoured to their jobs, and the woman was intrigued. When Natalia gave her a business card, she didn't expect her to call. But she did. And today, in just a couple of hours, she and her boss would be meeting with her and an architect to discuss design plans and budget for a new restaurant concept.

She couldn't deny the hint of excitement she felt, not only at the new revenue from this client but also at the design challenge. She strode into the office that morning, her loose black slacks flowing, her white blouse billowing. Having spent the last few evenings studying commercial design books, watching videos, and researching restaurant concepts, she felt prepared. One thing she wasn't going to do was let her sadness swallow her whole.

The meeting at the woman's office went exceptionally well. Shelly recognized the chemistry and rapport between them, which they both knew was essential to their success. "She took a liking to you," Shelly said on the ride back to the office.

"Yes, I really like her," Natalia replied, nodding. "She's so humble and down-to-earth considering she's so well-off. I was expecting her to be pretentious, but she makes everyone feel comfortable."

Shelly was still complimenting Natalia on her work ethic and obvious preparation when they rushed through the office doors side by side. They were heading toward the stairs when the receptionist called, "Natalia!"

She turned and raised her eyebrows in answer. The receptionist beckoned her over with a side nod of her head.

"What's up, girl?" Natalia asked as she leaned against her desk.

"There are two women here to see you. They've been waiting for a while." In a lower, hushed tone, leaning forward, she said, "I tried to get them to leave or come back after they had an appointment, but . . ." She turned her palms up to the ceiling.

Natalia swiveled to face the women. She'd been so absorbed in her conversation with Shelly, relishing the praise, that she hadn't noticed them sitting in the lobby chairs.

"No problem," she said to the receptionist over her shoulder.

But she was nervous, her hands shaking and her knees weak, as she walked over to the two white women. Her heels tapped loudly on the floor. She adjusted her purse on her right shoulder and shifted the notebook and folders she was carrying to the crook of her left arm. She recognized one of the women right away, the memories turning like keys unlocking doors. They were a homely pair, dressed like two old maids.

"Natalia Foster." It was a statement, not a question, spoken in a deep voice by the older woman.

Natalia froze as she saw the anger on the woman's face. Her jaw set tight like two locked gears, her eyes hard and steely like marbles. She glanced at the other woman, who immediately looked down at the floor.

"We need to have a conversation with you, *dear*," the older woman said, the last word stamped with superiority. "I don't know who you think you are."

Natalia turned to see the receptionist watching them, compelled by the approaching disaster. She was leaning forward in her chair.

"But you are not welcome near me or my family," the woman continued. "And you're certainly not welcome near my home. I don't know why you thought you deserved to be at my husband's funeral, but you are *not* a part of this family."

Confusion riddled Natalia's brain, a shooting target with this woman holding the rifle. She was silent as she gripped the notebook and folders to her chest and began backing away.

"Where do you think you're going?" Rosa asked, her voice rising two octaves as she stood up and moved toward Natalia. "I'm not done. We drove five hours to get this message to you. We wanted to make sure it was clear and that you understood."

Embarrassment and shame covered Natalia in a landslide. Her lips trembling, cheeks blazing, eyes watering, she blinked hard and fast as she looked down at Rosa.

"You may be Joe's child by blood, and he may have left you some money, but don't think for one minute that you're one of us," she spat. Literally. Natalia felt spittle land on her face with the hard enunciations of the woman's words.

Joe. Hearing his name brought Natalia back to her childhood, the aching for him. The conjured images. The curiosity. The hope that he thought about her as much as she thought about him. The hospital and her search for him. Not knowing her dad at all but hoping someday she would, then losing him altogether. A bomb had detonated, and she had somehow survived. But now she was facing the aftermath.

"I—I only wanted to meet him," she said softly, as if reminding herself.

"I am and was his wife," Rosa continued proudly, lifting her chin up as if it might add inches to her height. "You and your mother were two mistakes. You both disgust me."

First David's uncertainty and rejection—the severing of a connection she'd begun to rely on. A dream suffocated by the past. And now these two. Sitting on their high horses, spewing venom. The past again raising its heavy hand to punish her.

"Do you understand me?" Rosa asked slowly as if Natalia were mentally challenged. Natalia heard and understood the old woman's words, but they failed to fully register in her brain. She was stuck on "mistakes" and "disgust."

It all squeezed together, including her heart. So, when the tears came, they brought along everything else. The first one trickled down her right cheek. Joe. She would never know him. The second tear fell down her left cheek. Rosa. She was evil, full of hate. His family would never accept her. Then the rest followed, rushing out, taking her black eyeliner with them. David. He wasn't here for her. The love she thought she deserved was not meant for her to have.

Natalia bolted out of the lobby doors, dropping her notebook and folders, leaving a spread of papers on the polished floor. She had decided to take Joe with her wherever she went. She'd made several copies of the funeral program, and carefully cut out his photos from the collage, placing one in the notebook she used at work, another in her wallet, and two in picture frames on her office desk and mantle at home.

Her notebook photo of Joe slid across the floor as he smiled up at Rosa and Catarine.

Chapter 28

A cool breeze stirred the leaves of the live oak in Rosa's front yard. Sitting on her porch, bundled up in a black wool coat, gray scarf, and black boots, she rocked back and forth in her white rocking chair. With her hands perched on her worn purse that sat in her lap, her feet intermittently touched the surface of the stained concrete, its etchings running diagonally and horizontally across the rough surface. A large bouquet of chrysanthemums lay on the other rocking chair.

She stared up at the gray sky and hoped it wouldn't rain, not on this important day. Cars drove slowly by, none of them in a rush on this Sunday morning. As she waited for Catarine to pick her up for Mass, she waved at a smiling neighbor walking her three dogs. She hadn't stepped foot in St. Patrick's Church since she discovered her own son had also betrayed her. Her faith vacillated between fractional and nonexistent. But today she had no choice. It was All Saints' Day.

She'd spent yesterday preparing an elaborate meal intended to help celebrate Joe's life with her family on this special day. Though not enough time had passed to deem it a celebration in her mind, she'd decided to put forth her best effort and focus on Joe being in heaven. The starch-heavy meal included several loaves and biscuits, starting with Pane co'Santi. Standing at the massive island in the center of her kitchen, she'd struggled to knead the dough, taking breaks until the pain in her arthritic fingers subsided enough for her to continue. Her mother had taught her how to make the bread when she was just a child. She thought of her then as she poured raisins, figs, and walnuts on the flattened dough. She felt she was following in her mother's footsteps, a mirror of her life, as her mother had lost her husband when she was only sixty – even younger than Rosa. She never remarried and had spent the next twenty-seven years focusing on her children and grandchildren, volunteering at a homeless shelter and attending church whenever the doors were open.

Perhaps she was also destined to be a lonely widow. She couldn't fathom the thought of being remarried. Another man seemed as foreign as creatures on the bottom of the ocean floor. Adapting to someone else's moods and behaviors, meeting their needs and wants—these thoughts exhausted her. She wished she'd asked her mother why she'd never remarried but knew that she'd probably considered her dad her one and only true love.

True love. Was there such a thing? What made it "true"? Putting someone else's needs before your own. Carrying on even when the passion and romance fade away. Honoring your vows even when every fiber of your being wants to do otherwise.

She couldn't totally blame Joe for his infidelity. She'd tired herself of their predictable lovemaking many years ago. Always knowing what was coming had diffused any level of excitement. They'd let the spice leak out, and neither of them sought to bring it back. His ego was large, and she'd grown weary of stroking it. She knew there were women—there would always be women—who were willing, ready, and waiting to heed a married man's call. She'd seen how they smiled at him at church, at his stores, at the gas station, wherever the two of them went. He exuded a charm, a signal, that called out to them. See me. Want me.

Digging up subliminal images she'd brushed aside, she recalled his side glances at black women. As she thought more about it, she continued to wonder if Lisa had been the only one. She couldn't imagine Joe suddenly deciding to be faithful once he'd had a taste of new, younger brown flesh. Perhaps if she'd better maintained her own looks, he would have continued to focus on her. But she couldn't compete with what seemed to be his preference for black beauty. No amount of tanning would darken her pale skin enough. "I'm back on the wrong side of my thoughts," she said aloud. "I have to fight my way out of this. Focus on the good times we had. He stayed with me, after all. He didn't leave."

This was the pendulum on which she swung.

When she wasn't thinking of Joe, she found herself thinking of her own behavior and Natalia. The girl's sad eyes brimming with tears haunted her. Perhaps she'd been too harsh. A twinge of guilt gnawed at her, chiseling away at the hard being she'd become. She hadn't realized the girl never knew Joe. She assumed he'd been part of her life, even if on the periphery. She'd expected the girl to be more defiant, but instead she rushed away in tears. Tears Rosa had caused.

As she had continued to prepare for this day just 24 hours earlier, Rosa covered the dough with a towel, grateful for the chance to rest her hands. She hoisted herself onto a barstool and flipped absently through a home décor magazine, thinking again of Natalia and her career as she waited for the dough to rise, soft and bloated. She would break the mass into smaller, round pieces and coat them with a thin layer of egg yolk. Once baked, they would glisten enticingly on a white plate.

At least the girl had made something of herself. She had a career, which was more than Rosa could say for herself. *Joe would have been proud*, she thought as thorns of jealousy pricked at her. She saw his face smiling up from the floor of Natalia's office. But he wasn't just smiling. He was judging her. Something in his eyes had changed. How could she treat his child this way? Forget the fact that the girl had been conceived in sin. How could she treat anyone this way?

She had picked up the program and held it but the reception- ist had rushed over, grabbed it out of Rosa's hands, and stooped down to retrieve the rest of Natalia's scattered papers. When Rosa walked out of the building, she tried to keep her head high, but her own tears, warm and plentiful, poured out. Unleashing her anger hadn't given her the resolution she'd expected.

She bit her bottom lip as she swung open the refrigerator door hard, banging it against the wall. She needed the ingredients to make Joe's favorite dish: *il pan dei morti*, a sweetbread made with raisins, cinnamon, and chocolate. His mother had made and taken this bread to his father's grave on All Saints' Day for nearly thirty years following his father's death. She would do the same for Joe.

She was putting the loaf in their second oven when the door- bell rang.

"Hi, Mom," Catarine said as Rosa stepped aside to let her in. Her daughter carried plastic grocery bags in both hands as they continued into the kitchen.

Catarine had volunteered to help with the main course: ham baked in red wine and pasta con le sarde, and bucatini pasta with wild fennel, tomatoes, anchovies, cinnamon, golden raisins, pine nuts, nutmeg, and leeks and topped with bread crumbs. She placed her grocery bags on the side of the island away from Rosa and began unloading.

Rosa knew her daughter continued to judge her. She didn't have to say anything. Rosa could feel it in the way Catarine looked through her. She had expressed her embarrassment as they drove back from Houston to New Orleans. She never thought her own mother would behave that way, she said. Rosa didn't expect her to understand. How could she? Now a tension hung over their relationship like a thick fog, making it harder to breathe.

They each worked in their quadrants of the space, telling old stories about Joe. Like the time they were on vacation in San Francisco and Joe gave practically everyone on skid row a twenty-dollar bill. Or once when Joe sang in church. He knew he didn't have the best singing voice, but he didn't care. He belted out "Amazing Grace" as if he'd written it himself. The congregation laughed while they joined him.

Or the day Joe had an altercation with a crazy customer at one of the stores. Catarine had witnessed this one firsthand. The man was upset that he'd purchased an expired gallon of milk. Joe apologized and offered to replace it at no cost, but the man wasn't satisfied. He wanted something more to compensate for his second trip to the store. When Joe offered him a ten-dollar gift card, that wasn't enough either. He'd raised his voice, pointed his finger in Joe's face, and used several expletives. Joe's patience had diminished, his eyes darkening by the second.

"If you don't get your hand out of my face, I'm going to throw your ass out of this store," he'd told him.

"You ain't gon' do shit," the man yelled.

He had no idea Joe could have been a professional boxer if he'd so desired, and that he would lay him out on the store's floor in two seconds.

Joe felt bad after he'd knocked him out, and he apologized when the man came to, but the man wanted no part of it, storming out of the building. "He said he'd planned on just picking him up and throwing him out the front door, but his hands did otherwise," Catarine recalled, shaking her head. "He felt bad that I saw him hit that man." She stopped scoring the top of the ham, forming little diamonds across the surface, and smiled sadly.

"He was always dealing with crazy customers," Rosa said. "I was forever worried one of them would come back in with a gun."

"Well, Dad had his ready, too!" Catarine laughed.

After they'd avoided the topic of Joe Jr. for as long as they could, Catarine asked, "So, what's up with Junior? You two still aren't speaking?"

"Your brother did something that hurt me, but now I understand why he did it. So I'm going to fix all of it tomorrow at Mass. I have to."

Weeks had gone by, and Joe Jr. hadn't bothered to call or stop by. She knew he'd harbored the miserable secret to protect her, and Joe. Her original interpretation of its true meaning—that he loved Joe more than he loved her—had been a bit off, she realized. Why did she have to keep reminding herself that her son loved her?

Now that her anger had gone from boiling to simmering, she thought she could manage a conversation with him. She thought she was ready to let this other wound heal. Compelled by God, this was a reconciliation she had to fulfill. He was her son, after all.

"He's not the only thing you need to fix." Catarine peered at her mother as she chopped an onion.

"What do you mean?" Rosa asked.

"Natalia," Catarine said accusingly.

"I don't know how you expect me to fix that!"

"I don't think she's a bad person, Mom. You act like it was her fault, when it wasn't. If you want to blame someone, blame Dad. He was the one who lied and cheated."

Rosa was silent as she marched to the oven to retrieve the bread loaf, nearly dropping it on the floor as she pushed the door closed.

"She never even met him," Catarine said. "Can you imagine, not ever meeting your dad? Not ever knowing him? She was just trying to meet him before he died. And you acted so horribly toward her." She shook her head. "She's my half-sister—our half-sister—whether you like it or not."

Sister. Rosa winced at the word. That detail hadn't occurred to her. The word hadn't crossed her mind. *Illegitimate child, child conceived in sin* . . . but because she had no relation to Natalia, she hadn't advanced her thoughts beyond that. She hadn't thought about her own children.

"God, she looks so much like Dad. I just wanted to reach out and hug her. But instead you talked to her like she was nothing. I know Dad hurt you, and I know she's a reminder of that, but she's not the one you need to forgive. You should think about accepting her. It might help you heal. As a matter of fact, it might be just what Dad wanted, too."

Rosa thought of this now as she sat in her chair on the porch, pushing off with her feet, the curved rockers thumping rhythmically against the concrete floor.

Chapter 29

Sunlight twinkled through the blinds of Natalia's bedroom window. She squinted at the alarm clock on her nightstand: 7:15. As the rush of yesterday came hurling down on her, she shut her eyes and buried her head in the pillow. She spiraled down into a well, her breaths shallow, fresh tears flowing.

Rosa's face—white, worn, and wrinkled—was ingrained in her memory. The woman's words were carved in her brain. Anger circled around her like flies on a carcass. She was angry at everything. Rosa. Rosa's mute daughter. Herself. Her mother. Joe. They had all wronged her, as far as she was concerned. Why hadn't she been stronger? Why had she let that woman hurt her even more?

Her ruminations were interrupted by the harsh buzz of the doorbell. She ignored it, grabbing another pillow and pressing it over her ears to drown out the sound. But this visitor was persistent, ringing the bell repeatedly. *Damn it.* She flung the blanket off and stomped out of her bedroom toward the intercom near her door.

"Who is it?" she yelled.

"Pamela!"

Natalia pressed the button to let her in and opened her front door, arms folded as she waited. Pamela was bounding up the stairs two at a time.

"What the hell? I've been calling you since yesterday evening. I think your phone is dead."

"Yeah, probably." Natalia dragged her bare feet across the floor back to her room where she threw herself on the bed. "I had the worst day I've ever had in my life yesterday."

"What happened? David?" Pamela asked.

"No. Worse." Natalia stared up at the ceiling, her eyes puffy, lids protruding, as she explained how Rosa and her daughter had come to her office and verbally accosted her.

"I can't believe those bitches showed up at your office. What the fuck?" Pamela paced across the room, the wood floors creaking beneath her steps.

"Well, they did." Natalia propped herself up on her elbow.

"You must have been so embarrassed," Pamela said, sitting on the bed and placing her hand on Natalia's arm.

"I couldn't even think about that until I was in my car. I have no idea who saw or heard the conversation. Well, I wouldn't call it a conversation. I don't think I said anything. Our receptionist was sitting there, but I'm sure people could hear her upstairs. She had the nerve to get loud."

"She sounds like a terrible person. Mean and evil. Probably racist like her son."

"That's exactly what I thought. My mom warned me. She told me the woman seemed off. But I never thought she would confront me like that."

"Your mom is going to be furious when you tell her."

"I don't even know if I should. That could just make things worse." Natalia folded her arms and stared at the ceiling. "They're all horrible. The whole damn family."

"You got that right," Natalia agreed. "Why would I want to be part of a family like that?"

"I'm sorry I wasn't there for you," Pamela said.

"It's okay. I survived. I'm just mad at myself for crying. It was just too much. Everything came crashing down on me. And David," she groaned loudly. "I hate everyone." She sat up, grabbed a pillow, and pounded it with her fists.

"Except me, of course," Pamela said with a smile.

"Except you."

"We need to do something about this." Pamela formed a steeple with her hands. Then she stood up and paced the room again. "We can't let them get away with this, and they sure as hell can't have the last word. They think you're soft and weak, but you're not."

"Girl, I just don't care anymore. I'm worn out. I feel like a rag doll."

"You look like one, too," Pamela laughed. "I'll think of something. But you definitely need to tell your mom. I have a feeling she'd be willing to put her Christianity aside for this special occasion."

Chapter 30

Rosa's replay of yesterday in her mind was interrupted by the low bass from Catarine's car, which was pulling into the driveway. Rosa would never understand why her daughter liked music blasting in her ears that way. Rosa could hardly understand or hear the lyrics over the rattling speakers and wasn't sure how Catarine had acquired a taste for heavy metal and rock.

"Hi, Mom," Catarine said. She'd already adjusted the volume before Rosa gingerly slid into the front seat.

"Hi, honey," Rosa sighed.

"What's wrong? Oh, never mind. Joe Jr. I almost forgot. You know they may not even show up today," she observed.

"Well, it would just be postponed, then. It has to happen, though."

"I'm sure he would love nothing more than to be back in your good graces. This can't be easy for him, Mom. We already lost Dad, and now he doesn't have you either."

Rosa hadn't considered this. He had become an orphan. A forced isolation and disownment that prohibited all communication and any semblance of love from flowing between them.

"I'll make amends," she said. "I know this isn't right." She loosened and retied her scarf. She noticed the layer of dust across Catarine's dashboard and resisted the urge to tell her about it. "Honey, are you happy?" she suddenly asked. Catarine had no husband. No children. Just a semicircle of girlfriends—three, to be exact—she'd known since junior high.

"What? Why would you ask me something like that?" Catarine's face contorted and twisted.

"I just want you to be happy. We don't have much time in this world, and I don't want you to end up with regrets. You need to pursue your dreams. Follow your passions. I didn't, and now I'm old and on my way out."

"Mom! Don't say such things."

"It's true. I lived my life for everyone else—for Joe, for you all. I didn't take the time to follow any of my dreams or passions. I'm not saying I was unhappy. I just wish I had done things differently. I didn't take chances or risks. I became boring and predictable. I don't want that to happen to you. You're already past thirty."

Silence filled the car, an ominous overture of doubt. When it became unbearable, she touched her daughter's arm and said, "I'm sorry. I didn't mean to—I wasn't trying to hurt your feelings. I just want you to live your dreams."

"I'm not sure I even have any," Catarine sighed, her face now red and flushed. "I would like to meet and get to know Natalia, though. I can't stop thinking about her. Have you thought any more about what I said yesterday?"

"I have," Rosa said. "I do feel bad about how I treated her. It's starting to weigh on me. She was so upset and sad. But I'm just not ready. Let me deal with Joe Jr. One thing at a time."

They pulled into an already full parking lot.

"I can let you out at the entrance, then park," Catarine offered.

"No, no need for that. I could use the walk."

They sauntered in silence, arm in arm, toward the tall church. Its stained-glass windows reflected a lazy sun that had decided to show up, after all. A white cross rose stoically at the top, suspended almost in midair above the roof. As they walked through the double doors, Catarine took her mother's hand, guiding her through the crowd. They would sit in their regular seats in the fifth row, right side.

As they approached the pew, Rosa saw that Joe Jr. and his family had already arrived. John sat just behind him, saving their seats.

"Good morning." Catarine leaned forward, whispering the words to Joe Jr. and his wife. Their two daughters were already drawing pictures in a notebook.

When they turned to look at her, Joe Jr.'s smile caught a snag and a shadow of uncertainty crossed his face when he saw Rosa, who smiled and nodded solemnly at him. Her conflicting emotions were still battling with each other.

The sounds of the piano and a woman's clear mezzo-soprano voice brought their attention toward the altar and the opening hymn. Rosa focused on the words of the song, "You Alone Are Worthy."

One of the priests rose, a tall, thin man wearing glasses. "We pay tribute on this All Saints' Day to God for the grace of all those He has taken home to heaven," he said. "That is the very definition of a saint. Let us call to God for His pardon and His mercy for those times when we have deviated and sinned."

Mercy. A heavy word ladled with difficulty and resistance. *The root of my problem is Joe,* Rosa thought. *If I could truly forgive him, I could possibly forgive everyone.* She pictured Natalia, her eyes wide and afraid. Her lips shaking. She thought about Catarine. Her maturity and grace were effervescent against the backdrop of grief for her father. Catarine was right. Forgiving Joe Jr. was the pinnacle. Once she had accomplished that, she could toss aside her misery and ascend into relief and acceptance.

She rubbed the diamond on her engagement ring, lifted it to her lips, and kissed it softly as tears streamed down her cheeks. She would still give anything to see him again. To have more time with him. And with that certainty, she could forgive him. Not because he wanted her to, but because her love for him overcame his lies and mistakes. The cloudy, illogical nature of her thoughts shifted, making room for clarity.

The congregation piled into the aisles and spilled out of the massive front doors. Shades of dark blue, greens, and grays mixed with browns and oranges as the crowd dispersed into the parking lot. The cool breeze continued to sift in and out, lifting scarves and tousling hair.

Rosa wasn't sure how to begin with Joe Jr. as she followed her children to the parking lot. There were many ways one could start such a conversation. "I'm sorry" was probably the simplest. But when she thought about it, she wasn't sorry—but rather, exhausted and ready to live in peace. When it came to families, she knew all too well hers didn't fall into the category of apologizers. Their blood brimmed with stubbornness. They were far more likely to either hold grudges indefinitely or simply move on with no acknowledgment one way or the other.

She remembered Joe's anger when she'd refused to care for his dying mother. She wished that she had given him what now felt like a small favor. But at the time she was overwhelmed with the duties of putting her family first—caring for their children, who were all below the age of ten. Laundry. Meals. Homework. PTA. What had become obligatory sex. She couldn't carve out a sliver of time for herself. How was she supposed to find time for his mother as well? Why couldn't he just pay a nurse to help out, especially when they could afford it?

But that wasn't something Italian families did. Rosa was expected to carry out the caregiving tasks—bathing her, feeding her, talking with her. But she was indignant and adamantly opposed to doing it. She had been feeling unappreciated at the time. She was already bending and bowing from the load she currently carried. More weight would have immobilized her.

When she relented, he dismissed her like a judge sending a guilty criminal off with a life sentence. "Don't even worry about it," he'd said. So she didn't, and they moved his mother into an assisted living facility. But that anger stuck with him like a second skin for many years. She wondered now if that anger had driven him into Lisa's bed.

"Mom." Joe Jr. was at her side.

"Hello, son," she said, reaching up and around to hug him. She was like a small child in his embrace.

Funny how the roles reversed with age. She needed her children more than they needed her now. The progression of time was pushing her back into an infancy where she yearned to be cared for and looked after. She glimpsed her future and could see in ten years' time she would need assistance with simple things like getting into a car, taking a bath, and picking up the cast-iron pan, tasks she already struggled to do. Her mind was telling her one thing, but her body was not doing its job.

Her exhaustion, mental and physical, was palpable. She felt the creakiness in her joints and wondered how much worse they would be in time. There was no rewinding the hands of the clock. They continued to tick around, and with each rotation, she felt her decline. The inevitable descent into decrepitude beyond old age. A time when she would become a stranger to herself. A time when she would yearn for her younger years or the termination of her current ones.

She tried to think of the words to begin this conversation with her son as they stood next to Catarine's car, but her mind felt like outer space: dark, foreign, and filled with infinite voids.

"I wasn't sure if you'd be here today," Joe Jr. began.

"I didn't have a choice," Rosa confessed.

"Well, I'm happy to see you." He leaned in and hugged her again, for a long time, during which they communicated in silence. I'm sorry. I'm sorry, too. You know I love you. I love you, too.

"Hi, Grandma!" her youngest granddaughter yelled, interrupting their embrace. She was a spunky child with dark brown eyes and curly, tumultuous hair to match.

"Hello, sweetheart." Their hug was interrupted by the girl's older, quieter sister, who was tapping Rosa on her shoulder. At ten, she was already Rosa's height. Rosa squeezed her tightly before hugging Joe Jr.'s wife.

"We'll talk later," Rosa said to Joe Jr. as he helped her into Catarine's car.

She realized that so many words were left unspoken. If they weren't released, she would continue to smolder as she turned them over and over in her mind. She would take him to breakfast or lunch, or maybe dinner—a public place where they would be forced to behave civilly.

"Well, that wasn't so bad, was it?" Catarine asked after they'd shut the doors and started out of the parking lot.

"Better than I thought, but we still need to talk things over."

"I can understand that. Hopefully you can both move on after that."

"I hope so. I don't know how he lived with the secret for so long." Rosa wasn't sure if she was thinking of Joe or their son.

Greenwood Cemetery was in the middle of New Orleans on City Park Avenue. Rosa and her family filed through the wrought iron gates on Canal Boulevard where they were immediately greeted by the six-foot statue of a volunteer fireman and the large bronze statue of an elk sitting atop a mound of grass. The family was like a small army of sorts, carrying soft weapons—flowers, wreaths, and candles.

A third memorial, a masonry mausoleum atop a lower mound of grass, marked the mass grave of six hundred Confederate soldiers. Above these corpses, a statue of a Confederate infantryman stood on a marble pedestal, resting his hands on his rifle. Four busts of Confederate generals flanked the base of this pedestal: Robert E. Lee, Stonewall Jackson, Albert Sidney Johnston, and Leonidas Polk. Thousands of other known and unknown heroes and veterans—Confederate soldiers, army brigadiers and generals—were buried here. Their aboveground tombs extended for miles.

All that blood in vain, on both sides, Rosa thought. She could understand the fight for freedom. Battles fought by those who had less and were considered less than. But the whole idea of war made her question the very existence of humanity. Strife and torture. Supposedly right and allegedly wrong. Often at the root of it: money or power. The strength of it so overwhelming that segments of entire races could be gassed, lynched, burned, or hacked to death in the name of what was supposed to be a justified cause. Sometimes in the name of the Lord. And look where it got them. Dead and long gone.

Unlike cemeteries where upkeep was sporadic and dependent on volunteers, Greenwood was immaculate. Neat rows of tombs radiated out in all directions like spokes on a wheel. Freshly trimmed grass, recently swept concrete walkways, touched-up and scrubbed tombstones with clearly carved words indicating final resting spots. For those without families, the staff took care to place flowers on those obscure graves. They continued walking past the concrete police crypt with the starred badge and hat before turning right on Cherry Avenue.

Other families, old and young, gathered together. Some knelt quietly, alone, eyes closed, heads bowed. Others sat on picnic blankets cast near their loved ones' graves, eating sandwiches and drinking soda. At other graves, priests and archbishops blessed the tombs with holy water, leading families in prayer and worship. She recalled their trip to this cemetery last year. Joe, holding her hand as they took tepid steps toward his parents' grave. Little did they know that the deadly tumor had already rooted in his brain.

They turned left on Osier, passing more graves and more families who were bearing the loss and pain and had come out to celebrate these lives. They continued for three more blocks before they reached Joe's grave—next to his parents, John and Elayna. Wind and rain had washed away the black ink that had once filled in their engraved names and dates of life.

Joe's, however, was still fresh and new. The dark ink, the letters in all capitals, his birthday and death connected by a short, straight, abrupt dash that was meant to carry and mean so much. Joe's life lived not so straight but ending far too abruptly. Nearly seventy years and all that had happened in between. He could have lived another thirty years, Rosa thought.

Not nearly enough time had passed for dirt to cling to his tombstone, fungus to grow, or stains to spread. The white marble, framed by a dark gray border, sparkled as it bathed in a hide-and-seek sun, intermittent clouds passing by as if to say hello. A lone cross sat at the top, stern, steady, and strong.

Rosa reached out to touch the letters with her right hand, clutching the chrysanthemums to her chest with her left. As she expected, the stone was warm beneath her cold fingers. She placed the flowers in the empty granite vase set squarely in the middle of the headstones, then lowered herself onto the concrete step at the base of the grave. She leaned her head back, closed her eyes, and waited for the sun to touch her pale skin.

"Mom, you okay?" Joe Jr. asked cautiously.

She opened her eyes and watched as Joe Jr. kneeled in front of his father's tombstone.

"I was just thinking. So much has happened since Joe died, and so little of it makes sense. Well, it makes more sense. But I've had to work to put the pieces together. I'm not sure I'll ever understand the mind or inclinations of a man. But women—I can relate to them."

"What are you talking about?" Joe Jr. asked, a thread of irritation winding around his words.

"First, I went to see Lisa. You know—Joe's mistress. The one you met however many years ago." She paused to watch Joe Jr. clamp his lips firmly together, an attempt at keeping his mouth shut. She heard Catarine exhale before retrieving a blanket from her tote bag, spreading it out on the ground, and plopping down. She watched John settled down next her and grabbed a bottle of water and took a long swig. The audience of two prepared for the scene to unfold.

"She was not what I expected. She was . . ." Rosa paused as she searched for the right words. "She was prettier than I thought. High cheekbones. Doe-like eyes that made her seem almost innocent. Tall and lean like she could have been a model." She paused again, a memory rising up from the overgrown jungle that had become her brain. "Someone once told me that men don't cheat with women who are more attractive than their wives. Otherwise, they would be tempted to leave their marriages. I guess that was the case for your father. Anyway, she was also full of tempered regret. I think she felt bad about fornicating with a married man but blessed to have Natalia. It is quite a conundrum, wouldn't you say?" Rosa looked at Joe Jr. as his left eye began to twitch. "I was angry when I went there. So angry."

"As you should be." Joe Jr. squeezed the words out between clenched teeth.

"She apologized in her own way. She's a Christian now, you know. Married—a husband of her own now, too. But I was still angry when I left. So, I went to see the child in Houston. Natalia. I said some pretty nasty things to her. Told her she was a mistake and that she was not welcome in this family."

"Damn right! That black bastard has no place in our family," Joe Jr. railed. "You did right to set her straight. I already told her to stay the hell away from us. Niggers in this country think they can get away with anything these days. They actually think they're equal."

Rosa blinked rapidly as she processed her son's words. She felt blinded as she recoiled.

"Why would you say such a thing?"

"Because it's true."

"You are beyond ignorant!" Catarine spat. "Dad would be so ashamed of you."

"Who *are* you?" John asked, his head jerking backward in astonishment.

Rosa felt tarnished. Fearfulness skittered across her skin as she searched the compartments of her heart, recesses she hadn't visited in years. She tiptoed into the darkness, steps light and delicate.

The color of Natalia's skin hadn't mattered to her. But when she thought of Lisa, she found something there. A poisonous seed sprouting in the dark. A disdain that almost mirrored her son's. The disgust she felt moved from her stomach to her mouth as she dry heaved, her diaphragm lurching. The betrayal had been magnified when she discovered Lisa was black. That much was true. But as she continued searching, she realized she would have been just as upset if Lisa had been white. The horror had been the deceit. She recoiled in shame and hoped Natalia didn't think she was anything like her son.

"I don't hate them because of the color of their skin," Rosa said after she composed herself. "I hate what your father did. I hate that you knew and didn't tell me. I forgive you, and I forgive Joe. But I don't know how you call yourself a Christian while hating people who don't look like you."

She grabbed the top of Joe's tombstone for support as she rose to her full height. Her son reached out his hand to help her, but she swatted it away. She bowed her head and scurried away from Joe's grave. Away from a cemetery that seemed to be celebrating racism. She rolled her eyes at the statues as she ignored her children calling to her to slow down. Her steps propelled by scorn, this was the fastest she'd walked in years.

I'm a good person, she thought. Saddled with shame, she needed to remove the misunderstanding. To free herself from shackles of guilt and regret.

Chapter 31

Sometimes people deserve a second chance. Sometimes even a third. The question of whether people change—making them worthy recipients of that new chance—had always been up for debate with Natalia. She hadn't come across many who did. In most cases, their true colors emerged over time, revealing what had been there all along—shrouded in lies, covered by nice clothes, suppressed by novelty.

But with a concentrated effort, Natalia believed anything was possible. Armed with wisdom and hindsight, no one had to make the same mistake twice, especially if they learned something from it. No matter how long the indiscretion, it could be corrected—reversed. She watched her stepfather become regretful over time for the way he'd treated her. She witnessed her father live a lie and never acknowledge her existence but relent to remorse in the end. She also knew her mother had transformed from a mistress to a good and faithful wife.

She agreed to have breakfast with Tyler Saturday morning not because she believed he'd changed, but because she knew she had. If David could have dinner with his ex and press pause on their relationship, then why shouldn't she have a meal with hers?

I don't need to sit around waiting for him to make up his mind, she thought as she slammed her car door. *I'm free to do whatever I want,* she told herself as she drove up the busy streets of Midtown. They were meeting at the Breakfast Klub, a diner-style spot that had the best breakfast in the nation, according to all the major news outlets. She'd been before and could attest to the goodness, food so delicious it awakened taste buds you didn't know you had and made you close your eyes as you relished the flavors.

She wasn't surprised to see a line winding around the corner below the yellow awning toward the front doors. Luckily, Tyler had arrived before the restaurant opened and was already standing near the entrance. She approached him from behind, quickly grabbing his waist with both hands—an attempt to startle him.

"Hey, you," he said as he turned. She was caught off guard. His shoulders looked broader, his chest bigger and stronger, his cheeks fuller. She felt herself stiffen slightly in his embrace, her arms only halfway extending to his shoulders. She was accustomed to David's arms around her, not Tyler's. But she couldn't stifle the smile that spread across her face as she looked up at him.

"You look better. . . . Sorry, not 'better,' " she said. "That came out wrong." She shook her head. "Healthier? happier?"

"Dang, I must have looked like real shit," he laughed. "I do feel better. I think the road to recovery has finally ended. I got my bill of health—the cancer is in remission. Now I have to wait out the next five years, hope and pray it doesn't come back."

"Well, I sure hope it doesn't. But you can't live that way, thinking it might come back."

"I'll stay positive, but it'll always be a concern. Once you go through something like this, you realize how fragile we are. How little control we have over our bodies once a disease invades it."

"I know," she said quietly, thinking of Joe.

"I'm sorry, Natalia. That was . . . I'm sorry. I didn't mean to make you think of your dad."

"It's okay. I think of him every day on my own. No prompts needed." She attempted a smile.

"I'm sure you do."

They'd crossed the restaurant's threshold and were inside now. Tyler grabbed two laminated menus from a holder near the counter where they would order.

"I'm pretty sure I'm getting wings and waffles," Natalia said before scanning the menu. "I was thinking about this meal as I drove over here."

"Well, I'm trying to eat healthy, at least for the next five years. But I don't think the catfish and grits will hurt me this one time." He smiled and winked. Natalia's cheeks turned ruby red as she smiled, lowered her eyes, and looked away. He was still so damn good-looking.

They ordered and chose a table in the front of the restaurant near a large window. He slid a wooden chair back from the small table so she could sit down. The legs grated against the stained concreted floor as she scooted forward, with Tyler giving her an extra push from behind.

"I'm glad you decided to see me," he said as he sat down. "I thought you were mad at me. You weren't returning my calls."

"It's not that I'm mad at you or not mad at you," she said. "I told you I met someone. I was seeing someone."

"'Was'?" he asked, eyebrows raised.

She studied several paintings of women of color spread across the back and side walls: a woman playing a guitar, her hair in an afro-mohawk; another wearing a hooded purple veil, child-like eyes conveying her vulnerability; and an ebony-toned queen dressed in white, regal with her chin tilted upward.

"I don't want to talk about it. You said you wanted to talk to me about something?"

"Yeah, I, uh . . . I have some news. My wife is trying to get back with me. She wants to try to work things out. Move back to Chicago."

He glanced up as their waitress appeared with their coffee. She poured the hot beverage into black mugs she'd placed on the table. Her angle was too high and some of it splattered, creating small puddles on the walnut finish and dribbling down the sides of their mugs.

"Sorry about that." She smiled apologetically as she walked away.

"Could we get some sugar and cream, please?" Natalia called after her. The woman turned and pointed at a glass sugar dispenser, a bowl with packets of creamer next to it. Both were hiding behind a fake green plant in a silver metal pot. Natalia grabbed a napkin from the holder and wiped the coffee off the table, then dabbed at their mugs, lifting them to remove the round rings they'd created underneath. "Your wife wants to remain your wife?" She scrunched her eyes and nose together. Did he ask her to breakfast so he could tell her this? Was this his idea of playing another game with her? She decided to tend to her coffee before she said anything else. Three packets of creamer, two teaspoons of sugar measured carefully as she poured it from the dispenser. She wanted to toss the glass container at his chest, but instead she slid it over to him.

"I told her I needed to think about it." He waited for her to respond.

"So, your answer is based on what?" she asked as she vigorously stirred, the clicking of the spoon creating a tinny rhythm.

"Well, I wanted to see if we—you and me—if we have a chance at all?"

So, he was too much of a coward to tell his wife that he had feelings for another woman. Or to just leave, considering what she'd put him through. She felt her face warm and her stomach gallop as she took two sips of the hot drink, holding the wide mug with both of her hands.

"I don't even know what to say to you." She shook her head as she placed the mug back on the table. "You're basically saying that if you don't have a chance with me, then you're going back to her."

"I don't know, Natalia. I just know that I've always regretted not choosing you. And if I have the choice, if I can choose you now, then I choose you."

She thought of her own situation. What was she going to do if David decided to stay with his ex? She could end up alone with no one, at least for now. She'd be waiting for someone new to come along, starting all over. She faced the same predicament on two fronts—Tyler and David were both going back-and-forth between the past and potential new futures. She was tired of being jerked around on a yo-yo waiting for someone to stop yanking the string.

"My heart can only take so much," she said, looking out the window. "I have to be honest with you. I have strong feelings for the guy I've been seeing—or had been seeing."

"Yeah, you said 'was' earlier—like you guys aren't together anymore?" He tried again. "I mean, I knew you were with someone. But that didn't mean you were going to stay with him, or that things were going to work out. I guess I was hoping they wouldn't. What happened?"

She thought she would cry if she had to recount her conversation with David. "I can't—I don't want to get into any of that."

"So, you don't have *any* feelings for me anymore?" He sounded almost incredulous, leaning toward her, his arms folded. He was looking into her eyes as if the answer was sitting there, as if they were a chalkboard showing the solution to a complex mathematical equation.

"Tyler, you know I'll always care about you. I've told you this before. I never stopped caring about you. I'm not heartless. Maybe if I hadn't met David, I would be okay with us trying to pick up where we left off. I would have continued to think that we were soul mates just because we looked at each other and had an immediate attraction. But now I wonder if that's all it was. I wonder if you ever really cared about me the way I cared about you. You thought I was attractive, and you liked my body. But the entire time we were together, you never said you loved me. Because you were already in love with someone else. The woman you married."

Their waitress arrived with their meals. Crispy fried chicken wings encircled Natalia's golden-colored waffle topped with powdered sugar and one upside-down strawberry. A yellow circle of melting butter sat in the middle of Tyler's grits, his plate overflowing with crispy catfish, roasted potatoes, and toast. The smells hovered around them, intensifying their hunger.

"Can I get you anything else?" the waitress asked. They both glanced at the Tabasco and hot sauce and shook their heads in unison.

"You're right," he relented, mixing the butter into his grits and scooping up a mouthful. He finished his first bite before continuing. "I never told you I loved you, but that didn't mean I didn't feel that way. I still had feelings for Alicia, but I was definitely falling for you. I guess I was holding back because of her. When I moved back, it was easier to be with her again."

"Easier? First of all, you didn't *have* to move back. Second of all, you could have asked me to move with you."

"I know, Natalia." Pain flickered in his eyes again—currents of darkness battling each other. He inhaled deeply and took a bite of his catfish before speaking again. "I guess I've made my bed, now I have to lie in it?"

"That's one way to look at it. You chose her. Also, you have a child to think about—well, I'm not sure how y'all are handling that."

"I'm not either," he said, his face turning two shades darker.

"We can't keep doing this. We had our chance. Young love or lust or whatever you want to call it. Beyond that, we don't really have anything. I'll admit, when I first ran into you, I was elated. But I have to separate us from me and David. I have to draw some lines."

She studied Tyler's face, from his forehead to his eyes, nose, lips, jawline. His good looks weren't enough for her anymore. She needed his heart to be fully hers. With an ex and a child, it never would be. She would only have a piece of it.

"We could have created something," he said. "We still could create something."

She watched him toss the potatoes around as if he'd lost something inside the chunky pieces. She could see his resolve as he slumped back in his seat without taking a bite of anything. He was finally seeing that they wouldn't have a future together. His life would be as it was, maybe worse for a while. He would have to grapple with the pain of looking at a child that didn't share his DNA. He would have to try to love a wife who cheated on him. He would have to let Natalia go. "Maybe. But it wouldn't have been as it should have," she said after considering what they could have right now—today.

"What do you mean?" he asked.

"Well, let's start with all of the baggage. Like I said, we're not the same. You're not the same. You're broken, and you need to heal. When you come through this, you'll be stronger, though."

Now that they were moving the conversation ahead, she wanted him to focus on his future with his wife. She needed to get out of this circular conversation they continued to cycle through.

"Do you love this new dude?"

Her face flushed when she thought about David. His voice. His affection and respect for her. His care and concern for other people. His mind. His dreams. His devotion to Christ. But then his indecisiveness and the uncertainty of their relationship came rushing in—a stampede crushing those shining thoughts.

"I—I don't know," she admitted. "I think so."

"You're not sure? But your feelings for him are stronger than your feelings for me?"

This was not how it was supposed to be. Choosing between Tyler or David. All of this back-and-forth.

"I don't think that's a fair question, Tyler. We haven't really given each other a chance. I haven't spent much time with you lately. I don't feel like I know you anymore. I mean, I think I know your heart, and that's part of what draws me to you. But we don't really know each other at this point."

"Then we should start over. At least give it a chance and see where things go?"

She wasn't sure if it was the sweetness of the waffle dissolving into her mouth after the saltiness of the chicken or the questionable state of her relationship with David, but something had produced a simmering anger inside her. Why should she sit around waiting for David to choose her? And why should she consider a relationship with Tyler after everything he'd done and all the baggage he now carried? *I don't need either one of them*, she thought.

"No, Tyler," she said. "We had our chance. This back-and-forth, this indecisiveness isn't for me."

She felt light and free, buoyant like a hot-air balloon, as she bounced back to her car. *I'd rather be alone than take sloppy seconds or settle for someone who doesn't deserve me*, she thought. She turned the key in the ignition, cranked up the volume on her radio, rolled the windows down, and let the wind tousle her hair. Emotional freedom was worth fighting for. Tyler had hit her with a couple of arrows, but David had detonated a bomb. She would continue to nurture herself and fill the hole that his surprise attack had left behind.

Chapter 32

Another week went by with no word from David. No phone call. No text. No email. Nothing. Natalia accepted that it was over and began taking steps to repair her heart.

It was finally Friday. The end of a long week filled with demanding clients, unattainable deadlines, and not enough time to think clearly. To top things off, the powers that be had decided to move into a new building. Not to mention the talk of a new office opening in Dallas. The firm was growing, thanks to several new commercial clients. Unpacked boxes littered the new open work space and freshly painted bare walls stared back at them, but the floor-to-ceiling windows and glimmer of new wood floors infused Natalia with new optimism. She decided to stay late to finish unpacking—or purging—her files and reorganizing her desk: repositioning a gold-framed photo of Joe from the funeral program, a white-framed photo of her mom, and a blue-framed photo of her and Pamela, a close-up of them at a beach from nearly two years ago. She shoved the photo of her and David— the two of them dressed in black standing outside a theater, his arm around her shoulder, her arm encircling his waist—into a drawer. She was reaching for her purse when her boss appeared.

"You're here late," Shelly said, grabbing a nearby chair and sitting down next to Natalia's desk. "But I'm glad I caught you before you left. Listen, there's something I've been meaning to talk to you about. I was going to wait until Monday, but I'm so excited, I'd rather tell you now." She was breathless. "We're opening a new office in Dallas at the beginning of the year. We have lots of connections there and potential clients. The plan is for Jackson to run the office, but he's looking for a couple of people to join him right away. You don't have to decide now, but we'd like to promote you—have you join him and help build the team there. You would be a senior designer, and your raise would be worth it. I'm drafting an offer letter that I was going to give you on Monday, but I was so anxious to tell you. So, what do you think?"

Her boss's enthusiasm was infectious, and for a moment, Natalia forgot about her troubles with David. She felt her care-free spirit returning. A calling that beckoned her to be daring. To not live her life on other people's terms.

"I don't know what to say," she began. "First, thank you for choosing me. It sounds like a great opportunity." And, before she knew it, she was saying yes. A rebellion was taking over. She could create her own path. Her heart would mend itself, as it always had. A subtle scar might remain, but she would survive.

"You don't have to decide right this minute. Think about it over the weekend, and we'll talk more on Monday. How about that happy hour? We have an hour left." The team was celebrating their new office space and a client win.

"Yes, of course. We have lots to celebrate." *It's not like I have any other plans*, she thought.

"You doing okay? You seem a little . . . less like yourself lately. Is everything okay with your family?"

"Oh, yes. Everything's fine," she lied. "I'll see you there!" They left the office just before the sun descended and the sky turned a steel gray.

Happy hour turned out to be happier than she'd thought it would be. They chose a spot known for its margaritas and guacamole. A mariachi band performed: five men dressed identically in all black, ankle boots, large red bow ties, and straw sombreros. Their guitars, violin, trumpet, and accordion melded together to create a heavily syncopated, festive vibe, luring them from their barstools to the dance floor. They were a collection of disparate and uncoordinated bodies, drawing laughs from an audience she assumed to be regulars. One of them—probably feeling sorry for her—took her hand and began to guide her through the steps of a heel-and-toe, waltz-like dance. When perspiration and exhaustion took their toll, Natalia settled back onto her barstool while letting her margarita wear off and listened to her coworkers tell drama-filled stories about their friends and families.

Three hours later, she drove home. The neighborhood was eerily dark and quiet; one of the streetlights was out. She grabbed her purse and readied her house key for a quick entrance. As she approached the steps, she saw someone sitting on the top one, looking at her. While she couldn't decipher facial features, she knew from the silhouette who it was: David.

"Hi," he said casually. As if they hadn't gone two weeks without talking to each other.

"Hi," she returned, standing at the bottom of the stairs, uncertain of her next move. Should she continue up and invite him in, sit next to him, or continue standing awkwardly? Still simmering from their last conversation and tending to the hole in her heart, she folded her arms and decided to keep standing.

"I, uh, I was going to call you instead of just showing up like this. But I wasn't sure if you'd take my call. Plus, I wanted to see you—talk to you in person."

His face was dark, backlit by the dim yellow glow of the small porch light.

"I see," she said.

"First, I owe you an apology. I'm sorry for putting you through this. Dragging you into my past, making my baggage your baggage. I'm sorry I felt like I needed time to think. I just wanted to be sure about us, which meant I had to be sure about myself. I don't think I had true closure with Bianca, and I needed to have that before I could move on with you. I needed to be certain that whatever I felt for her wouldn't jeopardize or affect how I feel for you. Sometimes people think—well, I thought—it might be easier, safer to pick up where I left off with her. But the more I talked with her, and spent time with her, the more I realized my heart is yours. I've missed you, Natalia. I miss your smile, your sense of humor, the way you make me feel. No other woman can compare to you."

Her breathing had become uneven and ragged, coming in bursts as he continued to speak. She wanted to believe what he said, but how could she be sure?

"So you spent time with her. What does that mean exactly?"

He turned to watch a car passing by, the headlights illuminating his profile. She wanted to reach out, run her fingertips along his cheekbone, down his neck, across his shoulder.

"We didn't sleep together, if that's what you're asking," he replied.

"Of course that's what I'm asking," she snapped. "You think it would be okay for you to sleep with her, then decide to come back to me? Get a temporary breakup so you could have permission?"

"I didn't sleep with her," he protested. "We had lunch a couple of times, and we talked on the phone. I wanted to see where her head was, where my head was. It just wasn't the same. I didn't feel the chemistry with her that I feel with you. Our conversations were nothing like the conversations I have with you. We've both changed. You've never wondered about an ex before? Someone you loved or thought you loved?"

"Why does that matter?" she deflected.

"Because I want you to put yourself in my shoes. Maybe you can relate and have a better idea of what I was thinking. How I was feeling."

"I guess so," she relented. "But you're not about to sit here and make this about me and one of my exes. You're the one that just bounced because you thought you wanted *your* ex back."

"I know, I know. But I don't want her back. I just needed to clear my head completely. Not deal with both of you at the same time."

"'Deal with'?"

"You know what I mean. I wouldn't date you both at the same time. I'm not that kind of guy. Last week, I didn't see or talk to her at all. I must have worked seventy hours. I just spent time really thinking."

"So, what did you tell her, David? Does she know you're not going to be with her?" She wasn't sure what he even liked about this Bianca, who seemed to think far too much of herself. She was superficial, high-maintenance, and stuck-up, from what Natalia had gathered. "And how do you know you're certain about this, David? How do you know you won't change your mind?" Before he could answer, she continued, "Or how do I know you won't have another ex-girlfriend waltz into your life and make you sec- ond-guess our relationship?"

Fear kept her stoic as she continued to stand with her arms folded. She was tired of men. Tired of the lies. None of them could be relied on. Her stepdad had done nothing for her. Her own dad never acknowledged her. Tyler chose someone else when he could have chosen her. She never seemed to matter to the men who mattered to her. She felt left behind, unsure of herself. Like she was running a race she was destined to lose. Running out of breath and stamina, she wanted to just quit. She bit her lip to fight back tears, thoughts of the miserable two weeks without him reminding her of what she thought she lost.

"Because I love you. The thought of not being with you is unbearable for me."

Those three words jolted her back from the abyss. They were the hook on a pully tugging her back into the light. A portion of her pain dissipated into the dark sky that hung above them, still and silent. But her anger was still prickling. If he touched her, he would feel the sting.

"You love me? But you didn't know this two weeks ago? David, what you did was wrong. Just disappearing for two weeks without a word. I can't believe you didn't call to check on me. To see how I was feeling."

"Natalia, please."

"I'm moving to Dallas," she blurted out. She realized then that the decision was meant to get back at him. A jab with a sword meant to inflict pain. She was detonating her own bomb.

"You're what?"

"Yes, I'm moving. I got a promotion and they want me to help grow our new office in Dallas."

He leaned back, looked up at the dark sky, and rubbed his hands over his eyes. "Don't do this. I promise you, I'm yours," he said.

He sounded so sincere. But she couldn't see his eyes. Why did this two-week interruption into three months of bliss rattle her this way, creating doubt around all her decisions, questioning his honesty? Trees rustled, their leaves dancing in the darkness as a breeze floated by, shaking the branches.

He walked down the steps and tried to take her into his arms, but she pushed him away. She had already hoisted her sail, cruising out to sea, smooth, quiet, and unbound. She wasn't sure she was ready to turn her helm.

"Now *I* need time to think," she said.

Chapter 33

Not big on revenge, Natalia was more inclined to move on when people disappointed her, something she'd come to expect in life. Over time, she realized she was simply expecting too much, and she decided to lower her expectations to soften the blows. She would turn them over to God. Or, let karma have its way. In the end, she would rely on herself and her own independence.

Independent was the first four-syllable word Natalia learned—not in a history class discussion about the thirteen colonies severing their political ties to Great Britain, but in the kitchen of her childhood home when she was five years old.

"Work hard. Get your education. And make sure you never have to depend on a man to take care of you. I want you to be independent," her mother had said, looking into her eyes with a seriousness that made Natalia stand at attention. She was a small soldier following orders. "You don't want to end up like me. Independence means freedom. Making your own money can give you that."

Lisa's high school years had been interrupted by pregnancy, one that would not go full-term but led to her mother kicking her out of the tiny two-bedroom house she shared with her two siblings. She explained what life on the streets had been like. She knew what it meant to never have enough. To live life with your hand held out. Hoping. Pleading. Relying on men to help her make ends meet.

The lesson on independence occurred regularly. Whenever her mother was tired of James. Whenever they argued. Whenever they struggled financially. He didn't want her to work, so her days were spent keeping the house immaculate, preparing meals, doing laundry, and watching the news in between. Whenever Natalia needed money—for field trips, clothes, shoes, prom dresses—James either didn't have it or begrudgingly gave it. Asking him for money was a delicate dance that had to be practiced, then performed with the utmost care. Like unwrapping a present without ruining the paper, carefully peeling back the tape.

"Daddy?" She would begin with her voice barely above a whisper as she looked down at the walnut-stained wood floor. He would be sitting in his chair, the only La-Z-Boy recliner they owned, the threads worn bare where his elbows dug in and the wiry coils of his hair scoured the fabric.

"You must want something," he would reply gruffly. "What do you need money for now?"

If she was lucky, he would dig into his pocket and thrust the crinkled bills toward her. If she wasn't, he would say without consulting his wallet or pockets, "I don't have it." There was no continued conversation. No amount of pleading would change his mind or his heart. She learned that his decisions were often dictated by timing: if he was in a good mood, if he and her mother were getting along. So she always consulted with her mother before asking. Sometimes, Lisa would ask on her behalf. Sometimes they had success, but often, they didn't.

"I hate asking him for anything," Natalia had told her mother when she was fourteen and had made it onto the cheerleading team. The uniforms were three hundred dollars. The tennis shoes were a hundred dollars. And the pom-poms were fifty dollars.

"I know. You see why you have to be independent," her mother reminded her. "You don't want to have to do this all of your life."

"Are all men like this?" Natalia wondered aloud. "Are they all stingy? What am I supposed to do? He's the one who decided he wanted to raise me and take care of me. I bet my real dad wouldn't treat me this way."

Her mother shrank as Natalia hurled the words at her. "No, he wouldn't," she said sadly.

Natalia vowed that she would never have to ask a man for anything. Ever. She vowed that she would always make her own money, because money meant freedom. Money meant having a certain level of self-respect. You could hold your head high. Money meant you didn't have to grovel.

She got her first job at sixteen when she was legally old enough to work. She walked into Domino's Pizza, filled out an application, and was hired on the spot. When she opened her first paycheck, she felt the beginnings of liberation seeping from the paper.

She thought of those early years as she and Shelly sat in a meeting with two new clients, a couple whose child suffered from severe allergies. She listened closely as the wife expressed her concern over her child's health. Natalia recalled a recent article she'd read about green design, an approach that minimized harmful effects on human health and the environment. People could breathe easier with fewer irritants and toxins in their homes.

"The materials and chemicals used to create furniture and flooring these days can be really harmful to our health," Natalia explained. "It's hard to believe that it's legal for companies to make furniture and flooring with chemicals like formaldehyde, benzene, and perfluorooctanoic acid. I mean, these are known carcinogens. They get into our systems and stay there for years.

I'm not trying to scare you, but you should take every precaution you can."

Thinking of Joe, she wondered if any of these factors caused his cancer. How would she ever know? With Rosa's disdain and his son's hatred, she knew she never would.

"The cost can increase in some areas," Shelly explained. "But the money is worth it for your child's health and safety, and yours as well."

"We can definitely come back with recommendations and options that won't emit toxic gases into your home," Natalia said. "We can use sustainable, naturally sourced materials."

On the way back to the office, Shelly complimented her on her knowledge and praised her passion. Natalia enjoyed these habitual occurrences and worked harder to earn them.

Natalia's interest in the green interior design path crescendoed, the intensity building and spreading like wildfire. She wanted to create spaces that were better not only for people but also for the planet.

"I'm going to get my LEED certification," she announced as they walked back into the office. "I love that we can not only help people love their homes, but also maybe even help them be healthier and live longer."

"That would be fantastic," Shelly replied. "We only have one other person on our team who's certified on the commercial and construction side, but it's trending and becoming more important on the residential side. You could help us grow our business in that area. And it would fill a skills gap in the Dallas office once we launch it."

Natalia took the first step and signed up for the exam-prep training, spending fourteen hours over the next couple of weeks learning the ins and outs of water efficiency, materials and resources, and indoor environmental quality. She then devoted three hours a day for three weeks studying for the LEED Green

Associate exam. She ignored David's calls. She put time with Pamela on hold.

"Dang, girl. You don't have time to do anything anymore," Pamela complained when Natalia declined her invitation to a Broadway musical.

"It's just for another week. Besides, you know I'm not crazy about people singing when they should be talking."

"But I really want to go. You know I auditioned for this musical a couple of years ago," Pamela reminded her.

Natalia had forgotten her friend's prolonged misery when she didn't get a part. She apologized for being insensitive. "I'm just so interested in this," she said. "You wouldn't believe the amount of harmful chemicals we're breathing in, which, by the way, can cause cancer. Did you know we spend about ninety percent of our time indoors?"

"I wonder what my cheap-ass furniture is made of. Still, what can people do when they can't afford to buy better or safer furniture? And, hell, it's not like the air outside is much better. I mean, we don't know what we're breathing in. All that car exhaust and those damn chemical plants and refineries."

"Well, I at least want to do my part and educate my clients on their choices. There are affordable options out there, like bamboo and cork, but I'm still learning. My goal is to become a sustainable designer."

"I'm glad you're so excited about this. I'm sure your boss is pleased," Pamela said.

"I think this will open up new opportunities for me," Natalia said. "I'm just waiting for associate exam scores. Then I'm going to move on to the LEED AP Homes credential for single-family houses, multi-families, and low- and mid-rises."

"Look at you all focused and motivated. I'm proud of you, girl. Sooo, have you thought any more about getting back at that evil old woman?" she ventured.

243

"Nope. I'm focused on me and my career. If they stay the hell out of my life, I can easily stay the hell out of theirs."

"Well, what about David? Have you talked to him yet?"

"Nope. I texted him the other day and told him I was still thinking but also studying for this exam."

"Natalia, if you wait too long, you may lose him altogether."

"I just don't know if I can put myself in a position to be hurt again."

"Well, you need to tell him that."

"I know."

Later that week, Natalia arrived early at work to find a bouquet of sunflowers and congratulatory balloons on her desk with a card signed by her entire team. She'd passed the LEED Green Associate exam with a perfect score. When her cell phone rang, she was riding high—a hot-air balloon drifting in the clouds. She recognized the area code as New Orleans but not the number.

"Hello?" she said hesitantly.

"Hello, Natalia. This is Rosa. Joe's wife."

She didn't need to clarify that, Natalia thought. Besides, she recognized the deep tone of her voice, the lilt in the way she pronounced her name. What did this woman want now? And how did she get her cell phone number? When Natalia didn't respond, Rosa continued.

"Listen, I've been thinking a lot about the horrible things I said to you and how I treated you. And I feel terrible about it."

Natalia leaned back in her chair and rolled her eyes at the ceiling.

"Are you still there?"

"Yes," Natalia mumbled.

"Well, I want to apologize to you. I was angry and upset, but you're not to blame. What happened wasn't your fault."

"You said I was a mistake. And that my mother and I disgust you."

"I didn't mean the things I said. You must understand that I was—and am—still grieving. I was lashing out and misplacing my pain and anger. My husband had cheated on me and fathered a child outside my marriage, and I had no idea. All of this was a shock to me. You can't understand the pain of that kind of betrayal."

"And you can't understand the pain of not growing up with a father—your real father." Did this woman really want to talk about pain?

"No, I can't. But I understand pain and the wretchedness that comes with it. That ache and that yearning. I assumed Joe had also been a part of your life. And now that I know he wasn't, I know he endured pain as well. I can't imagine not raising my children."

An image of Joe Jr.'s angry, contorted face appeared before Natalia. His eyes wicked. His mouth vicious. His body rigid with a repugnance she had never seen before. She'd experienced subtle racism throughout her life—a white cashier who used a Kleenex to pick up a balled-up receipt she'd asked him to throw away, a white woman who'd said she was "pretty for a black girl"—but never such outright loathing.

"I'm embarrassed by my behavior, and I hope you can forgive me."

What would forgiving Rosa mean? And why did it matter now? Natalia found herself lost in a gray area where black and white was muddied by indifference. "Whatever," she said as she picked up a charcoal pencil and began doodling pictures of flowers in her sketchbook, their petals soft with detailed etchings.

"'Whatever'? Honey, are you listening to me?"

"Sure. Okay. I forgive you."

"I'm not sure you understand how badly I feel about it. I know you just wanted to see Joe. I would have done the same thing. Listen, I'd like to get to know you—we would like to get to know you. We can help you find out who Joe was. You don't have to decide now, but I'd like to invite you over for dinner. Christmas Eve. If you can make it."

Natalia tried to picture herself having dinner with Rosa and her family. The family Rosa had said she didn't belong to. She saw herself, black and out of place. Awkward and distressed.

"Um, I'll think about it," she said noncommittally.

"Okay. I hope you do. Just call me and let me know what you decide."

"Okay. I will."

After hanging up, Natalia sighed and stared at her computer screen. She shoved her sketchbook to the side, closed her eyes, placed her face in her palms, and tried to reset her mind. Maybe it wasn't such a bad idea. Maybe forgiveness could lead her to true freedom and perfect peace.

Chapter 34

The smell of sautéed salmon traveled from the kitchen across the living room as Natalia poured dressing over a kale salad. It was time to call her mom. Her mother would know what she should do. Her words of wisdom—and confirmation of what she'd already decided—were just what Natalia needed. Balancing the phone on her shoulder, she carried her plate and trudged over to her table, where she plopped down in a plastic chair. The line rang three times before her mother picked up.

"Hi, honey! What are you doing calling so late?"

Natalia shared every detail of the conversation she'd had with Rosa earlier that day.

"As long as it's not a trap," her mother said cautiously.

"A trap? That hadn't crossed my mind. Why would she bother calling if she hadn't had a change of heart?"

"Hmmph. I don't trust any of them."

"What about forgiveness, Ma? You're always preaching that God won't forgive us if we don't forgive others."

"Yeah, I know. That is the Christian thing to do."

"It had to have been hard for her to apologize. Admit she was wrong. That took some courage and humbleness. I'm sure she knows her son is a bigot who doesn't want me in their lives, but she's disregarding him. Or they're getting him professional help—I hope."

"Maybe you should go with David. After you forgive him and take him back," her mother suggested.

"Yeah, I do need to call him," she sighed.

"If you can forgive Rosa, then you can also forgive David. What is your heart telling you?"

David was in her heart. Her love for him was scripted there like hieroglyphics in stone. But. There was always a but with men. He'd hurt her, and he might hurt her again.

"David sounds like a good man," Lisa said. "We all mess up. We all make mistakes. He treats you well and respects you. He's faithful and he's a Christian. You can't ask for much more than that. But then on top of it all he's a doctor—he's made something of himself. And you say he's nice-looking?"

"Very."

"If he is what you say he is, then he sounds like a good catch. And remember, you don't have to marry him tomorrow. You're still getting to know him. You're giving him a chance, and he's giving you a chance. That's all you can do right now." Her mother paused and sighed deeply. "I just don't understand your generation. All this unnecessary back-and-forth with relationships. When I was done with someone, I was done. There was no looking back. It was over. Forward was the motion. But I think you can make an exception this time."

"That's what happened with you and Joe? You never looked back?" She'd tried in vain to get her mother to open up about her relationship with Joe. They'd always skimmed the surface, brushing over blades of grass, never actually digging down to the dirt where the truth lay undisturbed. She felt herself spiraling back down, sadness sprinkling over her like a fine mist, seeping into her pores, infiltrating her blood.

"Honey, you know he was married. I didn't want to break up his home. I thank God that I had you. I wanted you and we planned to have you. I just hadn't thought much beyond that. I didn't know God. I didn't know I was living in sin. I was only thinking of myself. Once I accepted God as my savior—and I met James—I knew what I had to do. I wasn't thinking how much it would hurt you. And I couldn't think of a way around it. You know how it all went."

"I know, I know," Natalia said on an exhale.

"What I did—what your dad did—was wrong. That doesn't change who we are, though, or who we became. He had a good heart. He was a good man. And he would have loved to raise you himself. But somebody had to lose. I do wish the circumstances had been different. But unlike you and David, we weren't starting with a clean slate. And I just didn't have Joe in my heart. But you. You listen to your heart. That matters. You and David can start fresh—no baggage."

She thought about her mom's words. They'd helped remove the wool over Natalia's eyes. Now that it was lifted, now that she had this clarity—this new insight and wisdom—she wouldn't make the same mistake twice. Nor would she let David pull the wool over her eyes again by not revealing the full truth. He had led her to believe he'd never been in love.

She would go in with her eyes wide open, her mind clear, and her heart ready.

Natalia awoke full of energy and fervor, in the mood for fall cleaning. As she swept and mopped, she realized it was time to spruce up her place—rearrange furniture and relocate pictures. The lemon-scented candle she'd lit was now making her nauseous. Where did this even come from? She blew it out.

She opened her living-room windows and balcony door to let in some fresh air. She stepped outside on her balcony and let the breeze tousle her unwashed hair. She listened to the sounds of wind and string instruments floating across the air from one of her neighbors' windows and imagined riding one of the notes to a place far away. She closed her eyes, leaned her head against the brick wall, and focused on the rise and fall of the notes in the song. The tune sounded so familiar, but she couldn't place it.

After a few moments lost in thought, she went back inside. She decided to rearrange her art collage. An hour later, she was pleased with her new wall. She'd taken pieces with similar colors and grouped them together, giving the arrangement a rainbow effect, ending with her black-and-white collection. She moved on to the photos on her mantel: she and her mom, she and her grandmother, two of her and Pamela. *Not one man*, she thought, shaking her head.

Joe. She still had two programs from his funeral; she could frame one of those. She rushed to her bedroom and pulled out the top drawer of her nightstand. She'd tucked them at the bottom of the drawer for safekeeping.

Back in the living room, she removed one of the photos of her and Pamela and replaced it with Joe's. Staring at it, she began to see the similarities. His lips were fuller than the average white person's, she thought. But then again, was he really considered white? Her mother had stressed that he was Italian, as if that precluded him from being Caucasian. His hair was full and wavy—borderline course. His nose strong and pointed. She placed the photo in the middle of the mantel, next to an arrangement of fake flowers.

She repositioned her kitchen table against the wall instead of in the middle of the dining area. Her intention was to have more of a work space. She put one of the extra chairs near her couch and another in a corner in her bedroom.

When her doorbell buzzed, she assumed it was Pamela, whose surprise visits had become more frequent as she expressed concern over her friend's woes. Natalia pressed her intercom button. "So you're gonna visit me every Saturday morning, huh?"

"Ma'am?" a man's voice responded.

"Oh—who is this?"

"I have a delivery for you, ma'am."

She rushed down the stairs, wondering what this delivery could be. *Maybe I ordered something for a client and used the wrong address*, she thought. They often sent deliveries to their warehouse until a client's house was ready. Or maybe one of the stores got it wrong.

She peeped through the glass window on the side of the door and saw a middle-aged white man standing outside with a large bouquet of flowers.

"Good morning," she said after opening the door, squinting her eyes from the glaring sun.

"Good mornin', ma'am," he said. "It is a beautiful mornin' indeed. Here ya go." He held out a clear glass vase filled with orange and yellow roses, red gerbera daisies, peach Asiatic lilies, burgundy mini-carnations, and red oak leaves.

She took the bouquet, then called "Thank you, sir" as she watched him head back down the short flight of stairs and climb into his white van.

The air was cool and crisp. Everything about the morning felt fresh and new as she listened to the twittering of birds, the sounds matching their fluttering wings and quick ascents to the higher limbs of the old oak tree. She didn't know who sent the flowers yet, but she could feel a new beginning.

The neighborhood was quiet. She imagined in some homes, people were sleeping in; in others they were having breakfast with boisterous kids; and in others, there were lovers, snuggled in bed together, bodies intertwined.

She ran back up the flight of stairs, inhaling the intoxicating smell coming from the delicate burst of colors. She placed the flowers on the coffee table in her living room before retrieving the tiny white envelope from the plastic stick.

Missing you. Immensely. Loving you. Only.

—David

Her heart began to dance. She smiled. Her defenses were worn down, and she was out of ammunition.

It was time to extend the olive branch.

"Hello, beautiful," David said, his face illuminated on her screen by light from his office window and punctuated by his shatterproof smile. She could hear the happiness in his voice. Like rising tides lifting her up. She could see it in his eyes. Like rays of the sun warming her soul.

"Hello, handsome. Thank you for the flowers. They're stunning." She smiled.

"You're welcome, babe. I hope that's not the only reason you called. Please tell me you're done thinking and you realize we belong together?"

"I've realized a lot of things. And one of them is that I love you. I'm just so scared, David. You really hurt me. I know life is about taking chances—especially when it comes to love and relationships. I'd let myself go with you and that's . . . that's rare for me. I don't want to ever feel that kind of hurt again."

"Natalia, believe me, I understand. And I am truly sorry. If I could do things all over again, I would do them differently. I think part of me was resisting how strongly I felt, how strongly I feel for you. It scared me. And I thought—well, I was considering a safety net. But that wasn't the right path. I have thought about you more than I've ever thought about a woman. I know my love for you is real, and I will prove it to you. This past month has been miserable without you. I literally worked every hour of the day trying to not think about you as often."

"Well, I did the exact same thing." She told him about her newly acquired LEED certifications. Her first encounter with Rosa. Rosa's ensuing phone call.

"I can't believe all of that happened and I wasn't there for you." He looked away, then down.

"I couldn't believe it either. I felt like I was living in a dungeon shackled by shame, pain, misery."

"Baby, I'm so sorry. How are you feeling now?"

"A lot better. You know—you learn and you grow. That's life." She paused as she felt her heart fill with joy—a warm elixir seeping over and throughout her entire body. "It's nice talking to you again. Hearing your voice. Seeing your smile."

"My thoughts exactly. I can't wait to see you again. What are you doing tomorrow?"

Natalia laughed. He wasn't wasting any time.

It was David's idea for her to meet his grandmother and attend church with them the following morning. "Of course, that makes perfect sense," she'd said in response.

He arrived at eight o'clock to pick her up. His punctuality was always a certainty. Perhaps it framed the life of a doctor whose daily reality was propelled by appointment times and tightly scheduled days. A world where every minute mattered and could be the difference between life and death. For most of his patients, time was always of the essence. With the ticking of the clock came the growth of tumors spreading into nearby healthy tissue.

"Cancer cells can't live without oxygen and nutrients. They send out signals to get new blood vessels to grow into the tumor," David had explained to her once. The cancer cells would then grow and divide and multiply over time to form a tumor. Time. The painful test and inevitable battle against which cancer often won.

She smiled as she slid her feet into a pair of black pumps. He was the most intelligent man she'd ever dated, and yet his modesty, at least when he was with her, always prevailed.

When she opened the door, she inhaled quickly at the sight of him, her stomach doing somersaults as they embraced. She didn't want to let him go, and he seemed to be feeling the same way, hugging her tight and close. When he released her, he tilted her chin up toward his face and kissed her gently. The sensation of his soft lips rippled down into her heart, stomach, legs, and feet.

"I missed you," he said, his smile matching hers. They stood in a capsule of delight.

Winter

Life can only be understood backwards;
but it must be lived forwards.

—Søren Kierkegaard

"The truth is rarely pure and never simple."

—Oscar Wilde

Chapter 35

Winter ushered in a host of new emotions dispensed sporadically in small doses. With the cold came a shroud of concern mixed with expectation.

Rosa couldn't be certain about anything anymore. She could only trust her gut and God. She knew dwelling on the past would only keep her chained there like a prisoner in solitary confinement. The dark, cramped cell would cripple her mind and body over time.

Forgiveness was something she knew she had to do. She only wished she could dispose of the memories, too. "Forgive and forget" was an oxymoron. They were a quarrelsome couple that would never see eye to eye.

She had finally talked with Joe Jr. She pictured him now, looking even more like his father as he grew older, sitting across from her in the well-lit café. He'd played with his silverware, cracked his knuckles, and rubbed his head while they talked about the weather, his job running Joe's grocery stores, his wife and kids—deferring the inevitable conversation that gnawed at them.

"I understand why you did what you did," she finally said. She was talking about the shameful secrets he begrudgingly kept for Joe. The deception he cradled like a grenade, keeping the pin in place all these years.

"Ma," he interrupted.

"Let me finish. I just want you to know that I forgive you." She had already decided it didn't matter what he said either way. Whether his decision was malicious or meant to protect her, the damage had already been done.

"Ma, I didn't have a choice. I didn't want to hurt you. I was angry with Dad for years. I couldn't understand it. I mean, he had just gone so far. Cheating. Fathering a child. And, she was black." He slowly shook his head from side to side as if his mind might give him the rationale he'd been missing.

She would get back to the black part.

"When I found out, I told him—and I told her—what I thought about it," he continued.

"And what was that?" Rosa asked, her fork in midair.

"That I didn't want anything to do with it. I didn't want to know her or her child. I couldn't believe what he was doing or that she was okay with the situation, knowing he was married."

Rosa's blood began to percolate, rising to her neck and face, warming her skin.

"You don't know how hard it was for me not to say anything, but I knew it would only hurt you. Not long after that, he told me they weren't together anymore. So I figured he had changed, confessed, and that he was gonna do right after that."

"Did he ever see the child?" she asked.

"I don't know," he said, looking down.

"You don't have to lie about any of this anymore," she reminded him.

"He tried to talk to me about it, but I felt like the less I knew, the better. I know he was involved when the child was a baby, but I don't know how long. I think the woman called things off, though. He was sad, upset about it."

Rosa sipped her cup of tea as she thought about her husband's pain over another woman and child he'd created. An entire life apart from her and their own children. "Well, it's done," she said. "He's gone, and I'll never know his side. I'll never know if he was sorry he cheated, or sorry that things didn't work out between the two of them."

"You can't think like that, Ma. Men do things—stupid things—because we're, we can be . . ." He paused to find the right word. "Weak. In the end, he provided for you, for us. He was a great dad and a decent husband." His voice rose as if he were asking her rather than telling her.

"Well, now that I've met the child and her mother, I'm not sure what to think." Knowing she had made that decision on her own, coming to terms with a truth that now obliterated her perception of her own marriage, emboldened her. The wool over her eyes completely dissolved, giving her new clarity and strength. She felt the spirit of the young woman she used to be rise inside her like an ocean tide.

She explained her intentions had been malicious initially, her pain driving every action she took. How she'd seen Natalia's photo. How she'd verbally abused her at her office, her jealousy and pain pulling and controlling her like strings of a marionette. How God had shown her what she needed to do.

"I don't know what to say. I don't think I could have done that," he said.

"Well, you didn't have to. I did."

Rosa scanned the garage for the Christmas decorations Joe normally dragged out every year. Bins, boxes, bottles, plywood, and tools were everywhere. She recalled the bins had been red, Joe's color-coded system of organization. She finally spotted them, four total, lodged behind a lawn mower.

She and her children had picked out a twelve-foot Douglas fir tree—a tradition they'd had for decades and decided to keep. John and Joe Jr. dragged it into the living room, leaving a trail of spindly needles from the car, up the stairs, across the porch, and through the entryway. The tree stood, large and lifeless, in front of the only window in the room, partially obstructing the view. They were all going to decorate it now.

"I need some help getting the decorations," she said when she walked back into the kitchen. John and Joe Jr. jumped up from their barstools, leaving their bottles of beer on the counter.

Christmas music flooded the living room as her sons returned with the bins and they set out to re-create a holiday that would never be the same for any of them.

"Your father loved Christmas," Rosa said as she picked up ornaments from one of the bins. "He bought all of this." Her arm swept across the piles of red, green, and silver now covering the floor.

"Yeah, it won't be the same without him," Catarine said, stroking the head of a gold angel ornament she held in her hands.

"I was thinking about inviting Natalia over," Rosa announced as though testing the idea out, though she had already decided she would.

Her children's eyes darted around at each other. No one wanted to be the first to speak.

"I'm going to invite her," Rosa said, hoping her clarification would provoke someone to say something.

"Well, if that's what you want, then you should do it," John said.

"But I want to know what you all think," she said. "Will you be comfortable? Do you want your kids to meet her?" She looked at Joe Jr.

"I don't know if it's a good idea," he said. "It might be weird. Besides, doesn't she have her own family?"

Rosa could tell he hadn't come around to accepting his half-sister. Blood relative or not, she was a reminder of something immoral and impure. Rosa knew he didn't want to confront the demons he continued to battle with every day, but if he did, he might find closure and peace and see that the color of someone's skin is just that—and finally forgive himself.

"I'm sure she does, but we're also her family now. She has the same blood running through her veins as you all do."

The silence reverberated around the room, drowning out the sound of Mario Lanza's "We Three Kings of Orient Are." Catarine placed another angel on the tree and walked over to her mother. She gathered her into her arms and squeezed her tightly.

"I would love to have Natalia join us," she said.

This was no surprise to Rosa. She could see that Catarine was pleased that her mother had decided to put away her bitterness. She turned and looked expectantly at Joe Jr., who was rummaging through one of the red bins as if he hadn't heard a word she'd said.

"Do you not have an opinion, son? You typically do."

"I don't see the need for it, but if it makes you happy, and they don't care"—he nodded his head toward Catarine and John—"then I'll keep my mouth shut."

Rosa caressed one of the branches of the large Douglas fir in front of her. Three needles, soft, tender, and smelling of pine, fell into the palm of her hand. She crushed them with the tips of her fingers, then dug her nails into each one, breaking them into tiny pieces.

"I think that would be best," she said, dropping the green pieces onto the floor as she left the room.

Chapter 36

The long drive to New Orleans created an atmosphere of calm in the car, inducing relaxation through the repetitive sound of rubber tires rolling across the rough asphalt of I-10. Trees blurred past at sixty miles per hour. An R&B station created low background noise, bass bumping periodically.

The route from Houston to New Orleans took drivers through a twisted topography alternating between long stretches of man-made canals and stagnant swamps. Bald cypress trees with knobby knees protruded from their roots, trunks submerged in the murky, vaguely reflective waters. Bare and exposed, their bland branches reached up toward the sky as if pleading for help.

Natalia fiddled with her watch as she bounced her right leg up and down. This was her first trip to New Orleans with David. Actually, it was their first trip anywhere together.

A soft patter of rain followed them as they drove across the Lake Pontchartrain Causeway. *Water all around us*, Natalia thought as she glanced at the lake stretching in all directions. Any trace of land was several miles ahead of them. Soon, they would be in her hometown. Soon, they would spend time with—what were they meant to be called—her other family? Her extended family?

"You nervous?" David asked, his lips stretching into a comforting smile.

"Yeah, I am. I don't know how Joe's crazy son is going to act—or react. Plus, what will they say when they see you?"

"Babe, you don't have anything to worry about. I'm here for you; we're here for each other. What's the worst thing that could happen?"

This question had become a running joke between them, meant to counter serious concerns with absurd ones.

"Well, let's see. The crazy son could physically try to harm us with a machete or one of the rifles on the back of his pickup. Catarine might have had a change of heart. After all, she was following her mom's lead. I haven't met the other son, but he could be worse than his brother."

"Relax. You told Rosa about us already, right? We don't have anything to hide. We could have met anywhere—church, the mall, a gas station—and I still would have been drawn to you."

"Oh, so you used to meet women at malls and gas stations, huh?"

They laughed.

He was right. She had already explained their relationship to Rosa. She recalled their conversation as she tried to detect any hint of emotion—concern, anger, happiness—across the phone line. But Rosa had responded almost neutrally.

"Hello, Natalia?" she'd asked hesitantly.

"Yes, hello?"

"This is Rosa. Your . . ." Her voice had trailed off. "Joe's wife."

Natalia had paused for several seconds, uncertain of where the conversation would go or what Rosa wanted from her. Then she said, "Uh, yes, hi."

"Listen, I—we were wondering if you'd given any more thought to our invitation. We'd like for you to join us for Christmas Eve dinner if you're in town. I figured you would be with your own family—with your mother, Lisa—on Christmas day. But Christmas Eve is just as big of a holiday for us. We'll have the Feast of the Seven Fishes."

Natalia inhaled, then exhaled deeply after she ended the call and wondered what the Feast of the Seven Fishes was. She sat in silence after she thanked Rosa and told her she'd think about. Her heart leaped at the idea of being in Joe's home. But then a leash of fear yanked it back. From stunned and confused to excited and hopeful, a volley of emotions surrounded her, making it impossible for her to decide on her own.

After several weeks and consulting with David and her mother, she'd called and told Rosa she would love to join them and asked if there was anything she could bring—dessert, sides—to which Rosa responded, "A side would be lovely." The word stuck with Natalia as she considered what side would fall into the category of lovely.

She and David had already planned to spend the holiday together. She quickly asked if she could bring a guest.

"Yes, of course," Rosa said decidedly. Natalia stuttered as she tried to explain who her guest was. "Well, I, um—I think I should tell you who he is. So—so you won't be surprised." Rosa was silent as she waited for Natalia to continue. "He's David— Dr. Duplessis." Rosa was quiet for the longest time. Long enough for Natalia to wonder if she'd heard her. "Hello? You still there?"

Rosa cleared her throat before she spoke. "Dr. Duplessis. He's a wonderful man. I think you two must make a beautiful couple."

"Are you sure it's okay? I don't want you all to be uncomfortable or even more aware of the fact that Joe isn't . . ." She couldn't say "with us" when the "us" didn't actually include herself. "Joe is dead" was much too harsh.

"We don't need a doctor to remind us of that. I feel it every day, every minute. Dr. Duplessis did everything he could to save Joe. It'll be good to see him."

Her second phone conversation with Rosa had created a conundrum ever since. Why hadn't Rosa asked more questions, like, How or where did you meet him? When did you meet him?

Then an image of Rosa's son surfaced, tall, looming, and angry. She hadn't been able to shake it ever since. She saw him when she showered and dressed. She saw him when she drove to work. She saw him when she cooked dinner. Each time he seemed to grow taller and angrier, and her fear was a juxtaposed counterpart. Her heart pounded in protest and her blood—a substance she thought she could feel—circulated faster, swishing and coursing with an uncertainty that surfaced through her body and made her skin prickle.

David spoke now, bringing her back to the rainy drive. "You don't have anything to worry about. If things do get crazy or uncomfortable, we'll leave."

They arrived the day before Christmas Eve so David could take in the city's sights. Though Natalia had assured him there wasn't much to see beyond the French Quarter and Saint Charles Avenue, he insisted on being a tourist.

By the time they pulled up to the Loews Hotel, the sun was casting its orange glow across graying clouds as if in defiance. Two bellmen dressed in all black were waiting to greet them, take their bags, and park David's car in a nearby lot. The recently remodeled lobby with its marble floor and crystal chandeliers smelled of magnolia—sweet, clean, and lemony.

Natalia waited patiently at David's side while he took care of the check-in. They'd chosen the hotel together after a long discussion about sleeping arrangements. Hesitant and worried about their "flesh" overcoming them, David thought he should stay in the hotel room alone while Natalia stayed at her mom's. She assured him she would be a good girl and suggested they get double beds. Besides, she'd spent the night at his place several times, and they'd both resisted temptation—though barely. Each time was becoming more difficult than the preceding one. Each encounter going further. A kiss. A deeper, longer kiss. Fondling—clothes on. Caressing with some skin contact.

"I don't know how much longer we can do this," David had said. "You don't know how hard this is for me."

"Um, trust me, it's just as hard for me," she'd told him. Her attraction for him was beyond anything she'd experienced with any other man. She felt it bursting through her pores, coursing through her veins like a fire that needed to be extinguished. His touch sent currents through her body—soft and tingly. Deprivation only intensified her desire for him, her imagination running wild with thoughts of their first time. When she was alone in her bed at night, her body ached for him—his smell, the firmness of his skin, the contours of his muscles.

They were like high school students fueled by hormones but restrained by invisible chains. Something would have to give soon, she thought, as David slid the room key into the slot above the brass handle.

New Orleans became a different city with David at her side. Every building, corner, and angle was brighter, sharper, more charming. Having grown up in the city, she never appreciated or noticed its beauty. But with David, she felt like a tourist.

They sat close together on the streetcar, their thighs touching, practically joined as one. David's arm draped around her shoulder as they listened to the wheels grating on the track and watched the mansions roll by through the open windows. Muggy air mixed with the smell of exhaust floated in and out as the trolley picked up speed for a few minutes, then came to a stop to pick up new passengers and drop off those who'd reached their destination. Natalia explained that, to her knowledge, no black people owned property on this street—Saint Charles Avenue. This was old money, passed down from who knows how many generations before them.

She leaned her head against David's shoulder, her body cradled in their seated embrace.

"Babe?" he asked.

"Hmmm?"

"What are you going to do about Dallas? Are we moving?"

Natalia laughed as she considered the implication of his question.

"Funny you should ask. I talked with my boss, and she said I could split my time between Houston and Dallas. A day or two in Dallas and the rest in Houston. It's such a short flight, she thinks we can make it work."

David exhaled and nodded.

"You seem relieved?" Natalia glanced up at him.

"I am. But I would go anywhere with you." He kissed her forehead and gripped her waist as she nestled her head on his shoulder.

When they reached downtown, they held hands as they walked toward Canal Street until they reached the French Quarter, where they turned left on Bourbon Street. It was crowded and already effusing the stenches of alcohol and urine. They watched street performers dance, sing, pantomime, juggle, play trumpets, drums, and guitars, their nearby cups beginning to fill with coins and dollar bills. Sketch artists drew exaggerated features of tourists who sat in folding chairs across from them.

She watched David taking in the madness, his jaw set tightly, eyebrows straightened as he maneuvered through the crowd.

"They say this place is haunted," Natalia said when they sat down for dinner. They'd chosen a popular Creole restaurant not far from their hotel: Brennan's. The bright pink stucco façade with its wrought iron balconies gave way to a fruity interior—apricot chairs and avocado leather booths. Gridded lattice, forest green and white, covered the ceiling and sections of the walls.

"You believe in ghosts?" he asked.

She shook her head. "Of course not. Well, maybe." She'd grown up in a city known for voodoo and horror stories. She'd heard about the LaLaurie mansion torture chambers and Delphine's supposed ghost now haunting it. She'd read about the St. Louis Cemetery No. 1, considered to be the most haunted cemetery in the United States, and the craziness at Hotel Monteleone, where a restaurant door supposedly opens and closes every night even if it's locked, and where the elevators have minds of their own, letting guests out on wrong floors.

"I'd have to see something with my own eyes to believe in ghosts," David said.

She had had encounters before but chose to ignore them, telling herself they were just coincidences.

She watched David's shoulders relax and his jaw loosen as his lips curved into a half smile. "What are you smiling about?"

"I'm just thinking about you, about us. And how much I love spending time with you."

"Likewise, sexy man," she said, winking at him. She watched the candle flicker on their table and she felt like the energy of the flame—erotic and daring.

Something shifted in the air as David leaned across the table and whispered in her ear, "I want you so badly." He kissed her neck softly three times before moving to her lips. She closed her eyes and momentarily forgot there were other people in the restaurant.

Natalia knew what was going to happen as she and David rode the elevator up to the tenth floor of their hotel. She wasn't sure if it was the wine, the humid night air that clung to her skin as they walked back, or Marvin Gaye's voice in the hotel's lobby—"I Want You." What were the chances? When she walked through the door of room 1001, she felt it had already been decided. A vision she'd replayed in her mind over and over again. And she knew David had, too. As if in a trance, she heard the click of the door and turned toward David as he fastened the second latch.

"Shower?" she asked, the word shaky as it fell out of her mouth. He nodded solemnly, as yearning spread across his face like a smoldering fire. His eyes were dark—murky with desire—as she touched his face with the palm of her hand. She could sense the torment as he gripped her waist firmly with both hands and pulled her toward him. They'd fought against their hormones and their chemistry for so long. But tonight, the stamina with which they'd fought had abandoned them.

She felt his hand slide up her back, pushing her cotton blouse away from her skin, as she untucked his shirt. She unbuttoned it rapidly, anxious to run her hands across his bare, muscular chest. The shirt out of the way, he stepped back momentarily to help her lift his T-shirt over his head.

Next, she was unbuckling his pants, listening to the clanging of the buckle as they fell to the floor. She was still wearing her blouse and skirt when he turned her around and pulled her blouse over her head. Her back against his chest, she felt flutters along her neck—gentle as a butterfly's landing—as he kissed her from her earlobe down to her shoulder, his hand under her skirt and moving up her inner thigh. Soon, her skirt was on the floor, a puddle of red, blue, and yellow.

She could feel her heart racing as David took her hand and pulled her into the bathroom.

Chapter 37

She wasn't sure when it started, but the habit was now firmly formed. It brought her comfort and gave her a sense of sanity. Perhaps it began in her head as thoughts she didn't verbalize. Scolding Joe for what he had done. The pain of his death—*why did you die so soon?*—layered with an affair—*how could you?*—layered with an illegitimate child who was now a young woman—*she has your blood coursing through her veins.* Now the thoughts spilled out of her mouth for anyone to hear.

"Your daughter will be here tomorrow. I invited her over for dinner. You won't believe this: she's with the handsome black doctor who tried to save your life. Can't you just see them together? I hope he's faithful to her. I hope she doesn't endure the sins of her father or her mother. Don't you hope that too, Joe?"

She felt his presence nearby. His spirit floating about the rooms and hallways of their home, infiltrating her lungs with every breath she took. She knew he could hear every word she said. So it was with sweet relief that she uttered them.

As she shuffled around the grocery store, she checked off the items on her list, tossing them carelessly into the grocery basket:

red wine vinegar, lemons, garlic, and purslane for the salad; spaghetti noodles and clams for the pasta; and shallots, mussels, sea bass, shrimp, and dry white wine for the stew.

Relieved to be responsible for only three of the seven courses for their La Vigilia, she hoped her list covered everything her pantry and fridge were missing. John would bring the first course: a salmon dip. Joe Jr. would take care of the third: grilled cod and possibly fried eel if he was up to it. Catarine would bring the sixth and seventh: limoncello gelato and rainbow cookies.

The mostly-seafood menu was meant to purify their bodies for the holiday. But Rosa could never comprehend how or when the purification process began when they indulged themselves for what seemed like hours. First and second servings of high-calorie but lightly seasoned food that anchored itself in the pit of your stomach long after you chewed and swallowed the last bite. They would be miserable and immobile after it was all over.

Seven courses for the seven sacraments. One in particular stood out to her now: marriage. It was meant to be an unbreakable bond of love between Christ and his people. A total union through which God's love was supposed to flow not only between the two of you but also through you to your family and others. Permanent. Faithful. Exclusive. Emblematic of God's unconditional love. Symbolized in sexual intercourse. They were supposed to be living in Christ, and Christ was supposed to be living in them.

But where had Christ gone when Joe was lured away from her into the arms of another woman? Could you love someone unconditionally but live another life in secret? Giving yourself to someone else, your body at least, shattered that sacrament like shards of broken glass, remnants of something once beautiful now turned into hard edges that would slice your skin.

She couldn't be sure what Joe had felt for Lisa. She might not ever know if he had stolen some of his feelings for her and bestowed them on his mistress, leaving her less loved, or if he simply had another vessel of love to pour from.

She continued to push the basket up and down the aisles of the grocery store, bright fluorescent lights beaming down everywhere she went. She wanted to dispel these thoughts. This anguish that lived in her mind, dominating how she felt: tormented.

She'd accepted the affair. She'd accepted his love child. But now she would live on a merry-go-round that asked the same question repeatedly: Did he love her? She wasn't sure if she was thinking of herself or of Lisa.

"Your total is $166.42," the cashier said, interrupting her thoughts.

Rosa's kitchen smelled of pasta, gravy, seared fish, and garlic—the smells of seven courses competing with each other rather than blending. The scents wafted across the kitchen and into the dining room, where she began methodically placing plates on the table in front of each chair. She paused when she reached Joe's spot as she thought about their last Christmas Eve together.

He'd seemed out of sorts, complaining of a headache but dismissing it while he downed each course as it arrived. She recalled his hand, subtle but sure, as he reached for his right temple, his face briefly contorted. After the pain passed, he continued to reminisce, telling sea stories from his navy days—like the time they thought they were going to die in a storm, the ship pitching, rolling, and yawing. Or stories about his childhood—how his parents rationed out their food, which was a good thing, because they had food when many of his friends often had to skip meals. He'd gone to bed early that night, exhausted from rounds of eating, she thought.

She hoped that by filling the table with others this year, his physical absence wouldn't be so pronounced.

"But you'll be nearby won't you, honey?" she said as she placed the final plate where he would have sat.

When her doorbell rang promptly at four thirty, everyone in Rosa's house froze for a moment as if they were playing Simon Says. Joe Jr. held a knife in midair, John stopped stirring a pot of boiling noodles, his girlfriend froze while hauling a bucket of ice, Catarine stopped dealing a deck of cards to her nieces. All of them looked expectantly toward a door they could not see. Rosa dropped the basket of dinner rolls she was carrying. Her hands shook as Catarine jumped up to retrieve the basket from the floor and scoop up the rolls one by one.

"Don't worry, Mom. We have more in the pantry," she assured her. "I'll get the door."

"No, no, no. I want to get it." Rosa pushed her daughter aside with more force than she'd intended. She shuffled as quickly as she could toward the entryway.

"Well, hello. Please, come in!" she said, stepping aside.

"Hello, Mrs. Russo." David spoke first and leaned down to hug her. Natalia balanced their store-bought side dish in the crook of her left arm and extended her right hand to shake Rosa's.

"How are you?" she asked.

"Oh, just fine, I think," Rosa replied, looking back and forth from Natalia to David. "Well, I must say you two do make a fine couple."

"Well, thank you. She makes me look a whole lot better," David laughed.

"Children, this is Natalia. And you remember Dr. Duplessis?" She didn't wait for a response. "Here, let me take this." She placed their mashed potatoes on the counter, then pulled an amber bottle of wine out of the bag David held out to her as she read the label: BADIA A COLTIBUONO CHIANTI CLASSICO RISERVA. "Very nice!" she exclaimed.

"We're not wine connoisseurs, but I asked around and one of the doctors recommended it," David said.

Before Rosa began the introductions, Catarine rushed to Natalia's side, hugging her warmly. "Our family already knows all about you, so don't worry," she said. "They know it's not your fault, and this kind of thing happens more often than people realize. But anyway, you're part of us—our flesh and blood—and we think Dad would have wanted it this way. So, relax." She squeezed Natalia's arms before rushing back to her nieces.

A series of nice-to-meet-yous followed as more guests arrived: Joe's brother, Benito, who went by Benny, and Benny's wife, Mary; Joe's sister, Elisa; Rosa's cousins, Antonio and Napoleon.

"Make yourselves at home," Rosa encouraged as she looked around the room to see if Joe was nearby. He would be so happy to see his child. All grown up and probably on her way to the chapel before long, judging from the way Dr. Duplessis was looking at her: eyes mesmerized, lips in a permanent smile. She hoped it would work for the two of them. Where was he? She checked her bedroom, the bathroom—no sign of him. She wrung her hands as she went from room to room. Maybe he went outside for some fresh air? But he wasn't there, either.

"Mom, what are you doing out here?" Catarine asked, her palms facing up toward the sky.

"I was—I was looking for your Dad," Rosa said. "He was just here earlier. I wanted him to see Natalia and Dr. Duplessis."

"Wait, what?" Catarine asked, confusion spreading across her face.

Rosa shook her head, ignoring her daughter. If she ignored Joe, she feared he might dissolve like a morning fog. She wished she could just pack her longing for him away in a small suitcase and place it high up on a shelf, hidden from herself and everyone else.

Natalia was pleased when John suggested that David bless the food. With grace and dignity, he acknowledged Joe: "While he is missed dearly, we know he's in a better place. Amen."

So far, so good, she thought, as she sat on the edge of her seat.

As she expected, dinner was a long affair with multiple conversations changing with each course. The men were loud and boisterous, often drowning out the women's voices: What would happen to our country now that we had a new president? Could you believe how many celebrities had died recently? Had anyone seen Martin Scorsese's latest movie? Someone said, "Joe would have loved it." Yes, they all agreed.

They avoided the topic of Joe's indiscretion, though Natalia was the living proof of it sitting among them. Rosa had introduced her as a new member of their family. She watched as everyone's gazes rove from her face—paused for a moment at her eyes—and continued down her torso to her legs and feet. She figured the eyes would tell them everything they needed to know.

"So, what do you think about the Black Lives Matter movement?" Benny asked, looking from Natalia to David.

They glanced at each other, a silent communication dance that said: *Did he just bring up police brutality and racial injustice? I can't believe he's asking us this; do you want to answer?*

"I know you know about all the killings—Alton Sterling in Baton Rouge," Benny added loudly.

"Oh, Benny, they don't want to talk about that," his wife said as she elbowed him.

"Sure, they do. Hell, I want to talk about it, then. It's a crying shame what's happening. I mean, at some point someone has to pay."

"I doubt that they will," David said, his voice low.

"But it's on video!" Benny shouted. "The shit was recorded! It's on a cell phone video." His eyes bloodshot, face oily, he'd clearly pushed the limits of his alcohol intake.

"Doesn't matter. It's almost always on video now," David said, shaking his head. "They're white and he's black. Or rather, they're police. Hell, some of the black officers do the same thing. That uniform gives them certain liberties."

Silence fell over the room like a lead blanket. They struggled beneath it as some of them grappled with the issues of right and wrong. Police and the use of force. Murder and self-defense. Courage and fear. Justice and corruption. Black and white.

"Ready for dessert?" Rosa asked as she stood and began taking plates away from her guests.

Natalia slid her chair away from the table, anxious to remove herself from this polarizing conversation. "Let me help you," she offered, thankful for a reason to leave the room. She tried to apologize to David with her eyes.

When they were safely in the kitchen, Rosa said, "I'm sorry, honey. You never know what people are going to say. Benny means well. He marched with Dr. King and is a big proponent of civil rights. He should have been a politician, although that probably would have corrupted him."

"Is he anything like Joe?" Natalia asked shyly, hoping the question wasn't too obtrusive.

"In some ways. Joe is also very passionate about certain issues, but he isn't a drinker, so his passion is more diffused. Benny is emboldened by the alcohol. They both have tempers, but usually they're justified when it comes to that. They both can be the life of the party—talkers. They can talk about anything and everything." Rosa paused and then reflected, "I think Benny has a thing for black women, too."

"Oh."

Chapter 38

Discomfort has a way of clinging to its victims like perspiration on a hot summer day—persistent and noticeable, finding its way around every curve and crevice. Natalia swallowed, an attempt to extinguish the malevolence she felt rising in the pit of her stomach.

At the dinner, Joe Jr. had looked at her as if she were a rat that needed to be poisoned. She'd hoped he would come around after his grief subsided, or after a rational conversation with his mother. But she could see his disdain in his turned-down lips, pressed together and punctuated by three curved lines on either side.

She was walking down the hallway after excusing herself in search of the restroom when she was sidetracked by a series of framed black-and-white photos hanging on the walls, crinkled along the edges and lined with sporadic cracks. The people in the aged photos—which almost seemed like jigsaw puzzles—appeared to be ancestors: women in long dresses standing on dirt in front of seemingly hand-built houses, close-ups of mustached men in dark jackets, children standing side by side, forming a chain with their arms looped together.

"What are you doing?" The words were spat out and rolled together on top of each other. Joe Jr. was standing inches away, looking directly at her with his hardened, beady eyes.

When she suddenly felt something warm pressing on her left shoulder, she was almost certain David had appeared at her side, that he'd somehow entered the hallway from its opposite end. But when she turned her head, expecting to see him, no one was there. She placed her hand on top of her shoulder, certain there was something pressing against it, and held Joe Jr.'s gaze for several seconds before she spoke. She didn't need to be afraid. The sensation was so strong, she thought she could hear someone saying it: "You don't need to be afraid. He'll get over it."

"I'm sure you can see that I'm looking at the photos on this wall," she said, wishing he'd go back to the dining room.

"Well, you don't need to. I know my mother has welcomed you into our family, but she's not in her right mind. She can't see that you don't belong here, but I do. You're just a bl— bastard child, an accident, and we don't need to be reminded of it."

The words hit her like cow whips, slashing and penetrating through her skin. She inhaled deeply as she studied his face: thick eyebrows formed a bridge above his small, sunken eyes; a pointy but prominent nose reached for her; thin lips pressed so firmly together they were barely visible.

"And what are you exactly? Something perfect and precious because you were somehow supposed to be born, and you believe I wasn't? Well, guess, what? They planned to have me." She paused when Joe Jr. raised his eyebrows. "That's right. I was planned. And even if I hadn't been, I'm here." She felt her cheeks warm and lifted her chin defiantly. "You can think whatever you want, but all I ever wanted, pretty much all my life, was to meet my real dad. I didn't have any control over what he did or who he slept with, and neither did you. So now I'm just trying to find out who he was, what he was like. From what I gather and what I've learned so far, you're *nothing* like him. And I don't mean that as a compliment."

She rushed past him, back into the dining room.

"We need to leave," she whispered into David's ear. "Now."

She could feel the confused eyes of the family on her, questioning the suddenness of their departure. As they approached the front door, Catarine rushed toward them, Rosa not far behind.

"What's going on?" Catarine asked.

"We shouldn't have come here," Natalia said, tears running down her face. She bit her bottom lip and gripped the handle of her purse tightly, angry that they would see her this way again—fragile and hurt.

"What happened?" Catarine asked. "Please. We want you here."

She shook her head, unable to speak.

David stood in front of her, his hands firmly gripping her arms, his face inches from hers. "Baby, tell me what happened." She glanced at Joe Jr., who was now standing in the kitchen, taking another swig from his beer bottle.

David practically ran into the kitchen to confront him.

"What did you do? What did you say to her?" he demanded.

"Oh, it's the hotshot doctor here to save the day," Joe Jr. said with a belch, then hiccupped before he continued. "She doesn't belong here and neither do you."

"Yeah, that's right. I'm a hotshot doctor. Call me what you like. But let me tell you something: you don't wanna fuck with me." David said this calmly, fists clenched. "You don't get to decide who belongs here and who doesn't. So leave Natalia alone and keep your ignorant-ass thoughts to yourself."

"Or what?" Joe Jr. taunted. "You think you're big shit because you're a doctor? You think you're smarter than we are? If you were so smart, why couldn't you save my dad? I told my mom we should have gotten a different doctor."

"That's enough," Rosa cried, her face and neck covered in red, splotchy patches. She tried to push Joe Jr. away from David and out of the kitchen, but she was far too feeble to make him budge. Joe Jr. yanked his arm away from her.

"Don't touch me," he yelled, spit flying from his mouth.

Natalia had followed David into the kitchen and she touched his arm. "Let's leave. He's not worth it."

"What? I'm not worth it? You uppity niggers think you're all that. Someone needs to teach you a lesson."

She wasn't sure if it was the "uppity niggers" or "teach you a lesson" part, but before she could blink, David took a step forward and punched Joe Jr. right in the mouth. The sound created a loud pop above the low hum of the Christmas carols piping through the ceiling speakers. Joe Jr. stumbled back toward the kitchen island, blood trickling down his chin. He touched his lips and looked around as if he didn't know where he was.

The entire family was now crowded in the kitchen, yelling. "What happened?" "What's going on?" "Oh, my God!" "What did you do?" "What the hell?"

David grabbed Joe Jr. by the collar of his shirt and whispered something in his ear before shoving him back toward the kitchen island.

"We need to leave. Now." Natalia was pulling David away from Joe Jr.

"Don't come back," Joe Jr. said. Natalia rolled her eyes at him.

"I'm so sorry," she said to no one in particular. The entire family was staring incredulously at them. One of the women went to the refrigerator to get ice for Joe Jr.'s lip while another dug a bottle of pain relievers out of her purse.

They were walking toward the front door, the family's voices still a chorus behind them, when Rosa appeared.

"I just want you to know that Joe and I are both upset about this. I'll take care of it. Please don't be upset. My son can't help himself. I thought I was clear with him and that he was mature enough to handle this, but clearly there's something else going on, and I'm going to get to the bottom of it." She looked so forlorn, Natalia almost felt sorry for her.

"Joe Jr. is . . . well, I guess you know what he is," she said.

"I apologize. I shouldn't have hit him," David said. "I lost it. I haven't been called a nigger since I was a kid. It brought me right back to that playground."

"He got what he deserved as far as I'm concerned. Maybe he'll keep his mouth shut next time," Rosa said.

"Or get professional help," Natalia recommended. "Thanks for inviting us. We appreciate the gesture."

"Of course, dear. Don't worry—we'll figure this out." She squeezed Natalia's shoulder, reminding her of the same sensation she'd felt earlier.

When they were in the car, Natalia examined David's hand, his knuckles slightly bruised. "We need to get you some ice," she said, kissing each knuckle softly.

"I'll be fine. Look, I'm sorry. I didn't mean to cause a scene, and I wish I hadn't hit him. Guys like that are usually all talk. Normally I have more self-control."

"He deserved it. Asshole," Natalia said. "And besides, you were protecting me. Standing up for us."

David shook his head. "It's crazy how you can grow up with nothing, struggling. Make it through high school, college, and medical school. Become a damn doctor . . . and still not get respect."

"He's not important. He doesn't even matter. Who cares if you get respect from him or not?"

David kissed her cheek lightly before starting the car. "Did you hear what Rosa said? About her and Joe being sorry?" He shifted from park to drive.

It hadn't registered with Natalia amid her intense embarrassment, but she considered it now. "Yeah, she was talking like he's still alive. She did the same thing earlier. Or do you think she meant Joe Jr.? Like she was apologizing for him?"

"Probably," David said, nodding.

On their drive back to the hotel, Natalia was thinking not of Joe Jr. but about the other person she sensed in that hallway with them: Joe. She thought back to his funeral and the shivers she'd felt when she stood near his casket and stared at his photo. *Has he been with me all this time and I just haven't noticed? Or does he come and go, appearing when I need him?* She was going to tell David, but it all just seemed too strange. She didn't believe in ghosts or spirits anyway.

Chapter 39

Rosa contained the steam she felt rising inside her. She waited until their family left and they had complete privacy. She walked past Catarine, who was putting the leftovers into Tupperware.

She found him in the backyard, leaning back in an Adirondack chair. His feet were crossed at his ankles, a half-full glass of whiskey set on his thighs.

"What did you say to her?"

"I don't want to talk about this."

"I didn't ask you if you wanted to talk. I thought we were clear on this before she even got here." The last words rose like octaves on a piano.

"You don't see what I see," he said as he stared at the concrete patio.

"And, apparently, you don't see what I see."

"I don't have to like her or get to know her if I don't want to," Joe Jr. said.

"Honey, I thought you were more mature than this. You sound like a five-year-old kid. How is it that you can forgive your father but not this child, this young woman?"

He was quiet as he took several sips from his glass, jiggling the ice cubes around after each swallow.

"I never liked or condoned any of this, and Dad knew that. I don't know why you think I'm supposed to accept her into our family just because he isn't alive anymore. If I didn't when he was alive, I'm definitely not going to now."

Reconciling the past with the present and future was proving to be more difficult that she'd anticipated. How did one selectively choose what to bring along and what to leave behind? She could see that her son was carrying a heavy load of hatred and unforgiveness. His hands were calloused from the weight, yet he wasn't ready to let go.

"You think I should ignore her and the fact that she's a part of Dad," Rosa said, a statement and a question. "He left part of himself behind with her. She's your flesh and blood. Doesn't that mean something to you?" She watched her son inhale and exhale deeply: no. How could she get through to him? Where was the hatred coming from? She needed to find the seed that planted it. "Son, it seems like you hate her because she's black. Are you telling me you'd be more accepting of this if she was white?"

He stared into his now empty glass. He shrugged his shoulders, leaning his head against the chair.

"I would still hate the fact that he cheated and fathered another child," he said.

"But would you accept that child?"

"I think so. I think I would."

"I don't know where this is coming from," she said. "You were not brought up to be this way. Where does this hatred come from? It seems like you have some insecurities about yourself that you need to deal with."

"You don't think they get handouts when they shouldn't? Hired for jobs they're not qualified for? Just to fill some quota?"

"Maybe some do. But so do white people—all races. You think every white person that's hired for a job is qualified just because they're white? No—we have privilege because of our race. I know you know that. You also know it's not easy for people of color in this country. Look at Dr. Duplessis. You think he became a doctor by pulling a degree out of his hat? I'm sure he worked hard in medical school and earned it. He's smart, intelligent. You can't take that away from him. You can't be angry because he doesn't fit your stereotype of what black people should or shouldn't be. And you certainly can't blame him for your father's death."

Joe Jr. stared up at the sky and sighed. "I don't think I can pinpoint one thing that triggered these feelings. I mean, we didn't have many black kids in our high school. Maybe if I'd been an athlete, I would have hung out with them since a lot of the black guys played sports. But my friends, we just didn't care for them. If you watch the news, they're usually criminals, doing things they shouldn't be doing."

It was simply wrong to stereotype people, putting them all into one bucket. Couldn't he see there were differences across all races? Didn't he want to be a good person? Not a hateful one? Why couldn't he see it wasn't about hate. It was about what was fair. It wasn't about people getting handouts or people getting jobs they didn't deserve. Did he think white people were somehow better than black people—or Asians or Hispanics or Native Americans? Couldn't he embrace those differences? What about the human race? We're all the same inside.

Soon an image began to emerge, and the picture became clear. Joe Jr.'s life hadn't turned out the way he thought it would. But until he realized that blaming others wouldn't make it any better, he would stay stuck. The wool over his eyes was adorned with thorns, inflicting pain that he cast onto others.

287

"Son, you need to get help," Rosa advised. "You need to examine your heart. You need to talk to someone to work these things out. Clear your head of the craziness and start all over." She stared into his gloomy eyes, looking for a sign of understanding, a semblance of agreement, a flicker that could ignite a spark and send him on his way. But all she could see was darkness.

Chapter 40

David lifted her black suitcase from the trunk of his car, and she followed him up the stairs to the front door of her fourplex. The drive back to Houston from New Orleans had been arduous as she replayed her second encounter with Joe's son over and over again. Each time she felt her blood turn hot at the thought of him, then cool when she recalled the pressure she'd felt on her left shoulder. She was certain someone had touched her; someone had been standing behind her. She had the distinct feeling it was Joe.

She wondered if ghosts or spirits could visit everywhere they liked. Would he roam around her apartment *and* Rosa's home? Or would he have to choose his domain?

"There's something on the door for you," David said, removing a white envelope that was wedged between the door and the frame. Her name was scribbled in a cursive handwriting she didn't recognize.

"This is odd. Someone other than the mailman actually put this on my door? They came inside this building?" She clenched the letter between her lips as she fiddled with the key to unlock the door.

"You gonna open it now?" David asked after they'd walked through the apartment and he'd placed Natalia's suitcase inside her bedroom.

"I guess so. Though I really just want to get in bed with you." She winked at him.

"I think that's a much better idea," he laughed. "You can open it later."

"Oh, let's just get it over with and find out what this is all about. It's probably from my landlord." She slid her forefinger along the seal to tear it open. When she saw the neatly written, blocklike letters—everything in all caps but sized like lowercase—she knew it wasn't from her landlord. Tyler was the only person she knew who wrote this way, giving every letter equal importance. He'd tricked her by writing her name in cursive on the envelope. Like those companies that send you mail that looks like a check, but when you open it, you find you can't take it to the bank, and it's worth less than the cost of the postage they paid to send it to you.

"It's from Tyler," she sighed. "I don't even know how he knows where I live."

"Google?"

She pushed him lightly in the chest and laughed as he feigned injury—his hand across his chest, body falling onto the couch.

Her palms felt sweaty, fingers shaky as she straightened out the two pages. He was sorry that she couldn't see they belonged together. He'd made a mistake and now he would pay for it for the rest of his life. But he understood and accepted her decision. He was going back to Chicago and was going to try to make things work with his wife. He wished her all the best. He would always love and care for her.

She folded the letter, tucked it back into the envelope, and placed it on her coffee table, resisting the urge to smell it. She felt the closure compress her heart and a surge of sadness from the scripted finality. She knew she would also always love and care for him.

As David lifted her off the sofa and carried her into her bedroom, she sighed, grateful that he hadn't asked her to throw it away. She would place the letter in her memory box with the rest of the special moments in her life.

The Future

"Love is the only future God offers."

—Victor Hugo

One Year Later

Painful memories cannot be forgotten. Though they may soften over time or cross paths with another recollection, they remain steadfast in their playback of feelings, sounds, smells, and tastes from moments that can only be relived in one's mind. To rewind the years was to see life with a new perspective: ill-informed decisions that could have been avoided, carelessness that seemed fun at the time, or irrational feelings that drove us to say things we didn't mean.

The problem with the past has always been its ability to hold us captive. The past is made up of moments in time that should be forgotten but continue to follow us like ants after the scent of sugar.

No one could know how things would play out. And that was the perplexity of the future—enticing with its catalog of possibilities, all contingent on decisions made today, right or wrong or in between.

Natalia and David had chosen each other. They were tucked away in the booth of the restaurant where they'd had their first date. She was sipping a glass of tea, watching him scan the menu, when he announced, "I'm not that hungry." He stood and took her hand, pulling her from the booth. Into her ear, he whispered, "Close your beautiful eyes," and he led her into the center of the restaurant.

Tilting her face up at him, she pursed her lips as she tried to decipher his motives. "What are you up to?" she asked, folding her arms across her chest.

"Just close them and keep them closed," he said, softly touching the tops of her lids with his long index finger. "Don't open them until I tell you to."

She relented and waited while she listened to the shuffling and tiptoeing of feet, the rustle of garments, and people bumping into chairs. She'd ascertained that this was a surprise, but the reason was still a mystery. Now she heard clicking noises. Shushing sounds.

"Okay, baby—open them."

The room, illuminated by candles on tables all around them, was full of people. She could feel their presence, but David's was the first face she saw smiling at her. Her body tensed and she was momentarily frozen.

"Look around," he laughed, as they all joined in.

Starting with her left, she scanned a semicircle of people: Catarine, John, Rosa, Joe Jr., David's grandmother, his brothers, her mom, Pamela, and Kevin.

Before she realized what was happening, David was on one knee. As he knelt, the room fell completely silent.

She watched his lips moving but couldn't make out the words right away. "Wait, start over," she wanted to say when her brain finally registered the words and what was happening.

"I didn't believe in love at first sight. But when I saw you—in all of your pain—I knew I couldn't let you go then, and I can't let you go now, or ever. I want to spend the rest of my life with you, Natalia. I want your face to be the first one I see in the morning and the last one I see at night. I want to be there when you're happy, when you're sad, when you're moody, when you're mad. I want to always be here for you. I want us to always be here for each other. I want to take care of you. I want you to do me the honor of being my wife. Will you marry me?"

"Yes!" The word burst out of her mouth like water from a fire hose. As he stood, she grabbed him and cried into his chest. "Yes!" Her body shook uncontrollably as she tried to rein in the feelings that overwhelmed her. Their love had grown into a beautiful sphere of comfort, trust, and permanence. She knew her heart belonged to him and his to her. Their souls were intertwined. She hoped the bond would be unbreakable. She lifted her face up toward his, cupped his face in her hands, and kissed him softly on his lips. Again. And again. And again.

The room erupted in cheers, whistles, and clapping. Confetti and balloons fell from the ceiling. Even the waitstaff joined in.

David slipped an oval-cut, blue-diamond ring set in platinum on her finger. Fresh tears formed zigzag paths down her cheeks as she thought back to a conversation they'd had last year about diamonds. They agreed they weren't worth the money people paid for them since they weren't actually rare. But colored diamonds—that was another story. And the meaning behind blue diamonds, folklore or not, fed into a silly superstition she found alluring.

"The blue diamond," she'd said, "is supposed to bring serenity, peace, and affection. It's also supposed to protect you from misunderstandings and fights in a relationship. In addition, it's supposed to bring you good health."

David had said the expectations were far too high for a stone, and they'd laughed.

"Well, at least it's different," Natalia had said. "Not status quo, you know?"

He'd nodded in agreement.

"Congratulations," Joe Jr. said later that evening. He'd approached her slowly, deliberately, while she was talking with Pamela.

"Thank you. I—I didn't expect to see you here," she said, still nervous being close to him.

"Neither did I," Pamela chimed in. Natalia gave her a look that said, "Stop it. Now."

"I didn't expect to be here," Joe Jr. said. "I realized I was angry. For so many years I was angry at my dad, angry at your mother, and angry at you. But I realize it's not your fault. You were just . . ."

Natalia raised her eyebrows as she waited to find out what she was.

"You were just, well, you're here because God wanted you here. He doesn't make mistakes, right?"

"No, I guess He doesn't. I never looked at it that way before."

But what about the color of my skin? she wondered as she watched him take a gulp of his beer.

Silence fell between them, a barricade to their voices. Thoughts and words left unspoken as they seemingly agreed to let Joe Jr. carry his racial hatred for others while making an exception for her—and presumably David. She'd seen the two of them talking moments earlier and couldn't imagine how they'd resolved the tension.

"See you at the wedding," he said lightly and quickly touched her arm. He nodded and smiled as best he could as he walked away.

"Well, I guess he's trying," Pamela offered.

"Yeah, that means something."

Natalia felt David's arm loop around her waist, pulling her close. "May I steal her away from you?" he asked, looking at Pamela.

"I guess so," her friend laughed. "I'm so happy for you both. To find true love is rare these days."

"Ain't that the truth," David said. After Pamela walked away, he asked, "Were you surprised?"

"Extremely! I can't believe you planned all of this and I had no idea."

"Baby, I bought the ring months ago. I couldn't wait to give it to you, but I wanted to share this moment with everyone who matters to us."

"It was perfect, and the ring is beautiful." She held her left hand up and watched the lights reflect the brilliance of the stone as it twinkled. "Our love is like this. Beautiful. Solid. Rare."

"I couldn't agree with you more. I don't think we ever had a choice in this matter. You are my destiny, and you will always have my heart."

She looked into his eyes and felt her own heart surge. She couldn't imagine her life without him. As tears began to trickle down her face, she relaxed in his embrace.

About the Author

Dione Martin was born and raised in New Orleans, where she spent much of her childhood and teen years reading. *The Wool Over Their Eyes* will be her debut novel. Dione earned her Bachelor's in English from the University of Minnesota-Morris and her Master's in Journalism from the University of Texas at Austin. She is currently a sr. communications director at Brinker International and is working on her next novel. She lives in Dallas with her two daughters and enjoys running, cooking, performing arts and attempting DIY projects.

Acknowledgements

I first have to thank God for giving me the inspiration and endurance to complete my debut novel. *The Wool Over Their Eyes* has been a labor of love. I spent years writing the draft and another year refining and polishing, working closely with my esteemed developmental editor, John Paine. We further developed the plot lines and transformed the overall structure of my manuscript. I also have to thank my editor, Susannah Noel, whose thorough editing and fact-checking added more punch and gave me such a sense of confidence and relief.

I also must give a big thank you to Inspire On Purpose for making the publishing process so seamless and painless. And I also have to thank Ascot Media Group for their behind-the-scenes work to publicize and share my story. Writing is such a solitary endeavor, but knowing that confinement results in a story and experience that can transport a reader makes it worth the effort.

And, I thank all of the influential writers who came before me and currently contribute to the literary world from Zora Neale Hurston, Toni Morrison and Maya Angelou to Brit Bennett, Terry McMillan and Ayana Mathis. I wish I could name them all. May we all continue to leave our marks, inspire others and live our dreams.

Made in the USA
Columbia, SC
29 May 2021

38725272R00173